The
Player
Next
Door

Elizabeth Davis is a full-time nerd whose interests include cold weather, rainy days, coffee, Minnesota Public Radio, and rom-coms where characters' homes vastly outstrip the income they would get from their jobs. Born and raised in suburban Milwaukee, she now lives in Minneapolis with her husband and two children.

To learn more, follow Elizabeth on Twitter: **@E_Davis_Romance**, and on Instagram: **@elizabethdavisromance**.

By Elizabeth Davis
I Love You, I Hate You
The Player Next Door

The
Player
Next
Door

ELIZABETH
DAVIS

HEADLINE
ETERNAL

Copyright © 2022 Elizabeth Davis

The right of Elizabeth Davis to be identified as the Author of
the Work has been asserted by her in accordance with the
Copyright, Designs and Patents Act 1988.

First published in 2022
by HEADLINE ETERNAL
An imprint of HEADLINE PUBLISHING GROUP

1

Apart from any use permitted under UK copyright law, this publication may
only be reproduced, stored, or transmitted, in any form, or by any means,
with prior permission in writing of the publishers or, in the case of
reprographic production, in accordance with the terms of licences
issued by the Copyright Licensing Agency.

All characters in this publication are fictitious
and any resemblance to real persons, living or dead,
is purely coincidental.

Cataloguing in Publication Data is available from the British Library

ISBN 978 1 4722 9756 3

Typeset in 11/14pt Minion Pro by Jouve (UK), Milton Keynes

Printed and bound in Great Britain by Clays Ltd, Elcograf S.p.A.

Headline's policy is to use papers that are natural, renewable and recyclable
products and made from wood grown in well-managed forests and other
controlled sources. The logging and manufacturing processes are expected to
conform to the environmental regulations of the country of origin.

HEADLINE PUBLISHING GROUP
An Hachette UK Company
Carmelite House
50 Victoria Embankment
London EC4Y 0DZ

www.headlineeternal.com
www.headline.co.uk
www.hachette.co.uk

Lindsey, this one's for you

Chapter One

The lives of millions of people hung in the balance. They were moments away from complete destruction, and the fate of the entire continent of Sulzuris depended entirely on what Clare did next.

But first, she needed Kiki to pee, and she needed her to pee *now.* "Come on, just get on with it," Clare said and tapped her foot, impatient with the little fuzzball's pickiness. "Everyone is going to kill me if I'm late." Normally she left herself plenty of time for Kiki's walk before a Quest—especially when they were about to pick back up on a cliff-hanger like Devi left them on last week—but she lived on the fifth floor and the elevator was out. Again.

Kiki sniffed the tree and circled it for the third time. Clare sighed. "It's the exact same spot you always pee in, you don't need to make this a whole production."

"Does that work?"

Clare spun on her heel and found herself face to face with none other than Mr. 6B himself, he of the unfairly handsome face and habit of eating out his lady friends on his living room couch. (Okay, it was just the *one* lady friend, and it was *one time.*

It wasn't like she was a perv. It was just that his living room was straight out her kitchen window, and she just *happened* to see it. It wasn't like she *watched*. Much.) "Does what work?" she asked and tugged at her sweatshirt, wishing she was wearing something—anything—a little more flattering than a hoodie with *Zutara Forever* written across the front.

Not that she was ashamed of her hoodie—Zuko and Katara should have ended up together, as anyone who had seen *Avatar: The Last Airbender* would agree—but when faced with a man who looked like he stepped out of a cologne ad, she wished she was wearing just about anything more sophisticated.

"Berating your dog into peeing."

Kiki finally got down to business. It was the exact same spot as when Clare brought her down earlier, the bark on the base of the tree still damp, and Clare had to stifle her sigh. "She's not my dog," Clare said stupidly, because, well, why was he talking to her? And how did people talk to him when looking at the handsomeness full-on was like staring directly into the sun?

He shifted his Smorgasbord tote into the other hand. She had heard a woman in the elevator call him Logan once, which fit. *Logan*s were insouciant, laid-back, and cocky, and 6B fit the bill all too well. His eyes were icy blue, a fact that was utterly irrelevant to literally everything, and wow, she needed to stop gawking at him. "You just go around, stealing other people's dogs, and then badger them into peeing faster?" he asked.

"I was not *badgering*," she protested, reminding herself at the last second not to use his name. She had no reason to know it and appearing to know it would make her seem like a stalker. Oblivious to her mental panic, Logan grinned. Clare had never actually been in the direct path of one of his smiles before and she really hoped he had a permit or something because that shit was deadly. "I was just getting her to hurry up, because Kiki is fussy."

"Still wondering how a dog that isn't yours ended up being your responsibility." He rested his shoulder against the young birch tree planted in the boulevard.

"Oh well, it's simple. I steal dogs, and take them on walks, and then ransom them back to their owners."

"Wouldn't opening a dog-walking business be easier? And less illegal?"

"But then where's the rush? No high to be had in following the law."

"Oh, I get it, you're an adrenaline junkie," he said with a soft laugh.

Part of Clare felt like she was floating above herself, and another part wondered if she was hallucinating. Was she really flirting with him? He was so far out of her league it wasn't even funny, but maybe that was it. He was so hot he barely counted as a person to her brain, more like a very sexy mirage who could talk. "That's definitely me. I'm an adrenaline junkie and criminal, definitely not a dork who lives for Quest for Sulzuris and dog-sits for her aunt."

"Okay, intrigued about whatever that quest thing is, but I see we're finally solving the mystery of the dog's ownership."

"It wasn't really a mystery, you just never asked who she belonged to," Clare volleyed back. This was almost as much fun as fighting off a pack of orcs, a reference Sir Hotness obviously wouldn't get, because guys with faces like that unfortunately did not play fantasy tabletop role-playing games. And Clare would know, because she didn't just play Quest for Sulzuris, she worked for it, too. An awful lot of the players, not to mention her coworkers, were the exact stereotype people first thought of when you said "fantasy tabletop role-playing game." She mostly worked with white dudes who had poorly maintained facial hair and assumed everyone in the world had an encyclopedic knowledge of *Lord of the Rings* and *Game of Thrones*, and yes, they could be exactly as annoying as it sounded. Quest Gaming was working on broadening their demographic—that was the reason she had wanted to work there in the first place—and there were a lot more people who played these sorts of games than most people assumed, but some stereotypes are hard to shake. Particularly when there's just enough truth to them to make them plausible.

"And is this dog-sitting business of yours free? Or do you charge your elderly aunt an arm and a leg for it?"

"I'm pretty sure she'd protest that *elderly* descriptor, but yes, it's free. It's a tale as old as time: girl loves dogs, girl doesn't have time for a dog of her own, girl agrees to dog-sit for beloved aunt and pretty much anyone else who asks."

"So if I got a dog, you'd walk him for free too? In the service of being a good neighbor?"

A flush started creeping up her neck, because it hadn't really occurred to her that he knew they were neighbors. It was obvious why she'd notice him, of course, but it never once crossed her mind that he might have noticed her too.

Clare made herself shrug lazily. "I'd probably charge you. No reason; I just want your money."

"You're a shark, aren't you?" he laughed and honestly, she'd pay him money to smile at her like that all the time. He straightened up off the tree and tipped his chin at Kiki, who was now straining at her leash toward the lobby. "Looks like your friend wants to go back inside. See you around, neighbor," he said, striding away like this was a totally normal interaction and not incredibly surreal.

"Come on, Kiki," Clare muttered to the dog, and watched Logan walk into the building out of the corner of her eye. "Let's get you home so I can get back to saving Sulzuris."

Chapter Two

Logan ran his hand down Amber's back, fingers gliding through the light sheen of sweat.

"Mmmm," she sighed happily as she rolled over. She swung her long legs off the edge of his bed.

"Where are you going?" he asked. Amber never spent the night, but usually she waited a little longer before leaving.

She grabbed her panties from where he'd tossed them earlier. "Early meeting," she said, and Logan didn't know her that well—they didn't exactly spend a lot of time talking—but he could tell it was a lie. She wasn't looking at him, and there was an urgency to her movements that was out of place. He stayed where he was, watching her shimmy back into her clothes at nearly record speed. Amber fluffed her nut-brown hair out from where it was caught in her T-shirt and turned to face him, unusually fixated on straightening the hem of her shirt. She took a deep breath. "Okay, there's no not-awkward way to say this, but tonight was the last time."

"You moving or something?"

Amber refused to make eye contact. "You know how I was seeing that guy from Tinder, right?"

Logan made a noncommittal noise because he couldn't say he remembered a specific guy, but he did know she was seeing other people. He was a lot more monogamous than most people thought, but when it came to casual sex partners he had no problem with them having other entanglements. Relationships meant having to care too much, in his opinion. His way meant getting laid regularly, but he never had to drive anyone to the airport.

"Yeah, anyway, I think he and I are going to go exclusive soon, so I probably won't be seeing you anymore."

Logan decided if he was going to get dumped, he might as well put his underwear on. "Probably? Or definitely?" he asked, pulling them on and picking up the jeans he'd been wearing when Amber arrived. He didn't bother with a shirt. He worked hard to look this good, and he believed in showing off the results of that work.

"Depends on how the conversation goes, obviously, but— yeah, this is the end."

Logan shrugged. He liked Amber well enough, but it wasn't like either of them were particularly invested in this. He couldn't even remember what her job was, although he thought it might be something that involved kids. Teacher, maybe? He didn't think she was a nanny, if only because he probably would have made several borderline dirty jokes about that. Either way, she definitely didn't have a meeting on a Sunday morning.

He realized belatedly she was waiting for him to have more of a response than just a shrug. "Okay then," he said. "It's been fun."

Her shoulders relaxed. "It has been, hasn't it?" she said, and he followed her out of the bedroom. "You might not be boy-friend material, but you're a hell of a fuck."

"I could be," he said, more because he felt like he should

protest that categorization than anything else. "I could be boy-friend material, I mean. If I wanted to be."

Amber laughed. "Tell me one thing about myself that doesn't have to do with sex."

"You like red wine but not white."

"Okay, fine—one thing about me that isn't sex or drinking."

Logan blinked, thinking hard. Everything that came to mind—her bra size, the fact that she liked to leave her heels on during sex—would make her point for her. "You're a teacher," he said finally, hoping he was right.

"What grade?" She lifted her chin, eyebrows raised, waiting.

Logan took a valiant stab in the dark. "Kindergarten."

"So close," she said, wrinkling her nose. "High school."

That rang a bell. "Oh right, you're an English teacher."

"French," she sighed.

This was not going well, so Logan did what he always did when things stopped panning out his way: he changed the sub-ject. Or more accurately, he poured on the charm to distract her from the discussion entirely. He grinned, the grin that worked miracles on anyone attracted to men, and cocked his head to the side. "Maybe you have a point," he said, and she shook her head fondly.

"Take care, Logan," she said, stepping back into her heels and brushing a kiss to his cheek.

The door clicked softly behind her. He stood there for a moment, chest oddly hollow. Then he shook his head and put Amber out of his mind. Logan never saw the point in dwelling on women. There were plenty of fish in the sea, after all, and he was fairly irresistible bait. There was no reason to feel like this, so he simply wouldn't.

Logan padded back toward his bedroom and noticed that one of the blinds was still open. He was high enough up that if he craned his neck, he had a view of the Hennepin Avenue Bridge from the windows on the other side of the apartment, but if he looked straight out this window it was into the units on the other side of his complex. Amber had a bit of an exhibitionist streak—and Logan was up for pretty much anything—so he'd gone down on her a handful of times on the couch that faced the window.

As far as he knew, none of his neighbors had ever complained, so either they hadn't seen, or they enjoyed the show. The unit straight across from his never, ever opened their blinds—he might have thought it was unoccupied if not for the string of Christmas lights that went up on their balcony last November and never came down—but the one just one floor down was occupied by The Nerd.

He sort of liked The Nerd. There was an air of geekiness that seemed to surround her in an unapologetic way that he admired. He saw her often enough around the building, either in the elevator or, if the elevator was on the fritz, in the stairwell. Once he watched her trudge across the lobby with an armful of medieval weapons, loudly explaining to everyone she saw that they were both fake *and* for work, and *please* no one call the cops on her.

He saw her sometimes out on the sidewalk too, walking that tiny, fluffy dog that he only occasionally saw in her apartment. To be perfectly honest he was most curious about that part, which was why he had stopped to talk to her earlier that afternoon. He had been delighted to discover she was funny as hell, if still a little puzzling to him. Where did she take her baking every Saturday afternoon? What was with the dog sweaters? And what sort of job required fake medieval weapons?

She couldn't be less his type, considering how much time he had spent wondering about her. He went for women like

Amber—tall, willowy women with cheekbones that could cut glass and attitudes to match. The Nerd was cute, although in an off-beat sort of way. She was shorter than most of the women he dated, and certainly a little mousier, but her chin-length blonde hair always looked soft to the touch. He wouldn't say no to fucking her, but he probably wouldn't pursue her, either.

There used to be a guy who hung around The Nerd's place a lot, some skinny, glasses-wearing dude who had once set up what appeared to be a diorama of a battle in the middle of her kitchen, but Logan hadn't seen him in probably a year. He wondered about that too—did she dump him? He looked boring, so he hoped she had, for her sake. She'd been really funny about those weapons.

The Nerd was still awake. She baked a lot, sometimes late into the night. Logan liked to watch when she did, although not in a creepy, lurking sort of way. Mostly he'd just glance out his side window and try to guess what she was making, and then an hour or so later he'd see if he was right. But she wasn't baking tonight. She was watching something on her TV—it featured lots of swords and possibly a trebuchet, so maybe medieval weapons were both a hobby and a job for her. He shook his head and spun the blinds closed. Whatever was wrong with him, spying on his neighbor was not going to fix it.

Chapter Three

"Yaen, what's your decision?" Devi prompted.

Clare's palms were sweaty but she squared her shoulders and kept her voice even. She had been playing as Yaen for years. She knew exactly what Yaen would do. "I kiss him," she announced.

"You're sure?"

"Positive." Clare ignored the sharp intakes of breath from her left and right.

"Roll for success, then," Devi instructed her, and Clare held her own breath as the dice skittered across Toni's dining-room table. She'd rolled a twelve and the entire party gasped. "You grab Ildash by the robes, kissing him despite everything he's done. Your lips meet and for a moment, it seems you've failed. He goes still and you wonder if he'll go through with it anyway, casting the spell that will rip the continent in two. Rain pours down around you, soaking you both—"

"Oh my god, a rain kiss?" Toni interrupted.

"You're goddamn right it is," Devi replied without missing a beat. "Slowly, Ildash lowers his hands, cupping your face as he returns the kiss. With tears pouring down your face, you watch as he pulls back and gasps, violet eyes flying open. The rain stops and a ray of sun breaks through the clouds."

"Wait, he was *cursed*?" Clare gasped.

"Shut up and let me tell you. The golden light dissipates and Ildash is left standing before you, blinking like he's never quite seen you before. He looks down at his hands, bewildered, and then back at you. 'Where am I?' he asks. 'And what was I about to do?'"

"Oh my god, he was cursed," Clare said again, a huge smile on her face. "Did my kiss break the curse?"

"Is this just *Beauty and the Beast*? It feels like *Beauty and the Beast*," Annie pointed out.

"I'm getting there, and no, the Beast was dying so that's different," Devi said with a long-suffering air. "Do you guys even want me to keep going, or are you just going to keep interrupting me?"

"Sorry, continue," Clare said.

Devi cleared her throat. "You explain everything to Ildash— the war he started, the spells he cast, the bargain he made with the Orcling King—and with each new revelation he looks more and more horrified. 'How can I make things right?' he asks, and you wonder where to even begin. It seems, however, that for now, Sulzuris is saved." Devi sat back, apparently finished.

Clare preened in her chair and reached for one of her brownies. She baked for every game day and these were a particular favorite, fudgy and delicious, and she wasn't about to deny herself some victory chocolate. But then she caught the way Devi was smirking. "Wait, *seems*? Oh shit, what did we miss?"

Devi leaned forward and so did Clare, Toni, and Annie, breath bated. "With Ildash freed, it seems Sulzuris is saved . . . but over on the eastern shores of Noet, an eerie calm has fallen over the land. The waves seem smaller and softer than usual, as if magic is smoothing the way for something. Even the ravens have gone quiet, their raucous calls silenced. It should feel peaceful, but there's something sinister about the stillness. Just past a rocky outcropping that surrounds the deep, calm waters of Firesand Bay, the prow of a ship appears. And then another, and then another. The ships crowd the bay until there's hardly any water left, it seems, just wooden vessels of war, all of them flying the same flag."

Toni gasped and Devi sent her a stern look, the rest of the table silent as a tomb. Devi returned to her Game Master voice. "The Dragon Army has arrived."

She may as well have dropped a bomb. "We defeated them months ago!" Annie exploded, while Clare and Toni shrieked in surprise. "They're back?"

Devi grinned and tossed her hair over her shoulder. "You defeated some of them. But no one ever said they had entirely given up, and Ildash has a lot to answer for still. But that will have to wait until next time."

"Fuck," Annie muttered. "I wish you weren't so good at this."

Toni frowned. "Degar didn't even get to do anything. I maintain my potion would have worked."

"Probably," Devi conceded, closing up her iPad with her notes. "It would have killed Ildash, but then you would have had to fight the king's minions, and with all the damage you took storming the castle I'm not sure it would have worked. You'd be betting a lot on the dice, which is risky. Plus, Ildash-on-a-redemption-quest will be a powerful ally if you let him join you."

"Fair enough," Toni said. "Chase is going to be pissed he missed this, though. And I can't believe Yaen is getting the villain romance of Clare's dreams. How long have you been angling for this?"

"Since forever," Clare and Devi said in unison. "It's all I've ever wanted," Clare added.

Clare had been playing Quest for Sulzuris since her freshman year of high school, so that wasn't much of an exaggeration. Her first group had been a bunch of quiet, nerdy boys, but they had universally looked down on Clare's love of romantic storylines. *It cheapens the game*, they always said, and she had given up on making those choices for years, even after she'd left that game in a somewhat explosive fashion. But their mockery and her subsequent humiliation had stuck with her, and it wasn't until she met Devi her first month of college that she'd found another girl who played, and who similarly thought romance adventures were actually more fun than regular ones. It was hard—okay, nearly impossible—to play Sulzuris with just two people, but they managed, coming up with solo quests for each other and trading off as Game Master until Devi met Annie at a Young Democrats meeting on campus and hit it off. Toni and her twin brother Chase joined them their first year out of undergrad, when they were all still living in shitty student housing in Dinkytown and working terrible jobs that were only tangentially related to their degrees.

Now they were on their fourth campaign together, although Chase traveled a lot for work and thus was more of an auxiliary member now. But love for Quest for Sulzuris had been a defining feature of Clare's life for a decade now, which was why being hired by Quest Gaming two years ago had been such a momentous occasion for her. There had been some ups and downs working there, but she was creating a world that other people would get to lose themselves in, and that was enough.

"Look on the bright side," Clare said to Toni, who was a

touch bloodthirsty when it came to these decisions. "I'm sure Degar will get to kill a lot of dragons on the next campaign."

"You will, I promise," Devi said, and lifted her brownie toward Clare in a silent salute. "What's new with you?" she asked Clare.

Clare busied herself picking up some minuscule crumbs and shrugged. "Not much," she admitted. Her life had been quiet lately, and while that wasn't unpleasant it was also, well, a little boring. She went to work, which she loved but where she still didn't have many friends, she baked, she walked Kiki occasionally, and she came to game day. They were gearing up for a new edition at work, which would be exciting, but that pitch meeting wasn't for weeks, and there was no guarantee her idea would be chosen.

Clare's life was very safe, but it was also monotonous. She didn't even have a boyfriend or crush to break up the routine, not since Reid left.

She had been with Reid for nine months, just long enough to start making long-term plans. They met at a party at Chase's boyfriend's apartment; some guy in the room made a disgusting joke and Reid had rolled his eyes at her, thus signaling he was one of the good ones. She asked him for his number and within a week, they were dating.

Clare had been trying to work up the courage to broach the "should we live together?" discussion when Reid abruptly announced he had taken a job at a company in Phoenix. There was no conversation about her joining him, or them even trying long-distance. Just *Sorry, you know how I feel about Minnesota winters* and *I think I want to make a fresh start,* and that was that.

She'd been sad about the breakup, but not particularly devastated. However, lately she'd felt a little bit itchy to change things up, if not quite itchy enough to download a dating app. Clare didn't have a problem with using dating apps in general, but she found the endless *Hey there cutie* ☺ attempts at conversations to be soul-sucking. She wanted a connection with someone, and yeah, sex would be nice—better than nice, actually, she really could use a good lay—but Clare had never been one for casual relationships. She was a girlfriend-girl and always had been. In fact, she'd never even had sex with someone she wasn't already dating. And that meant she was more or less treading water, hoping for something or someone to come along and liven things up a bit.

Devi frowned at her. "Are you okay?" she asked, and Clare belatedly realized she had been staring blankly at a pile of crumbs for a little too long.

Clare blinked and straightened. "Oh yeah, totally fine."

"Really?" Annie asked. "Because you sorta zoned out hardcore there."

"It's nothing," Clare shrugged. "Life is just, you know, kind of . . . boring?"

"Good boring, or bad boring?" Toni asked.

"Just boring boring," Clare replied.

"Well, don't tell your boss that or he's going to give you one of his weirdo assignments," Annie said drily.

"They're not that weird," Clare protested.

"They're a little weird," said Devi. "Most people aren't required to go whitewater rafting for their job. But are you sure you're okay?"

"Positive." Clare pushed a smile on her face because really, she had nothing to complain about. She helped herself to another brownie. She had just saved the world, after all. She could handle a little ennui.

Chapter Four

Logan
Things are over with Amber

Sam
Who the fuck is Amber

Logan
Met her at Pour. You were there.

Sam
Why do you think I keep track of the women you fuck? I have much better ways to spend my time
Like letting my mom lecture me about finding a nice boy and settling down
Like going on Tinder and actively soliciting dick picks
Like letting my nieces give me a manicure with permanent marker

Logan snorted at his phone. Sam never bothered to try to spare his feelings, which was the main reason he was friends with her. They had met in college at a frat party, both of them drunk, and proceeded to have what was, to put it mildly, the worst sex of their lives. Sam had rolled over after, looked at him, and burst out laughing.

Logan had joined in, and they'd been friends ever since.

Logan
Yes I get it, I sleep around

Sam
You do, tho
Not like, in a slut shamey way, just like, as a description of your habits in general.

When was the last time you had anything resembling a date that wasn't just meeting for drinks before you had sex so she was sure you weren't an axe murderer?

Logan
I resent that
No one has suspected me of being a serial killer in YEARS

Sam
Which means your last date was YEARS AGO bud, keep up

But to be serious: you have never bothered to update me on the end of a fuckbuddyship. Is everything okay?

Logan frowned. Everything *was* okay, but Sam was right. He rarely bothered to tell her about who he was seeing, since there wasn't much to tell. But for some reason, he had felt like talking about Amber today.

Logan

I guess I thought you cared about me?

Sam

That was your first mistake.

He snorted again and pocketed his phone. It was time for his meeting with Peggy Roth, which did have him a little on edge. Maybe that was why he'd somewhat idiotically reached out to Sam for reassurance. It wasn't 4 p.m. on a Friday so he wasn't getting fired—he didn't think—but there was no way to fight the drop in his stomach the second he saw a request for a one-on-one with the VP.

Because in addition to being unceremoniously dumped by Amber, Logan had been unceremoniously dumped by several clients in the last month. He had managed to find a few new ones already, but that amount of churn was usually a bad sign for a financial advisor.

Logan was fairly good at the winning clients part of his job as it exploited his two main talents: flirting, and reading the room. A lot of people assumed investment was a math and economics game, and it was, to a certain extent. But a lot more of it was gut feeling; reading the writing on the wall and convincing people he was the right person to trust, and then making the right choices with their money. It wasn't all that different from picking women up in bars, quite frankly.

But much like his hookups, clients tended to leave him just as easily. It wasn't that he was making crappy choices with their money, as his metrics were more or less the same as the rest of his colleagues, but rather that there was something about

Logan that made people want to move on. He had managed to keep enough clients to stay off Peggy's radar for a while, but the massive departure in the last month was enough to warrant this meeting.

He should be safe so long as he kept the Schneider account, though. John Schneider had made his money in off-brand cereal, which was boring but highly lucrative, and was one of Loyalty Investment's oldest clients. Logan had inherited him when a senior advisor retired last year, and it was both a major coup for Logan and an easy way of keeping his metrics solid. He just had to keep things steady and not make any risky moves; Schneider was a very conservative, risk-averse client.

Logan stood, pushing his chair in. The Aidens were both in their cubicles one row over. The Aidens had been college roommates and were basically interchangeable, down to getting the exact same job right out of college. Even they admitted it; they were both tall and blond with light hazel eyes and a sort of Instagram-ready handsomeness that drew women to them without much effort. By virtue of having a slightly longer last name, Aiden Gerrick got to go by his first name while Aiden Brooks was resigned to using his last. They weren't the worst— Logan had *some* standards—but they were, in Sam's eloquent phrasing, "slightly sketch." Brooks was on the phone with someone, his voice in the rare "I'm doing actual work" register while he threw a baseball up in the air repeatedly, catching it with a loud *smack* in his palm each time. Logan couldn't hear Aiden, but he was probably one of the many people clicking away at his keyboard.

Logan made his way through the maze of identical grey cubicles to the hallway that held the actual offices. He knocked and waited for her response before entering. Peggy Roth did not look like one would expect the Vice President of a wealth management firm to look, because she dressed like a wacky English professor, complete with curly salt and pepper hair and turquoise glasses—but she had put in her dues and despite the staid dress code at Loyalty Investments, no one was about to tell Peggy Roth she had to retire the bangles.

But even though her clothes said *I'm a quirky aunt*, her demeanor when Logan walked through the door reminded him strongly of his middle-school science teacher. He had a bad feeling he was about to be told off for doodling when he should've been paying attention in class.

Unfortunately for Logan, he was right. Peggy fixed him with a look and gestured for him to sit down. "Mr. Walsh, thank you for stopping by," she said sternly. She peered down her nose at her computer, her glasses pushed to the top of her head. Her fingers clicked across the keyboard and she turned to face him. "I'm guessing you know why you're here today."

"I know I lost the Miller and Yang accounts, but—"

"And the Chaudhary account," Peggy interjected.

Okay, maybe this was going worse than he expected. "And the Chaudharys, yes. But I have brought in two new clients in the last three weeks, which brings my metrics back up to where they should be." He was fudging it a little, since he was technically down about a hundred grand in total client investments, but it was at least *close* to where he should be.

"It seems you're close to meeting this month's metrics, yes, but you aren't yet. Your client portfolio is about $100,000 short."

Logan hid his wince. "I've got a few leads, and—"

"It's more than that," Peggy interrupted. "It's the Schneider account as well."

Logan's stomach plummeted. "Schneider is leaving?"

"Not yet," she said, voice grim. "But he has complained. And he's making noises about leaving us for Marc Wimberley."

This time, there was no hiding his grimace. Wimberley worked at Confidential Wealth, their main rival in the Twin Cities. Logan and the Aidens played basketball against him occasionally and, quite frankly, he hated the smug bastard. "Schneider hasn't said anything to me," Logan protested.

"Well, he has doubts about your trustworthiness. His portfolio is performing adequately, but he reached out earlier this week to express some concerns about your . . . personal life."

Logan immediately ran through his mental rolodex of recent hookups. He wasn't the best at getting last names, since that was usually beside the point, but he was fairly sure he hadn't slept with anyone related to Schneider. He hoped. If he had, he was fucked beyond belief.

Wimberley, though. He would know about Logan's dating habits, thanks to the Aidens and their big dumb mouths bringing it up all the time, and was just shady enough to use it against him. Of course, Wimberley had been married to his high-school sweetheart since they were right out of undergrad, and thus was the exact type of *traditional family man* Schneider would want.

Yeah, Logan was in serious, serious trouble.

"My personal life?" he asked, waiting for the hammer to drop.

She appeared to choose her words carefully. "Mr. Schneider has said he would be more comfortable with someone a bit more . . . traditional. More settled."

Fuck. This was *bad.* "What do I need to do, then?" He tried thinking of leads he had on new clients, wondering if any of them would have a portfolio large enough to replace the Schneider account. He suspected they didn't, which was also very bad for him.

"Your personal life is your business, but I want to emphasize how important Schneider is to this company," Peggy said. "I want to see you taking concrete steps to keep him. But there are several problems at play here. Schneider would like to see proof you're mature and trustworthy, and we would like to see significantly less churn among your other clients. Your problem is not bringing in new clients, since you bring in more clients than most in this firm. But you also lose more clients than almost anyone else. Your churn rate is—well, it's bad. No point in mincing words here. Clients don't stick with you, and that's a problem. And it goes without saying that if we lose Schneider, we will likely be letting you go."

Logan knew better than to try and charm her, but he had to say *something*. "But if I'm bringing in new money, isn't that enough? I could find someone to replace the Schneider money, if I have enough time."

"To put it bluntly, no. That is largely the reason you're not being fired today, but the firm cannot tolerate this sort of revolving door of clients. We're named *Loyalty Investments* for a reason, Mr. Walsh. We want a client base who trusts us, rather than clients who feel they've been neglected after a year and move on."

"I touch base with clients on a—"

"You like the chase," Peggy said, apparently uninterested in anything he might say in his own defense. "That's, shall we say, readily apparent. But then you lose interest and are off chasing the next client, rather than taking care of the ones you have. I suspect that is at the root of Schneider's displeasure as well, but I'll be frank: he is a man who likes to be wined and dined by his financial advisors. His portfolio might be performing adequately, but if he does not take a shine to you—and soon—you will be in serious trouble." She looked him straight in the eye, taking her glasses from the top of her head and folding them in her hands. "I need to see more maturity from you. Some sort of proof that you're someone that Loyalty Investments wants on their team, someone clients can trust."

"Maturity?" Logan asked.

"Maturity. You're very charming, of course, and that's a useful asset in a business like this. But charming only gets you so far. I need to see that you're dependable, someone people would trust *long term*. Client–advisor relationships are more like a marriage than a courtship, and I'm going to need you to demonstrate you understand that."

It was fitting, really. Amber had moved on because he wasn't boyfriend material, and now he was in trouble at work because he wasn't husband material.

"And if I can hang on to Schneider?"

"You need to hang on to Schneider and slow the rest of your churn, or else our next conversation will go very differently. Show me you've grown up, Mr. Walsh," Peggy said, and just like that, he was dismissed.

Chapter Five

Clare filed into the conference room after Noah and Derek and took her usual seat, halfway down the table on the left, just under the painting of Golgath the Destroyer. He was one of her favorites in Sulzuris's bestiary, a squid-like beast large enough to pull entire cities into the sea. She liked to think sitting in front of him gave her a little extra boost of confidence; her own personal tentacle-monster buddy.

And she was going to need it, because it was time to pitch their ideas for the new adventure. Being hired as an Associate Game Designer on the narrative team was literally her dream come true: a chance to worldbuild a sandbox for everyone else to play in. She got to create characters, develop new worlds, and write templates for new adventures. Sulzuris was a collaborative storytelling game, so Clare's job was less to create a defined narrative than to give players exciting tools to create their own stories. She built guardrails and paths and then stepped back so players could take over. Every game had a Game Master, who was the person who directed the shape of the narrative, while individual players made choices and then rolled dice to see how successful their choices were. That meant if a Game

Master wanted to entirely ignore every rule, character statistic, and option Sulzuris put in front of them, they could. Or they could take a world Clare herself had built and turn it into something new and exciting, perfectly tailored for the rest of the players in the group. Sulzuris was a game of endless possibilities.

It was an especially exciting time to work for Quest Gaming, because they were in a "time of transition," as the CEO had said in a speech shortly after she was hired. Tabletop role-playing games had exploded in popularity in the last decade—"Thanks, *Stranger Things*," Clare always said when she brought this factoid up—and Quest was in the process of retooling some of their products to appeal to a wider demographic.

These sorts of changes were always a tricky line to walk. Clare personally still held a grudge against the Third Edition, which had cut her character Yaen's perception abilities almost in half by requiring her character's class to use lower-value dice before an attack, so she understood why long-term fans were wary of any sort of revisions. But Clare also knew that there were thousands of people out there who might be interested in playing Quest for Sulzuris if they could just convince them that it wasn't *just* tentacle monsters and demons and inscrutable rules written in a confusing shorthand.

One of the easiest ways to get into a game like Quest was a one-off adventure campaign, where the Game Master used prepackaged materials and a self-contained narrative for their group. Once groups got a feel for the world of Sulzuris they could branch out, and these sorts of introductory campaigns were the perfect way to get people hooked.

But tabletop role-playing games also had a certain reputation, one which tended to scare off a lot of women, in particular. There was a strong segment of players who disdained anything that challenged the privileged position of white cis men, and who really felt women playing Sulzuris sullied the game's purity. It was the "nerdy guys in their basements" stereotype, and while that wasn't exactly *wrong*—Clare had played her fair share of campaigns in basements with a bunch of dudes—Quest for Sulzuris could be so much more than that. There were a lot of ways to broaden their appeal and shed that stereotype, and Clare was sure that romance was the perfect angle.

It wasn't that there weren't romances in Sulzuris. Game Masters and players had been running romance storylines as long as the game existed, and there weren't any rules against it. But there was a big difference between something that happened amongst players and something that was encouraged by the game itself, and Clare wanted to bring that element into the sun as a way of catching new gamers.

Clare just had to convince her coworkers of that first. The pitch meeting was their first chance to throw out storylines and characters that could be incorporated into the general "travel" brief leadership had outlined. Each team in narrative and character development had a name that corresponded to a type of character within the game. Leadership felt this added to a sense of camaraderie within the teams, and gave them some friendly rivalries to spur on creativity. Clare was part of the Mages, and while she wished there could be at least one other woman on the team, she also knew she was lucky to be here.

Because there was a lot more riding on the all-teams pitch meeting than just a chance to help shape the direction of the new edition. Everyone knew that Noah was interviewing for Narrative Lead on the Dragon Army team, and that would leave an open Senior Game Designer on the Mages. Clare knew everyone would be gunning for that spot, but she wanted it more than the rest of them, she was sure of it.

Craig, as Narrative Lead, was in charge of the pitch meeting, and that meant he was her first hurdle. Craig had been the one to hire her at Quest Gaming, and Clare would always appreciate him for being the person to give her a shot at her dream job. The company was dominated by men at most levels, and she was grateful Craig had been willing to push back on that. He had taken her under his wing and pushed her to expand her horizons to strengthen her writing abilities, and while it had been a little embarrassing to carry a crossbow, sword, and mace through her building's lobby, one weekend of practice on the rooftop lounge had given her a deeper understanding of how to wield those weapons. Devi had pointed out that it wasn't like Clare didn't already know everything there was to know about weapons in Quest for Sulzuris, but as Craig had said, there's a difference between knowing and *knowing*.

Craig himself had plenty of life experience, having spent two years in the Peace Corps in Namibia right out of college. He spent another year after that backpacking through other African countries, and had worked odd jobs in Eastern Europe for a while before going on what he called a "spiritual quest" in Southeast Asia. He had seemingly endless anecdotes about outrunning a mugging in Romania, losing all his possessions in a flash flood in Thailand, and performing karaoke for money in Kenya. He'd lived a life of endless adventure before returning to the US and taking a job with Quest Gaming, and Clare's life path to Quest—suburban childhood, followed by state college and a stint as an administrative assistant at the YWCA—was comparatively dull. Craig was larger than life, but Clare was depressingly life-sized, if not smaller.

But he was the first person she had to convince. Craig wasn't one of the Neanderthals, and he was completely on board with the "time of transition" mode the CEO wanted to follow, but he was a cautious man when it came to demographics. He was careful about not alienating their old die-hards, and Clare understood his position to a certain extent. Those were the people they could count on as customers, and it wasn't good to drive them away. But Clare was certain there was an audience out there that was different from the lifers, and she could bring them in without driving long-term fans away.

Craig came in and the room instantly quieted. "Right then, let's get started," he announced, turning to Noah on his left.

Despite her nerves, Clare loved these sorts of meetings. Everyone fired off ideas, bouncing things back and forth, while Clare kept track of everything suggested on the smart board. The goal was to have a catchy pitch for the team to present at the all-hands meeting next month, when the other narrative teams would present their ideas and leadership would pick the ones they wanted to develop further.

At her turn the room's attention shifted to her and Clare took a deep breath. "Okay, how about this: a Non-Player Character named Captain Ellis Ravencroft, a half-elf, sometime pirate, sometime merchant—it really depends on her mood and how law-abiding the Game Master wants her to be that day—as a guide. She'd be a Rogue, with high perception and above-average hit points, but—" she took another deep breath "—the real key is that she's got a man in every port. Anywhere the parties go, she'd have a built-in connection for them. That would serve as a launching pad for the adventures, and we could write some backstories for her love interests or make it possible for players to romance her if they want. This would give Game Masters a nudge toward more romantic—"

"Sorry, just so we're clear: this is a female character?" Craig interrupted.

"Yes. I'm thinking sort of a lady James Bond type, or maybe

Indiana Jones, where she's deadly and dangerous and hard for anyone to resist. It'd be a lot of fun, and I think newer players, especially ones who are maybe looking for something more romance-oriented—"

"I'd be wary of launching something with explicitly romantic storylines," Craig said.

Clare had expected some resistance, but not necessarily from Craig. Her money would have been on Derek shooting it down. "Captain Ravencroft wouldn't necessarily have these encounters while the teams are playing unless that's what the group wanted," she said as cheerfully as she could manage. Craig always liked upbeat pitches, after all. "It would just be a background runner, one element of her character. I think Game Masters could have a lot of fun with it, and if someone *did* want to go the romance route—"

"Would women want to play with that sort of character in the story?" Derek asked, right on cue. "It seems like, if you're looking to bring romance in, they wouldn't want competition. Shouldn't it be a guy?"

"That's not how female players operate," Clare replied. "Besides, women who are attracted to women play too. Some players might not be interested in that angle, but I think a lot of others would find it enjoyable, and it would set a tone that they could follow."

"What kind of tone?" Noah asked. He and Derek were the star writers on the team, and she wasn't surprised they weren't on board with a romantic angle, but she had hoped Craig would support her more visibly.

"Something light-hearted, you know? We could have a few stories available that would be more like a rom-com, even. Stumble into a tavern and be offered the chance to fake-date a barmaid who was jilted by her fiancé, that sort of thing."

"This is Quest for Sulzuris, not *You've Got Mail*," Craig said, shaking his head. "And I just don't know if you'd be the right fit for that sort of character, either."

The rest of the team laughed, and Clare did her best to join in. Craig was always reminding her to be a team player, after all. "What do you mean, not the right fit?"

Craig leaned back in his chair. It squeaked as he rocked back and forward, chewing his lower lip and running his hands through his thinning hair. He was maybe fifteen years older than her, and Clare was at an age where that felt both like not that much and a lot. The necklace he said he'd gotten in Namibia peeked out from near his top button. "I don't mean to be inappropriate, but, well, we're like family here, and we all know you're—let's say monogamous," he said with a chuckle. "You had that boyfriend for forever. Randy?"

"Reid." She would hardly characterize nine months as *forever*, but she also didn't feel like correcting him.

"He's right," Derek chimed in. "You're the kind of girl who puts *looking for something real* on her dating profiles." The rest of the table chuckled.

That was uncomfortably close to the truth, but Clare wasn't ready to give in. She almost never challenged Craig's decisions, but she really did believe in Captain Ellis. "Okay, so? It's just a character."

"You're just—you're not the type," Craig said again. "Writing a character like that takes a lot of life experience that you don't have."

"What—exactly are you saying?" she asked, doing her best to master the ball of nerves in her stomach.

"Oh, don't be like that," he said genially. "We're just tossing around ideas here, and it's my job to keep you focused on what you can achieve. A character like that—one who sleeps around—well, you're not really the type to handle it, not without you going out and getting a whole lot more experience. I'm sorry, Clare, but it's just not happening right now."

Clare sat quietly as Derek started his zombie pitch, listening and willing her stomach to rise back up from the floor. Craig rarely turned down a pitch that bluntly, and it stung. Usually he'd hear her out, and on more than one occasion he'd been willing to help her punch it up a little before going in front of the group. He'd never been quite so blunt about her personal life, either. Clare had learned to handle the jokes the rest of the team threw her way, usually about her being a woman. Even when the jokes were kind of mean, she had gotten good at fake-laughing until the spotlight turned away. It was just how the team operated, she reminded herself, even if this felt different; more pointed. But she had realized very early on that pointing out unequal treatment would just get an eyeroll from everyone else. The key to getting by was to just let it all roll off her back, and she was pretty good at that. That was what it took to succeed at Quest, and Clare was going to succeed no matter what.

But she wasn't always the most confident in front of the rest of the team, either, a fact Craig never failed to point out in their one-on-ones, so maybe her pitch hadn't been as good as she thought. It was something she needed to work on if she wanted to be considered for Noah's job. The meeting continued—Derek's plan had a lot of support from the other guys, although Clare personally thought it sounded like a rip-off of *The Walking Dead*—and she gave herself permission to check out mentally once the meeting wound down and the rest of them started talking about Call of Duty. They all played it on the weekends, and Craig had told her to "jump in" whenever she wanted, but she had never been much of that kind of a gamer. She liked things like Animal Crossing, but while she could be almost as bloodthirsty as Toni when playing Sulzuris, first-person shooter games never really appealed to her. The first few months she worked at Quest she had tried to join them, but she lost interest and no one else on the team seemed to notice when she stopped.

The meeting finally wrapped up without a real decision having been made, although a few possible storylines were emerging. Craig caught her eye as they left, motioning toward his office, and Clare decided she was going to take a second shot. All she had to do was convince him it was worth trying. He'd hired her because he believed in her, after all.

Craig closed the door behind him and sat down at his desk. Like all the offices at Quest, his office had a playful, laid-back vibe. Action figures lined the bookcases behind him, along with a couple of drones and remote-controlled cars, and the desk itself was just a plain faux-birch table with a sleek monitor perched on top. Artifacts from his travels decorated one wall, a sign of how much life he'd lived compared to her.

"How was your weekend?" he asked.

Clare took a seat across from him. "The usual. Campaign is progressing nicely, and I got to spend some time with my aunt's dog."

Craig smiled indulgently. "How is Kiki?"

"She's good," she shrugged. She was used to making small talk with Craig but needed to figure out a way to bring it around to her pitch.

Craig tipped his head toward the door. "Derek broke up with his girlfriend. Again," he said in a hushed, confiding tone. "So I'm sure you understand why I had to go easy on him in there."

Clare searched for the right diplomatic response. "I thought his idea was good, I just think we're leaving money on the table. If we're serious about broadening our appeal, we can't just do what we've always done. I think that's what Leadership wants."

"Even if you're right, I'd assign this Captain Ellen—"

"Ellis."

"Captain Ellis, sorry. I'd still assign her development to someone else. Maybe if we switched the gender, made her male, that might make more sense. Captain Elliot, or something. You could even keep the rogue angle, have him have a female in every port."

"Those sorts of characters already exist," she argued. "Captain Ellis, female, would be different. And as I created her, I think I'd be the perfect person to build her into the narrative."

"I don't know about that," Craig said contemplatively. "If we did someone like that, I'd give it to Derek, probably. I know you want Noah's job, but to be Senior Game Designer material you have to be more of a go-getter."

Derek was a serial dater, but as far as she knew, his girlfriends never lasted longer than three months because he was a mansplainer of the highest order. Not exactly the love-'em-and-leave-'em type Craig was implying, but he did date a lot, she'd give him that. Clare shifted uncomfortably. "Because I'm not the type to have a one-night stand, you mean?" she asked.

"I don't know if I'd put it quite that crudely, but yes, that's the essence. You just don't have the experience."

"How—how could you be sure of that?"

"Don't be like that," he said with another wave of his hand. "No reason to take this so seriously. I'm just offering a bit of guidance."

"Guidance," she repeated dully. Craig was always offering her guidance and pushing her to think bigger, she reminded herself. This might be a little more personal, but it was in the same vein as when he wanted her to practice with the weapons to get a feel for them.

Right?

"Writing a character takes life experience," he said.

"I don't mean to be argumentative, but I don't have a lot of life experience as a tentacle monster, either."

Craig laughed, and a little of the tension in the room bled away. "Touché. I just feel—this sort of character and storyline might be a tough sell, and if you're serious about it, you'd need to do it properly. Prove you know how to handle something like that."

"But if I can prove that to you, you'll seriously consider it? Including Captain Ellis in the new adventure, and letting me write her?"

He scratched the side of his nose. "You know what, yeah. If you go out and get yourself some real-life experience, I'll consider it."

"I just have to prove to you I can—I can, um, have a one-night stand?"

Craig smiled. "I knew you were a smart one." Clare shifted and reminded herself that he meant that as a compliment.

He leaned forward, a conspiratorial grin on his face. "You know I'm just looking out for you, right? I don't want you to pitch something you can't handle and fall on your face again. Remember the fiasco with the online teaser?"

Clare smiled back weakly. She had jumped at the chance to work on that project her first two months at Quest, but it had landed with a thud with their audience. It wasn't entirely her fault—she personally felt Noah had escaped without shouldering his share of the blame—but it had been humiliating. After the fact, Craig had pointed out that as someone who had never been in a kayak, she probably wasn't the right person to handle a story about a river adventure and sent her out to try her hand at it.

He'd been right on that account, she had to admit. It was a lot more strenuous than she'd expected, and even though that didn't have a ton to do with whether or not the audience responded to a teaser, she deferred to his experience there.

And she didn't have much experience with one-night stands of any kind, that much was very true. She'd always been a girlfriend-girl, but if she wanted to be a serious writer, maybe she did need to push herself out of her comfort zone, get some more exposure to things she hadn't done before. Working for Quest was Clare's dream, after all. *Achieving your dreams means thinking outside the box, right?* "I see your point," she said, and Craig's smile grew a touch warmer.

"It's just about life experience, kid. Nothing more. And if you want that job . . ." he said, trailing off pointedly, "well, you're going to have to prove it." Maybe his kindly tone didn't land quite right, but she knew what he meant.

And she also knew what she had to do.

Chapter Six

"Hold the door!" Logan called, jogging through the exposed-brick lobby toward the elevator. He had been Instagram-stalking Amber as he walked, eyes barely lifting from his phone. She had posted a photo of her with a bland-looking guy, grinning cheek-to-cheek as they squinted into the sun. The man could have been anyone—a brother, even—but Logan knew instinctively it was the guy she wanted to date.

Logan just didn't get it. They were both white guys who looked good in a suit. All that guy had that Logan didn't was a face that was a seven out of ten at best, while Logan was frequently told he was a nine or nine point five.

Am I too good-looking? Is that it?

He couldn't say for sure, and the fact of the matter was, no woman in the last ten years had given him so much as a glancing consideration of being the sort of man you took home to meet your parents. He could hardly say he was blameless in this, but still. Amber saying it so blatantly had wounded his considerable pride, and he was fixating. He glanced up from his phone long enough to hit the button for his floor and then clicked over to Amber's new boyfriend's profile, but it was private.

"Dammit," he mumbled, and the person next to him snorted.

"Instagram-stalking not working out for you?" The Nerd asked, grinning up at him.

"Didn't your dad teach you not to read over people's shoulders?" he replied, unable to stop his own smile.

"Your phone was practically in my face, there were no shoulders involved," she said as the door slid shut. "Besides, you're like a foot taller than me. I'd never be able to see over your shoulders." She hit the button for the floor below his and cocked her head. "Who were you looking up?"

"No one," he said, pocketing his phone. "No dog today?"

"Just coming home from work. I'll have Kiki next weekend, though."

"Should a dognapper be broadcasting their plans?"

"You going to rat me out?" she said without missing a beat.

The elevator juddered to a stop and Logan's retort died on his lips. "Are you fucking kidding me?" he grumbled. The building had two elevators, each of shocking unreliability considering how much he paid in rent. Plenty of times he just took the stairs to avoid this possibility, but six flights was a long-ass walk, and he was tired today.

Clare already had her phone out. "Yeah, it's 5D," she said without preamble. "Elevator's stuck again." She paused and jerked her chin at Logan. "Which one are we in? I wasn't paying attention."

"West," he said, and she relayed the information.

Logan pried the doors open a few inches, only to find solid, bare wall. "Between floors," he reported, and she glanced up at the screen above the door.

"Between four and five, no way out," she told the super. She paused, listening, and rolled her eyes. "I appreciate it, but also . . . come on, this needs to stop. This has got to be an ADA violation. Yeah, yeah, I know." She hung up and sighed heavily. "The super is going to call the fire department and reset the system in the meantime. If the reset doesn't work, the fire department should be here in twenty minutes."

"We pay entirely too much to deal with this bullshit," he said, taking off his messenger bag and setting it by his feet.

"We do, but I'd say even people in cheap buildings deserve functioning infrastructure no matter their socioeconomic status," she said, and he realized belatedly she had scolded him, just so gently he almost missed it.

"Fair enough," he said, glancing around the elevator to cover his embarrassment. "But that still means we have twenty minutes to kill."

"That we do," she agreed, because the super always promised to try "resetting the system" when the elevator failed, but it never worked. She leaned back against the side of the elevator, looking up at him.

She was cute, for sure. Not his usual type, but appealing. And she was funny, that much he had established during their first short conversation. There were far worse ways to spend twenty minutes.

"So what do you do? When you aren't dognapping, obviously," he said, leaning against the other side.

"I'm a game designer for Quest Gaming," she replied.

"Oh, so like . . . video games?"

"Tabletop role-playing, actually. There is a video game division, but I'm on the tabletop side, which is way bigger."

Logan wasn't entirely sure what that was, to be honest, but the way she said it seemed like she expected him to know, so he nodded. "Impressive."

"It is," she said cheekily. "You?"

"Not very impressive, sorry to say." He waited for her

chuckle, absurdly pleased with himself when she did. "I work in finance," he said vaguely. That was all he said usually, since the women he was talking to normally didn't care.

"I have an aunt who works in finance," she replied. "It always sounds so interesting."

"It isn't," he said honestly. "But I make a decent amount of money doing it, so I guess I don't really care."

She gave him a small grin and once again, he felt stupidly proud of himself. It didn't seem that hard to make her smile, and yet he felt like he deserved a medal. Her phone rang and she grimaced at the number. "Yeah?" she answered, and then sighed. "Are you kidding me?" Another long pause. "Yeah, I'll tell the other tenant stuck in here with me. And seriously, if you don't get this fixed, I'll be talking to my lawyer." She hung up, looking disgruntled. "Fire department is busy on an emergency call, and since we're safe, we're stuck until they can get to us. Probably going to be a while. More than twenty minutes, I'd guess."

"You have a lawyer?" he asked.

"What? No, that was just a bluff. But I might start calling around, because I hate this." And with that, she sank to the floor and opened her Minnesota Public Radio branded tote bag. She stuck her bare legs out in front of her, crossed at the ankles, and rearranged her bright blue skirt above her knees. "Good thing I have provisions."

Logan watched as she pulled out a bottle of white wine. "Too bad you don't have a corkscrew."

Clare laughed and cracked the top with a twist of her wrist. "Bold of you to assume I buy anything more expensive than ten dollars," she said, and took a pull straight from the bottle.

"You're just diving right in, aren't you?"

"I was going to get drunk in my apartment, but since I won't be getting there for at least another hour I figure why not get drunk in the elevator with my neighbor?" She shrugged and pulled a second bottle out of her bag—this one red—and held it out to him. "Want some?"

Fuck it. It wasn't like he had anything better to do. "Sure," he said, taking the bottle and twisting off the cap as he sat down next to her. It was, he quickly discovered, absolutely terrible wine. "You paid ten dollars for this shit?" he coughed.

"I said I don't buy anything that costs *more* than ten dollars. That one cost me seven."

"Tastes like it," he said. Logan made a face and took another drink. "Wait, no, I think you got ripped off."

She tipped her head to the side. "Are you a wine snob?"

"Apparently," he said. "And it seems we've established you're not."

"I'm economical with my money," Clare said primly, her tone at odds with the healthy swig she took from her bottle.

"And careless with your tastebuds," he muttered, but still went back for more. "Bad day?"

"A usual day, more like," she said, and leaned her head back against the elevator wall. "I work with a lot of men. It's exhausting sometimes."

He thought about Sam and similar complaints he'd heard from her. He had a strange feeling these two could be friends, even though Clare was all optimism and friendly banter and Sam was, well, Sam. She was mean as hell and he liked that about her, but she was an acquired taste. "I work with a lot of bros," he said, and his gaze landed on her ankles, delicate below her shapely calves. "We're a lot to deal with," he agreed.

"You know, you could do something about that," she said, closing her eyes. He wished she hadn't, because he hadn't yet decided if her eyes were green or brown. "Agreeing that men suck is not actually the same thing as doing something to make your workplace more friendly for people who are not cis men."

Logan couldn't help but nod. Her cheeks were pink, flushed from the alcohol, and he fought the urge to reach out and straighten the folded-up corner of her Peter Pan collar. "How long did they say we would be stuck here?" he asked.

"Sick of me already?"

"Wondering how much time I get to spend with you," he said before he realized what he was doing. His mouth had a way of going on autopilot before his brain caught up, and maybe this was his problem. But he couldn't really help it, flirting came as naturally to him as breathing.

She turned to look at him, her nose just bare inches from his. She licked her lips, looking at his mouth, and then lifted her eyes to meet his gaze.

"Do you even know my name?"

Chapter Seven

He blinked, and Clare cursed herself for interrupting what was looking to be a promising moment. But she couldn't help it. She had never kissed someone whose name she didn't officially know, and his overt flirting had caught her off guard.

Maybe Craig had been on to something. The part of her who had been a shy, awkward nerd in high school—or maybe not shy, just not as comfortable in her own skin as she was now—kept wondering *why* this was happening. But the part of her who wanted to experience new things told her to stop thinking too hard.

But still. Logan was too handsome, too charming, too used to women who looked like underwear models to be interested, even slightly, in someone like her. *Reasonably cute* was her usual league, the sort of guy who would hardly stop traffic but who looked adorable in glasses, and probably had a poster of the Periodic Table in his apartment, and at least one *Doctor Who* mug in his cupboard.

Logan looked like he just walked off a movie set where he played a character who was technically a villain but actually just deeply wounded; a sensitive, dangerous soul with a smile the screenwriter would call *wicked* at least once.

He was the sort of guy who would ask her to tutor him in physics even though she wasn't that great at STEM stuff. (Guys like him just assumed all nerds were math and science nerds. The existence of English nerds was, apparently, still undiscovered by cool kids.) He'd flirt with her as a thank you, and then forget her name before final grades were posted.

Logan smiled at her, dark and, yes, a tiny bit dangerous in a way that *shouldn't* be sexy but *was*, and cocked an eyebrow. "Do you even know mine?" he asked.

A nervous giggle escaped her throat, puncturing the bubble of tension surrounding them. "I'm Clare," she said, and he—very regrettably—leaned away.

"Logan," he said amiably. "Sorry if I crossed a few lines there."

Clare was both relieved the world was returning to its axis and a little disappointed he had given up so easily. "We're two twenty-somethings stuck in an elevator; I think some hanky-panky can only be expected." She winced the second the words *hanky-panky* came out of her mouth. She might as well wear a sign that said *Prospective Mediocre Physics Tutor: No Sexual Interest Required*.

But Logan's eyes twinkled at her anyway. "You're saying it's the environment, not me? I'm hurt," he teased.

"Stuck in an elevator is a time-honored trope, I probably would have been disappointed if you didn't even try," she said, matching his tone. Perhaps the universe had been trying to do her a solid by throwing a one-night stand into her lap. Weirder things had happened, although she couldn't think of any at the moment.

"Well then, I'm glad I didn't let you down," he said. "Tell me, Clare, when you aren't stuck in an elevator, what do you do?"

"I already told you, I'm a game designer." She was disheartened he had forgotten that part of the conversation quite so quickly, but perhaps the universe wasn't as much on her side as she thought.

"I'm not so stupid that I forgot what you said five minutes ago," Logan replied. "I meant for fun. You walk your aunt's dog, and you said something about . . . a quest? Is that the same game you work for?"

Clare honestly couldn't believe he remembered that. "It is, yeah. Working for Quest Gaming is like, a dream come true for me. I've been playing Quest for Sulzuris since high school."

"Is that like Dungeons and Dragons?"

"Yes, but full disclosure—us Sulzurian nerds get really annoyed with that comparison. Tabletop RPG is a whole genre, not just one game."

"Understood. Are you, like, an elf?"

"In Sulzuris? I'm a human," she said, with a touch of unease. She had a pretty good sense of humor about herself generally, but guys like Logan—hot guys who liked sports and shit—generally found gaming mock-worthy. Clare wished the fire department would hurry up and rescue them already. The longer this conversation went on, the better the chance he would hit a nerve and she would wreck this fun-banter thing they had going.

"I didn't realize those games had regular humans in them," he said genuinely.

"I mean, I'm not *quite* a regular human. I'm a tavern wench whose mother was a Mage, so I have magical powers, but they aren't as strong as a full witch."

He nodded, seemingly processing it. "And you fight what, dragons?"

"There is a dragon army, yes, but there's a lot more to it."

"Like?"

She tipped her head to the side. "Are you really interested? Or is this building to some sort of weird massive humiliation where you mock me for this?"

Logan turned, surprise written all over his handsome face. "I would never!" he said, and he looked so honestly put-out that she would suspect him of anything like that, she had no choice but to believe him. Maybe he really wasn't like the guys she'd known in high school. "Has that really happened?"

"I mean, not on a grand scale or anything, but let's be real— guys like you have one interest in women like me." He lifted his eyebrows eloquently and she flushed. The universe was handing her a hot guy flirting with her on a platter the same week her boss had challenged her to find a one-night stand, and here she was, trying to talk him out of it by driving home just how big of a dork she could be. "Homework."

"You lost me."

"Guys who look like you want me to do their homework, and they think what I'm into is dorky."

He furrowed his brow. "Well, good news, I haven't had homework in a solid six years, so you're safe there."

"And playing a tabletop RPG?"

"Is something I am unfamiliar with, and I like learning new things."

She narrowed her eyes at him, scanning for any hint of mockery. But either he was a better liar than she had ever encountered, or he was legitimately interested.

Clare took a deep breath and launched into an explanation of the game. "It's the sort of thing that's easiest to understand while you're playing it, but it's basically telling a story as a group. There's a Game Master, who explains what's happening and offers players choices. So, for example, if you're in a party that's walked into a tavern, the GM will ask if you want to order a drink or go sit by the fire. One of the players will answer, and if it's a choice that has a couple of possible outcomes—like, say, you decide you want to attack an orcling with your sword—you roll dice to see how successful you are. There's more to it, like how good your character is at things like swordfighting, or magic, or whatever, but that's the gist. Our group has been on this really long campaign that is way too involved to explain right now, but long story short, my character just saved the world by kissing the villain and breaking the curse he was under."

"I see, so you like saving villains with the power of love," he said, but the glimmer in his eyes was friendly, not teasing.

"When they're hot and it's fictional, yes."

Logan grinned at her and was about to say something when a loud *bang* startled them both. "Fire Department. You okay in there?" a female voice called.

"Alive and well," Logan yelled back. "Looks like our rescuers have finally arrived," he said, standing and offering her a hand to pull her to her feet.

Clare wished her heart didn't do a silly little flip at his touch, but it did. "Thanks for listening to me ramble." She really should have taken the chance and kissed him when it seemed like he was going to—or at least would be amenable to it—earlier. It would have been the perfect opportunity to show Craig she was capable of casual sex. Logan, quite frankly, was the perfect opportunity to experience some casual sex. But the moment was dissipating like fog on a bright morning.

Logan held up his bottle of wine. "Thanks for the shitty wine. I owe you one," he said, just as the elevator began its slow, lurching descent.

* * *

The fire department was going to "check out" the elevators, which meant, after all that, Logan and Clare still had to take the stairs. She didn't mind as much as she normally did, though, because it meant spending just a little longer with Logan. But the steps were making her flushed and sweaty, and she wished she had at least half of the elegance and swagger of the women he brought home. Especially since he didn't seem to have any desire to bolt, which meant maybe she could put her slowly burgeoning plan into action.

One of the things that had always held Clare back from one-night stands was feelings: both hers, and the other person's. She didn't want to accidentally lead anyone on, but that felt like less of a problem with Logan. Having seen his revolving door of partners, she knew she wouldn't have to worry about him wanting anything more.

On the first landing Logan gave her a crooked grin that made her stomach flutter. "Here, let me take that," he said, slipping the tote bag off her shoulder. The now half-empty wine bottles clinked together as he climbed the stairs. She couldn't tell if he was just genuinely nice, or if there really was flirting behind it. And if there was flirting, was it just mindless flirting because Logan couldn't contain himself, or was it flirting with intent? Flirting with intent would make all of this much easier. She started trying to figure out a subtle way to invite him in, and then considered that maybe subtle wasn't really his style anyway. Maybe she should just ask.

They reached the fifth floor and Clare put her hand on the door to the hallway, half-expecting Logan to hand back the bag and continue on his way before she could figure out the least awkward way to say *Want to hook up?* But instead he shrugged. "I've got it," he said, and held the door open for her.

Clare did her best to control her glee while the handsome

guy walked her to her door. But being, as she had said earlier, nearly a foot taller than her, Logan's strides outpaced her and he drew to a stop in front of her door just before she did.

Clare had been rummaging for her keys in her purse, but she stopped short and frowned. "Wait, how did you know this was my door?"

Logan set the tote down and leaned his shoulder against the jamb. He lifted an eyebrow, eyes dark. "Are we really going to pretend we can't see into each other's apartments?" he asked. She wondered if he'd pitched his voice low to keep the neighbors from hearing him, or if it was just to make her lean in closer. Either way, it worked. A blush started crawling up her neck and she looked down. She really couldn't believe it was this easy. "I—I mean, I guess—"

He tilted his head. "Do you mean to tell me you haven't noticed me?" he asked with a softness to his tone. "I'm wounded."

"I think you're well aware that people notice you," she said, licking her lips. "In fact, I think that's something you're proud of. Too proud, even." It felt surreal to be standing in front of her door, flirting with Logan like it was the most natural thing in the world, and even more surreal that she was able to keep up with him.

This is really happening, she thought to herself. All she had to do was close the deal.

"You're not wrong there," he said, shrugging one shoulder. He tucked a lock of hair behind her ear.

Clare swallowed and laughed nervously. "Is that a line?"

"Do you care if it is?" he asked.

She chewed her lower lip, deliberating. It was a risk, since he was her neighbor and if things got awkward, she would still have to see him all the time. But on the other hand, the words *Logan* and *awkward* didn't really go together. Clare thought about the way Noah, Derek, and the rest of them had chuckled at Craig's insinuation that she wasn't the type to hook up, and gathered her courage. Logan was the perfect opportunity and she wasn't going to pass him up, nerves be damned. She was going to make this happen.

"Not really, no," she admitted, and rolled up on her tiptoes to kiss him.

Chapter Eight

Huh. Clare watched the light under the door in her en-suite bathroom shift as Logan moved around in there.

She officially had a one-night stand. And it was . . . fine? To be perfectly honest, she thought it would be a little better.

Not that sex with Logan had been bad. In fact, it had been quite good. He obviously knew what he was doing and had been more than sufficiently focused on her pleasure. It was fun and she enjoyed herself, but . . . well, *but*.

It wasn't exactly spectacular, and she had, perhaps wrongly, assumed that sex with someone as experienced as Logan would involve fireworks of some kind. Instead, it was just barely-above-average sex. But then again, she'd only ever had sex in relationships. Maybe this sort of hookup just didn't work for her.

Logan emerged from her bathroom and she forgot her doubts, because damn. He really was the hottest man she'd ever slept with, so she mentally upgraded the sex they'd just had from a six point five to a seven. His smile made an absurd pack of butterflies explode in her stomach, and to her surprise he slipped under the covers with her. "Hey, you," he said, with the exact right fondness-to-raspiness ratio.

He really did know what he was doing.

Clare looked down shyly. "Hey," she said softly. She had sort of assumed, when he'd gotten up to throw away the condom, he would be on his way out the door. She figured he would head out eventually, but for now she wasn't going to deny herself this.

Logan settled on the pillow next to her, his nose mere inches away. Just over an hour after she had officially learned his name, he was stretched out in her bed, naked.

Suck it, Craig.

"So I take it I can officially borrow a cup of sugar from you now?" he asked, eyes gleaming in the dim light.

Clare snorted, any lingering bashfulness forgotten. She made an exaggerated grimace and wrinkled her nose. "Actually, my bar for that is three orgasms, neighbor," she said, far too delighted when he threw his head back and laughed.

"You're funny, you know that?" he asked.

"Yes," Clare deadpanned, and they both burst into laughter again. Maybe it was for the best that the sex was only so-so, she thought, because if it had been good she would have been in a lot of trouble. Logan was a genuinely fun person to be around, in addition to looking like a prince who had gone undercover to escape the pressures of royal life. If that had been combined with mind-blowing sex, she probably would have gone and fallen in love with him.

This way, she could tell Craig she understood Captain Ellis Ravencroft well enough to write her, and maybe she and Logan could stay on good terms. Chats in the elevator, jokes in the lobby, that sort of thing. But first, she needed to figure out a way to get him out of her bed, because sleeping over seemed against the whole spirit of a quickie hookup.

Logan yawned and she fought the urge to reach out and

brush his dark hair off his forehead. They were flirting, sure, but that felt a little too tender for the moment. And she was supposed to be figuring out a way to kick him out. "You tired there, old sport?"

Okay, maybe not the best start at getting him to leave.

Logan narrowed his eyes. "Who you calling old?" he replied playfully. *Okay, so* Great Gatsby *references go over his head. Got it,* she thought, and then he yawned again. "But yeah, I am, actually," he said.

Clare hesitated. It was as good of an opening as she was going to get. "It is a real long walk back to your place," she said, hoping her dry tone softened the message.

"Too long," he said, either not picking up on her subtlety or ignoring it. *Not picking it up,* she decided. "Are you . . . staying?" she asked.

If she was going to start having one-night stands, she was going to have to get better at this part. Logan opened his eyes and studied her for a long moment. "Yeah, I think—I think that would be nice," he said.

Oh. He wanted to stay, and with every passing second she was losing any will to make him leave. Her eyes drank in the planes of his cheekbones, the faint stubble on his cheeks.

Fuck it. It still counted, even if there was a sleepover after. "G'night, neighbor," she said as playfully as possible.

Logan closed his eyes, a soft smile on his face. "Night, Clare," he whispered.

The next morning, Clare woke up before Logan. He was still on the other side of the bed, facing her. The only difference was his hand, which was now lying outstretched on her pillow, almost like he had been reaching for her. She gave herself a moment to study him, taking in the way sunlight painted the sharp planes of his face and softened them. When he was awake there was a sardonic edge to everything he did or said, but asleep he looked . . . not younger, exactly, but more vulnerable.

Clare brought that train of thought to a screeching halt and decided to get up. She had to keep this casual, and her usual instincts were rearing their heads.

She eased out from under the covers and dressed quickly, being sure to leave Logan's clothes on the floor, as that would only delay his sure-to-be-hasty exit. She hesitated with her *Zutara Forever* hoodie in her hand, and then remembered that a) he'd already seen her in her dorky-ass sweatshirt, and b) he'd already slept with her. No point in trying to pretend she was someone she wasn't.

Out in her kitchen, she felt better. It was her safe space, the place where baking replaced work stress with a peaceful vibe, like waves on a shore. When she was baking, she didn't have time to ruminate over how frustrated she was at work, or that there was an exceedingly handsome, naked man in her bed and she didn't know what to do about that. She really should have told him to leave last night, rather than letting him stay. In the cold light of day, she wondered if maybe he had stayed out of pity.

For the second time that morning she shook her head and forced herself to stop thinking that way. She started pulling out the necessary ingredients for blueberry muffins, and got the oven preheating. Muffins didn't take too long to make, so they'd either be almost ready by the time he got up or she'd have extra blueberry muffins for game day. The group wouldn't complain about that, at least.

The rhythms of baking—measuring, pouring, mixing— settled her down, and she had just slid the trays into the oven when Logan walked out of her bedroom.

Shirtless.

Thankfully, she could pretend it was the heat from the oven making her blush. "Morning, neighbor," he said easily, like this was a totally normal thing.

Well, for him it probably was.

She narrowed her eyes at him even as a smile threatened her face. "Are you calling me that because you forgot my name?"

Logan chuckled and rolled his eyes, sliding onto a stool at her kitchen counter like he wasn't wearing jeans designed by the devil himself, and nothing else. "No, I haven't, *Clare*," he said pointedly. "What's for breakfast?"

"What gave you the impression it's for you?" she teased. *Please don't stay for breakfast; just let this be what it was and go.* She had been counting on Logan's natural instincts to be to run, and now that they weren't, she was not mentally prepared to ask him to go.

"Probably the fact that we had sex last night," he said nonchalantly.

Clare laughed and checked her phone when it buzzed on the counter. *Oh right, Kiki,* she thought. She'd forgotten what day it was, but this was a perfect excuse. He wouldn't want to have to meet her aunt. "Just a heads-up, my aunt is bringing Kiki over now," she said.

"Are you kicking me out? Without even any—" he sniffed the air, "—blueberry scones?"

"Close, muffins. And I didn't mean—it's just, a year ago she walked in and my ex—well, he wasn't my ex then, he was my boyfriend, but he's my ex *now*—was here, and he was only in his boxers and—"

Logan had slipped off the stool as she rambled and approached her, silencing her with a gentle finger to her lips. "And you'd appreciate it if I'd go put a shirt on?"

Honestly, she'd rather he never wear a shirt ever again, especially now that he was standing close enough that she could feel the heat pouring off his body, but really the best option was for him to leave. Aunt Peggy might be the coolest aunt around, but she did have some limits. She could probably handle walking into a morning-after situation, since she understood Clare was most likely not a virgin. But he should at least be dressed, especially if Logan was so determined to stay.

Clare sighed, giving in. She didn't really want him to leave anyway. "Yeah, I think that'd be for the best. And she doesn't live too far away, so maybe now?"

Logan gave her a mock salute and headed for her bedroom. He moved with an easy, unconscious grace; as she watched his backside, Clare wondered idly if he'd ever taken dance classes.

Blinking herself out of yet another reverie, Clare checked the muffins and pulled them out to cool. Logan took his time in her room, and she wondered if maybe he was hiding from Aunt Peggy. That wouldn't be the worst thing, but Aunt Peggy tended to be very perceptive and would probably notice his shoes at the door. She'd put two and two together fast enough.

But Logan proved her wrong yet again as he strode out of her bedroom in the long-sleeved, button-down shirt he'd been wearing yesterday. It was considerably more crumpled than it had been in the elevator, but there was no helping that. He picked up a muffin, juggling it from hand to hand because they were still hot, and grinned mischievously at her just as Aunt Peg's key turned in the lock.

Kiki's nails pattered against the hardwood floor as the dog trotted in happily, her owner close on her heels.

"Sorry I'm so early, but I thought I'd get a start on—" Aunt Peggy stopped, a curious expression crossing her face.

"A start on what? And Aunt Peggy, this is my, um, neighbor Logan," Clare said, glancing over at Logan.

He looked like he'd seen a ghost.

Chapter Nine

There wasn't anything Logan could do except stare, because this wasn't happening. It couldn't be. This was a nightmare, and at some point he would wake up in his own bed, relieved to discover it was all a dream and that his boss hadn't just walked into the apartment of his latest hookup.

Logan blinked. Peggy Roth fixed him with a stern look and no, this wasn't a nightmare or a hallucination. This was real, and this was hell.

"Good morning, Mr. Walsh," she said coolly.

"Morning, uh, ma'am," he said. Logan rarely ever used her name in the office, never quite sure if Ms. Roth, or Peggy, or Madame Vice President was more appropriate. "Ma'am" seemed sufficiently deferential though, and Logan was prepared to do his best impression of a private greeting a general if necessary.

Why the fuck didn't I leave last night? he thought, annoyed with himself for being so sappy. Clare had been so cute he hadn't wanted to, even though he almost never bothered to stay the night with anyone. And now the universe was making him pay for that moment of sentimentality.

Clare looked between them, clearly bewildered. "Wait, you know each other?"

"He works for me," Peggy said. "I take it you didn't know that," she added, with a look askance at Logan.

He was completely fucked.

"Definitely not," he said as quickly as possible, just as Clare shook her head *no* to her aunt's question. "We're, uh, neighbors. Like she said." *Please don't ask why I'm here at nine in the morning in the clothes I was wearing at the office yesterday, please don't ask why I'm here at nine in the—*

"I see," Peggy said in a tone that indicated she knew *exactly* why Logan was there at nine in the morning in the clothes he'd been wearing at the office yesterday.

You like the chase, Mr. Walsh. Perhaps Peggy had a point, and not just about his work.

Clare's smile wavered. "So, you're off to Duluth?" she said to Peggy, clearly struggling to sound casual. Logan was no help, because his mind was just a steady stream of *fuckfuckfuckfuckfuckfuckfuuuuuuuuuuck.*

"Little farther this time; going up to Bayfield. There's some good camping around there in the National Forest," Peggy said with yet another side-eye toward him.

"Aunt Pegs likes camping," Clare said, and then furrowed her brow. "Or I guess . . . you'd know that?"

The barest glimmer of a smile flitted across Peggy Roth's face. "I don't really talk about my hobbies at work, so he probably doesn't."

"That sounds, uh, fun," Logan said unconvincingly. He briefly wondered why she wouldn't take her dog camping—as far as he knew, dogs loved that shit—but as always, Peggy Roth was one step ahead of him.

"Kiki gets carsick on long trips," she explained. "And Clare loves her, so she stays here."

Logan made an understanding noise and for two painful hours—or maybe just ten seconds—the three of them looked at each other. "Well," Peggy said, clapping her hands together. "I guess I'm off then."

Clare moved over to kiss her aunt on the cheek, walking her to the door and closing it behind her. She bent to absently scratch Kiki's head on her way back, while Logan's heartbeat tried and failed to return to normal.

"Well, that was awkward as hell, sorry about that," Clare said with a grin that Logan desperately wanted to return. But the easy banter of just a few minutes ago had evaporated, because all Logan could think about was the conversation he'd had with Peggy the other day. About how immature he was, how he needed to stop playing the field and settle down.

And now he'd gone and fucked her niece.

Logan headed off the court to the bench where they stored their water bottles. Once a week he played a pick-up basketball game with some of his coworkers at an outdoor court just across the river from downtown. To be perfectly honest they weren't the best group of guys, but they were probably the closest thing to a group of friends Logan had outside of Sam. Well, Vince was decent, but he only played occasionally, thanks to having a brand-new baby at home.

Being in his late twenties was strange, sometimes. It was perfectly normal and acceptable to have friends with wives and babies and mortgages, like Vince, and friends who still lived in slightly shitty bachelor pads, like the Aidens. Logan felt like he was somewhere in the middle, since he had a decent apartment that didn't reek of cologne like the Aidens', but he and the

Aidens did share the same hobby of sleeping around. But some-times he didn't like having that in common with them, as there was a mercenary bent to the way the Aidens approached it that made him vaguely uncomfortable sometimes.

"Almost had you this time," Vince said genially. He worked with Logan and the Aidens at Loyalty Investments, and had just gotten back from his paternity leave. Vince used his shirt to mop his face, his dark brown skin shining with perspiration, and tossed Logan his water bottle.

Logan caught it with one hand. It was only May, but already the heat was borderline oppressive. "Next time it'll be you and me against those two assholes," Logan suggested. "They won't stand a chance."

"Doubt it," Brooks said, collapsing onto the bench. His blond hair was dripping, and he was breathing hard, skin flushed. He pulled out his phone and held it up for them to see. "Left or right?" he asked, showing them a picture of a leggy blonde.

"Right," Logan and Aiden said, just as Vince said "Left."

Vince shrugged. "There's a million other white girls who look exactly the same."

"Yeah, well, not all of us are lucky enough to be married to a woman like Nicole," Logan said, and Vince grinned proudly.

Brooks looked back at his phone. "Right," he said, more to himself than anyone else.

Aiden flopped onto the small patch of grass behind the bench. He had a terrible sunburn on his face in the outline of sunglasses, giving him the impression of a red-and-white rac-coon. "I'm sick of dating apps," he whined. "Want to go out this weekend?"

"You're just hoping Logan will chum the waters for you," Brooks said, still flipping through his phone.

"And? Not my fault women flock to him. I'm just taking the path of least resistance."

"Like a parasite," Logan said, draining his water.

"I prefer to think of it as a symbiotic relationship," Aiden said, arm now draped over his eyes. "Like those birds that live in alligators' mouths, or whatever."

"Plovers, and they don't live in alligators' mouths. They ride on crocodiles' backs and sometimes clean their teeth," Vince explained.

"How do you know that? Do they have biology requirements in MBA programs and I missed it?" Logan asked.

"Nicole and I had a lot of time to watch nature documentaries while she was breastfeeding," he explained. "PBS is free, you know."

"Whatever," Aiden said. "I'm just a baby bird, looking to get laid."

Logan rolled his eyes. He had spent plenty of Friday nights moving from club to club downtown with the Aidens, usually in search of someone to take home, but the way they were talking about it was annoying him for some reason.

"I'm in," Brooks said, because of course he was. "Logan?"

Logan made a noncommittal noise. "I don't know," he said.

Aiden frowned at him. "What's got your dick in a vise?"

Vince grimaced and stood. "On that awful image, I have to get home and get dinner going," he said, picking up his bag. "See you guys later."

Aiden turned on him the second Vince was gone. "Seriously, you got the clap or something? Because my doctor—"

"I do not have an STI," Logan interrupted. "I just—I sorta fucked up this weekend."

"Condom broke," Brooks said understandingly. "It happens to the best of us."

"It wasn't that. I, uh, well, Roth sorta chewed me out in her office the other day about how my clients don't really stick around, and she kept bringing up my *maturity*."

"So, you banged her," Brooks said. "I get it, she's kinda hot for an old lady."

"Jesus. Fucking. Christ," Logan said, Sam's words running through his head. *The Aidens can be utter cavemen, especially the not-Aiden one.* He would probably regret telling them this, but Sam would tear him a new one and he was looking for at least a tiny bit of sympathy. "I didn't sleep with my boss. I slept with her niece," he said, and regretted it the second the words came out of his mouth.

Both Aidens cracked up and Brooks even tried to high-five him, clearly not grasping the severity of the situation. "No, it's bad," he tried to explain over their wheezing laughter. "Roth came by the next morning and caught me there."

That was the wrong detail to add, because they just laughed harder. Aiden even had tears streaming down his face. Logan wished Vince was still there to be the voice of reason, but as his dad would say, if wishes were fishes, or whatever. Logan never really understood that one.

Brooks calmed down first. "Okay, aside from being fucking hilarious, what's the problem? So she knows you fucked her niece; it's not like she can fire you for that."

"No, but she already thinks I'm immature and untrustworthy, so what's she going to do when she realizes it was just a fuck?"

Brooks shrugged. "Then fix it."

Logan rolled his eyes. "How? I can't unfuck her niece."

"If only that were possible," Brooks said wistfully. "There's so many women I'd unfuck. But no, you date her. Or make an attempt, anyway. How hot is she?"

Logan hesitated, because while he thought Clare was

pretty damn cute, he knew the Aidens probably wouldn't agree. They regularly swiped left on women more traditionally hot, largely because they had a slightly inflated sense of their own handsomeness.

Brooks read his hesitation wrong and made a face. "That bad, huh?" he asked.

"Fuck you," Logan snapped. "That's not it."

"You're the one who implied it."

"I did not."

"Did too," Brooks said petulantly. "But whatever, especially if she's not that hot, just take her out for a few drinks then let her down easy. If Roth asks her about you, she'll probably be all excited someone so hot dared talk to her, and then you won't be in trouble with Roth. A few dates later you tell her you think she deserves someone better than you, and you're letting her move on. Boom, problem solved."

Logan thought about it for a second and shook his head. Clare was too smart to fall for that.

"You could still come out with us, you know," Aiden wheedled. "You don't have to bring the niece, you could just come and hang out, and let us benefit from your face."

Logan considered correcting him and telling them Clare's name, but then he thought better of it. He shook his head and started packing up. "Not up for it this weekend," he said. "Maybe next."

Aiden nodded. "Count me in," he said to Brooks as Logan headed out. "And let's just hope Logan doesn't turn into another Captain Boring like Vince," he added.

Logan had almost made it to his car when someone called his name. Recognizing the voice he swore and turned around. "Wimberley," he said in a cheerful voice he reserved for his most annoying clients. "How've you been?"

Wimberley had his own bag slung over his shoulder, although he'd chosen to get it monogrammed with *Girl Dad*, as he clearly thought constantly telling people he had daughters made him a feminist. Marc Wimberley was an absolutely insufferable asshole Logan had known since college; he had been with the same woman since high school, a bland but pretty blonde who could have been his sister, given the resemblance, and whom Wimberley frequently referred to as "the missus." Wimberley shook Logan's hand, like they were meeting in a conference room for the first time, and Logan barely managed to stifle his eyeroll. "Oh, you know. Wife and kids keeping me busy," he said, finally letting go of Logan's hand. "You?"

"Oh no, my wife and kids are giving me a lot of free time," Logan replied and right on cue, Wimberley chuckled like Logan had said something funny.

"How's work?" Wimberley asked, and Logan's antennae went up. In addition to being a smarmy bore, the man had a reputation. But where Logan's reputation was the relatively harmless "enjoys giving women orgasms," Wimberley's was "will steal your clients like a fucking snake." That smiley, white Americana, polos-and-boat-shoes motherfucker was the dirtiest player in the game, and Logan knew exactly what he was up to.

Logan affected an unconcerned frown. "The same."

Wimberley's eyes gleamed and Logan curled his hand into a fist. "Big stuff in the works, but I can't say anything," Wimberley teased, tapping the side of his nose.

Does he think he's being subtle? Logan smiled and readjusted his bag, grinning at the man who was trying to get him fired. "Happy for you, man, but I have to get going."

"Got a lady friend waiting for you?"

Lady friend? Was he born in 1940? Jesus fucking Christ. "Going to visit my dad," Logan replied. *Two can play at that wholesome shit*, he thought viciously, and then realized he *did* owe Burt a visit sometime soon. He made a mental note of that and waved to Wimberley. "See you around," Logan said, but in his mind, he was already vowing to grind that jackass into dust.

Chapter Ten

Logan had arranged the wine ahead of time with the waitstaff, since Schneider was notoriously picky and rude when a bottle didn't live up to his expectations. Logan knew the staff at Red Steer well, and he didn't want to expose them to one of Schneider's scoldings. He was in for one himself and there was no point in putting anyone else through it, too. He knew Schneider's tastes well—something he prided himself on—and made sure to be sitting at the table a good ten minutes before their agreed-upon time, just to be safe.

This was the first step in his mission to save the Schneider account. He hoped a lunch and some good old-fashioned wooing would be enough, because if it wasn't, he was screwed.

Within three minutes of Schneider arriving, Logan knew it wouldn't. Schneider barked orders at the server, and then eyed Logan suspiciously when he tried to be nice to put the server more at ease. "This is what I mean," Schneider grumbled under his breath as she left.

Logan pretended not to hear him. "How are things, John?" he said in an attempt to control the tenor of the conversation. He needed Schneider to like him more than he did right now, that was all. He could do that. "Now that it's ice-out up on Lake Superior, are you going to be taking the *Gertrude* out?" The *Gertrude* was Schneider's schooner, named after his beloved and long-deceased mother. It was large enough that sailing it on most of Minnesota's lakes wasn't possible, and he owned a summer home up near Grand Marais for the sole purpose of having a private launch for her.

Schneider harrumphed, which was never a good sign. "Neighbors complained about some work we were having done on the shore, and now the county's involved. Enough to put me off it entirely. Might sell it all just so I can stop dealing with their nonsense."

Okay, so they weren't off to the best start. "I'm sorry to hear that. How's Theresa?"

"Spending most of her time down with the grandbaby in St. Louis."

Right, his daughter had just had a baby. "Boy or girl?" he asked, leaning back to let the server nervously place a refill of the bread on the table. Logan smiled at her, which led to another *harrumph* from across the table.

"Boy. But I think we need to cut to the chase here. We have a problem."

At least he wasn't wasting Logan's time. He sat up straighter. "I have heard that you're unhappy, and I asked you here to—"

"It's that business," Schneider interrupted, waving his hand at Logan and the empty space where the server had been. "You're too much of a pretty boy. I want someone I can count on, someone reliable. A family man."

Logan really hadn't thought he would be this blunt, which meant things were dire indeed. He also hadn't been flirting with the server in the slightest, but arguing that point would get him nowhere. He put on a smile and kept his voice soothing. "I'm very sorry to hear that, and while it's true I'm not married, I can assure you, I am working with your best interests at heart." When Schneider didn't so much as crack a smile, he decided to try another direction. "But if you'd be happier with someone with a family, my colleague Vince is an excellent financial advisor and new father. I could put you in touch with him, because above all else we want you happy at Loyalty." Losing Schneider would be terrible for his portfolio, but maybe if he could keep Schneider at Loyalty Logan wouldn't lose his job immediately.

"I already told Roth I'm not interested in switching. You're the third advisor I've had there, and what I want is stability. Stability, and values. Like Marc Wimberley over at Confidential Wealth, for example. You know him? Married, three kids, pretty wife."

Fucking Wimberley. "Values," Logan echoed. He had an idea of where Schneider was going, but quite frankly, he was going to make the man say it himself.

"Values. *Family* values."

Logan made himself nod, as if he was taking this seriously. He was, in the sense that his job was on the line if he couldn't convince Schneider he was steady enough. Sometimes, though, with prospective hookups and with clients, the best way to handle things was to give them another option. "What's stopping you? If you're unhappy and he's the kind of advisor you want, I know he'd happily take your business." *Please don't fall for it, please don't fall for it, please don't fall for it,* Logan mentally chanted as he waited.

"I was with Loyalty when it started. I value that."

Well, that was a reason, at least. "As I said, I understand that my marital status is giving you pause, but—"

Schneider waved his hand and tucked into the steak in front

of him. "I don't care so much about the vows; I just want to know you're settled. Not playing around. Committed."

Logan desperately wanted to ask him what the hell his dating life had to do with his ability to invest money, but he had to get out of this somehow. "As it happens, I am seeing someone." Sam would kill him for this, but desperate times called for desperate measures, or whatever. They had been friends long enough that if Schneider called his bluff and demanded a dinner, they could fake it.

Getting through dinner without Sam peeling Schneider's face off with her bare hands was not going to be easy, but Logan had to get through this meal first.

Schneider looked at him suspiciously. "You are?"

"I am," he said with a confidence he did not feel. If Schneider even suspected he was winging it, he was done for.

"Then I'd like to meet her," Schneider replied.

"She's a busy woman," Logan evaded.

"If she wants you to keep your job, she'll find time," Schneider growled. He eyed Logan again. "I've heard stories about you."

"Stories?" Logan asked mildly.

"About your . . . dating habits."

Fucking. Wimberley. Out loud, Logan merely said, "I'm not sure where you got that information, but I assure you, I've turned over a new leaf."

"Then prove it. Dinner with me and Theresa and this woman of yours."

"Clare," Logan corrected automatically, and his stomach jolted. *What the fuck did I just say?* He had meant to say Sam, but his brain, which had been insisting on thinking about how cute Clare had been that morning before Peggy arrived and it all went to hell, had gone and fucked it all up. Now he was going to have to either get Sam to pretend her name was

Clare—and she would like that even less than spending time with a guy like Schneider, so that plan was looking less and less viable by the second—or he would have to do what his idiot friends suggested, and make this thing with Clare real. He watched Schneider chew the last bite of steak, considering Brooks' words from the basketball game. While he didn't really like the way Brooks had talked about Clare, it wasn't the worst idea.

It wasn't the best, either, but Logan was desperate. And now that he'd gone and told Schneider that his girlfriend's name was Clare, his options for fixing this had narrowed to basically one. He had to get Clare to date him.

It couldn't be that hard. She was already into him, and he didn't mind spending time with her. Who knows, maybe she would even get bored with him the way most women did eventually. She might even end up dumping him first; he just needed to make sure it was after she agreed to have dinner with Schneider.

Oh, he was so, so fucked.

Schneider just grunted. "The wife wants me down in St. Louis with the grandson for a few weeks, but I'll be back next month. Call my secretary and set it up." He threw his napkin down on the plate and leaned back, clearly thinking he had set a trap for Logan.

Logan just hoped he could get out of it.

Chapter Eleven

Clare loved the rain. Which sounded maudlin and emo, for sure, but she did. Especially thunderstorms on humid summer days, when she could sit inside her dry, cozy apartment with the sliding door open to her tiny deck, smelling the petrichor and listening to the soothing slap of raindrops on cement.

Thunder cracked and a distant siren wailed, but otherwise the streets were quiet. She rested her feet on the chair next to her and breathed in. The half-eaten pan of brownies lay nearby on the table, and the horn-tipped hood from her onesie flopped back off her hair.

A unicorn onesie was annoying as hell to pee in, but whatever, it was cozy and fun and she was an adult and there was no one in the world who could stop her from buying it, so she had, and had zero regrets. And tonight, she wanted to bake brownies in a unicorn onesie and then eat them fresh from the pan, all on her own.

Besides, she felt good. She had managed to have sex with a super-hot guy, and now that she had that experience under her belt, she figured she should be able to land at least one more, easy. Then she could tell Craig in no uncertain terms she was, in fact, the person to write Captain Ellis Ravencroft. It was awkward to more or less announce to your boss that you'd just had sex, but Craig was the one who told her to go get some life experience. She knew there was a gap between who she was at home and who she was at work—Clare-who-played-as-Yaen always spoke her mind and didn't care what others thought of her, while Clare-at-work was much less confident—and she hoped this would be the start of a new version of herself at work, one that was more like her non-work self. There was still the matter of getting Captain Ellis integrated into the pitch, but she had weeks to cross that bridge. Even if Leadership shot it down, it was worth the effort.

And while it was odd that it turned out Logan was Peggy's employee—making last Saturday way, way more awkward than it needed to be—it could have been worse. When Peggy came back on Sunday to pick up Kiki, they had talked things out, with Aunt Peggy admitting she wasn't expecting to see any man, much less her direct report, in her niece's kitchen on a Saturday morning. Peggy had seemed wary of Logan, although not outright disapproving. It was probably his reputation, but the fact that his reputation was why Clare wanted to sleep with him was probably more detail than either of them wanted to get into. She agreed to give Peggy a heads-up on unexpected house guests—including names—in the future, and that was that. All things considered, her life was going pretty well.

Someone knocked on her door and Clare put her feet down, smothering a sigh. It was probably Jennifer from two floors down, who sometimes got her mail. She didn't love the idea of a neighbor seeing her dressed like this, but the alternative was making Jennifer stand in the hall for an absurdly long time while Clare changed into normal clothes, all for a thirty-second exchange.

"Hey," she started, swinging the door inward, but then her mouth went dry and every other thought in her head flew away like a Sulzurian faerie caught in a hurricane.

Because standing on her threshold was Logan. After the other night it was somehow even harder to look him in the eye, but she made herself do it, realizing way too late what she might look like to him.

But he just grinned that cocky half-grin, like she wasn't standing there in a white, pink, and purple fuzzy onesie with a rainbow mane. "What's with the get-up?" he asked, stepping past her into her apartment.

"What do you want?" she said, more out of shock than anything else. When he'd left on Saturday, she'd sort of gotten the impression he wasn't planning on seeing her ever again.

Which was fine. That was the whole point and Clare was fine with it. Totally, completely fine.

"I owe you for the wine."

"Um," she said eloquently.

Logan dropped a ten-dollar bill on her counter. "I'm overpaying you in the hopes you buy yourself something slightly better next time. And do you wear that all the time? Is this like, a thing I should know about?"

His gentle teasing pulled her out of her stupor. "Only if you're going to be showing up at my door randomly."

He shrugged, so apparently he would be. "Do you have a matching one? I'm feeling left out."

"Everything I have will be about a foot too short for you, so no."

"But there *are* other onesies, got it."

"Just a Chewbacca one," she muttered.

"There's a Chewie one? That's settled, I need to try it on. Where is it?"

"Shut up, it's only for nerds."

Logan looked affronted. "I like nerd stuff," he protested, and Clare rolled her eyes. "What? I do. I like *Star Wars*," he insisted.

"Everyone likes *Star Wars*," Clare countered. "My *mom* likes *Star Wars*."

Logan leaned his elbow on her countertop. "Prequels, originals, or sequels?"

"Sequels. She's really into Kylo Ren. I think it's the hair."

"He does have excellent hair," Logan said thoughtfully.

"Not that I'm not enjoying this banter, but did you really come over to pay me for the wine?"

"Is that such a surprise?"

"Well, you hated it. So yeah, kind of."

"I don't like having debts," Logan said. "And besides, you're fun." He glanced around her apartment like he was looking for something. "No Kiki today?"

"I only have her when Aunt Peg is out of town, so no. But did you . . . want something?" Clare said, deciding to cut to the chase.

Logan looked startled. "Want something?"

"I know you said before you didn't need me to do your homework, but seriously, why are you here?"

"Can't I just want to hang out with you?"

"I mean, no offense, but isn't that like . . . your whole thing? Not returning to the scene of the fuck, or whatever?"

Logan laughed and shook his head. "Couldn't I have another reason? Don't you have, like, friends? You can't play that *Sulzuris* game alone," he said.

"Of course I have friends. They just don't look like *you*."

"What, devastatingly handsome?"

"In a word, yes." Silence surrounded them and Clare cursed her inability to keep her damn mouth shut.

Logan, however, looked delighted. "You think I'm handsome?"

"You have a mirror."

"I do, but it doesn't tell me I'm handsome nearly enough."

"Something tells me you don't need a lot of verbal reassurance," Clare said, unable to stop her grin.

"That doesn't mean it isn't nice to hear," he said, and he winked, like that was a thing people actually did. "But you're right, I did have an ulterior motive for stopping by. I'd understand if you're, uh, busy—" he gestured at her onesie then, "—but if you're free, I was thinking of going out tonight with a few friends."

Clare raised her brows. "Define 'going out,' because I don't know if you've caught my vibe, exactly, but it's not really 'clubbing.'"

He leaned his hip against her counter, arms crossed. "We're not going clubbing, just out for drinks," he said. "And you're more than welcome to wear that, if you want."

"And who is 'we'?"

"Myself, my friend, Sam, and Brooks. Well, his name is Aiden, but we call him Brooks, because there's another Aiden too. And one of Brooks' friends, I dunno who he is."

Clare mentally counted on her fingers. "So, me and four guys?"

"Three. Sam's actually a Samantha."

"And two are named Aiden?"

"Sometimes. I mean, sometimes there's two guys named Aiden, but tonight it'll just be one, and he goes by Brooks."

"This feels unnecessarily complicated."

"And this feels like stalling," Logan said, cocking his head to the side in an imitation of her posture.

"Where would we go?"

Logan grinned like he'd just won something. "Pour. The one on Hennepin and Lake."

Clare sagged exaggeratedly against her couch. "Oh no, no. Please, no. Don't make me go to Uptown."

"What's wrong with Uptown?"

"Everyone there is named, like, Chad, or whatever."

"Not true. Sometimes they're named Aiden," Logan said. "But are you in?"

Clare couldn't tell if this was him asking her on a date. Drinks was date-like, although drinks with three other people was less so. She decided once again to cut to the chase.

"It's not a date, is it?"

"Do you want it to be?" he replied, with just the barest bit of hesitation before responding.

Clare realized belatedly he might have thought she *wanted* it to be a date, which in addition to being untrue would probably come across to him as clingy. "Not really," she said, and Logan lifted his eyebrows again.

"Is that a yes?"

"Okay, fine."

"Fine? Come on, show a little enthusiasm," he wheedled with a devastating grin.

She put on an overly bright smile that made him snort. "Yay, Uptown!" she cheered. "Is that sufficient?"

Logan's eyes flashed with heat and she momentarily regretted her sarcasm, because he clearly didn't play fair. "We'll work on it," he said in a low voice. But then his gaze cleared and his voice returned to the teasing tone he'd had before. "Did you want to go get changed? Or are you wearing this, because honestly, I vote for this."

Clare rolled her eyes at him and went to change, still not quite sure what she'd gotten herself into.

Chapter Twelve

Logan was so fucking stupid. He wasn't sure what the hell he was thinking, bringing Clare out with his idiot friends. It should have been just the two of them. *That* would have been an actual date, a way to make his straight-out lie to Schneider something slightly more plausible; a way to set the stage to beg her to come to dinner with his obnoxious client. Clare had said she didn't want it to be a date, but there wasn't a lot of conviction behind it, so Logan was sure he could make this work, or could have if it had been a one-on-one thing. Instead, he was stuck watching Clare flirt with *Brooks* of all people.

Brooks, that piece of shit, had spent the entire night fawning over Clare. He knew exactly who she was, and while he didn't have much in the way of brain cells he could probably figure out why Logan had brought her with him, but that didn't matter to Logan's so-called friend. The second they walked out onto the still-damp rooftop patio, Clare dressed in jeans and a soft blue V-neck shirt that was plain but did wonderful things to her curves, Brooks' eyes had lit up. He could be reasonably charming when he wanted to be, and tonight he wanted to make Logan's life hell.

"It's a video game, right?" Brooks said, leaning down close to Clare's ear while she sipped her gin and tonic.

She shook her head. "It's tabletop role-playing."

"Like Monopoly."

Christ, Brooks was even dumber than Logan thought. "No, like Dungeons and Dragons," Logan said, probably more tightly than either of them were expecting, given that both of them sent him slight eyebrow raises.

"I'm killer at Monopoly," Brooks said with a wink. He touched Clare's arm lightly, turning her away from Logan and plastering an interested look on his stupid face. "We should play sometime."

Oh, Logan was going to *kill* that jackass.

Sam nudged Logan's arm. "What's your deal?" she asked, throwing back a tequila shot and setting it down on the table. They moved a few steps away; not like Clare and Brooks would notice.

"No deal."

"Yeah? Because you look like you're about to shit diamonds."

"Why are you so crude?" he whined. His rum and Coke was finished, and he slammed the glass down hard enough to draw looks from the table next to them. They'd lost track of Brooks' friend a half-hour ago, leaving Logan nothing to do but watch as his so-called friend deliberately made his life more difficult.

Sam shrugged. "I just am." She nodded to Brooks and Clare, who still had their heads close together. "I thought she came with you?"

Logan's shrug was almost imperceptible. "She did, sorta. It's . . . complicated."

"As in you fucked her and now Brooks is trying to?"

"Something like that."

Sam made a face. "Weird, she seemed smarter than that."

"What do you want, Sam?" he sighed. The server brought over another rum and Coke for Logan, but he didn't have the energy to muster his usual charm to thank her, and instead just nodded politely.

"I wanted to know what's bugging you, but now I do." She pulled her long dark ponytail over her shoulder, her smile poisonously sweet. "You've got a cruuuush."

He shook his head, because that wasn't it. He was annoyed with Brooks because he had a plan, and Brooks was deliberately fucking it up. Plus, Clare deserved better than Brooks, who was, at best, a bit of a dick. "Like I said, it's complicated."

Sam frowned. "I really don't think it is, but sure, if that's what you need to tell yourself."

Logan downed half his drink in one gulp, earning him yet another eyebrow raise, this time from Sam. He decided to try and redirect the situation. He stepped over to Clare and Brooks, letting his slightly broader shoulders nudge his so-called friend to the side. Behind him, Sam rolled her eyes and headed toward the restroom. "How's it going, Clare?" he asked, ignoring Brooks entirely. He was going to get a truckload of shit from the Aidens at work on Monday, but he'd deal with that later.

It was hard to interpret Clare's expression. He was usually better at reading people. There was something different about her; something that made him second-guess himself.

Brooks answered instead. "I'm trying to get your girl here to agree to play me at Monopoly," he said with a leer over Clare's head at Logan.

Logan could not believe they were still talking about fucking Monopoly, but then again, it was Brooks. He didn't have a lot of conversational options. "Don't. He'll cheat," Logan warned her with a grin that he knew from experience made her ears go red. Right on cue, the tips of Clare's ears pinked up and suddenly, Logan felt a bit better. Her smile warmed his belly, and he was feeling pretty damn pleased with himself when Brooks spoke again. "Logan's just a pussy who can't take losing."

Clare grimaced at his phrasing, and for the hundredth time Logan kicked himself for thinking this was a good idea. Maybe if he could get Clare to talk to Sam more, it might give off a better impression. At this rate, Clare was going to think his friends were creeps and tell her aunt to fire them all.

"Logan's a poor sport, you mean?" she said sweetly.

"One time I crushed his ass in one-on-one and he was mad at me for days," Brooks bragged.

Logan had been mad because Brooks blatantly fouled him and denied it, but sure, he could tell it that way if he wanted. Logan shrugged like he didn't give a shit. "Like I said, he cheats."

Brooks looked annoyed. "I did not," he argued.

Logan downed the rest of his drink, belatedly remembering it was his third and his dinner had just been a frozen dinner from Smorgasbord when his stomach gave an unpleasant lurch. "Agree to disagree," Logan said tightly, acutely aware Clare was watching them closely.

Brooks rolled his eyes and turned back to Clare. "So how about it?" he asked.

She looked confused. "How about what?"

"That game of Monopoly. Logan's got his panties in a twist, so we could get out of here. Go some place quiet."

Logan's jaw fell open, because even by the Aidens' standards, that was low. Sure, Clare had specified she didn't want it to be a date, a fact Logan was still trying to find a way around, but he had brought her with him. For Brooks to offer to take her home was a betrayal.

Clare looked at Brooks for a long moment, almost like she was considering it, and then shook her head. Her blonde hair swished back and forth with the movement. "I think I need to get going, unfortunately. Thanks for all your, um, thoughts on board games." She turned to Logan, examining him critically. "And I think you need to get home, too. You look kind of . . . green."

He *felt* green. Chartreuse, to be specific. Anger and too much alcohol and not enough food was a bad combination, and Logan realized belatedly he had driven Clare there. Normally he just took a RideShare, but he'd wanted this to feel as much like a date as a not-date could. Except now he was too drunk to drive, making him look like he hadn't thought about getting her home.

But Clare was, as usual, a step ahead of him. "Why don't you give me the keys," she said when Brooks was distracted by the return of his friend. "I just had the one gin and tonic, and it was weak as hell."

Logan frowned. "I'll talk to Kay about that," he said.

"Sorry?"

"Kay. The bartender. She's, uh, a friend of mine." He knew he probably shouldn't say *I fucked her too*, but Logan was very out of practice at this and *friend* was the best he could come up with on the spot.

"Mmm. A friend. A friend you made the same way you met Sam?"

Leave it to Sam to tell my date that we fucked. "Yep."

"And me."

Logan wanted to protest, but she was right. She was right and his brain was too muddled to muster a coherent argument, so he just followed her to where Sam was talking to a journalist friend Logan vaguely recognized. She was a lesbian though, so at least he hadn't fucked her, too. He was not making the best impression on Clare, but he was also now too drunk to fix it.

He dimly heard Sam offer to drive him home, but Clare brushed her off by explaining she lived in the same building. Sam looked far too interested in that detail, but Logan would also deal with that later.

Future Logan was going to have a lot of problems, the poor bastard.

Logan leaned on Clare a little as they weaved through the crowd. She was the perfect height for that, all short and cute and shit. She didn't seem to mind, and they had made it down the narrow staircase and through most of the downstairs bar before she stopped short.

"Noah?" he heard her say. Great. Another guy who was going to try and sleep with her. Logan put his arm over her shoulder and looked down at the guy, who was a few inches shorter than Logan with sandy-brown, curly hair. His shirt said something in what looked like runes, so clearly a nerd friend of hers. Logan wasn't used to competing with that demographic, but he was pretty sure his face would win out.

He had a damn good face, after all.

"Didn't think this was your scene," Clare was saying.

The guy shrugged, a microbrew in his hand. "More mine than yours," he said. "Who's this?"

"This is my, um, friend."

Logan waved lazily, now leaning more heavily on Clare. *Fuck, I am drunk. Why the hell did I get this drunk?*

Noah gave him an odd, searching look. "Guess you're more surprising than we thought," he said, and Logan didn't know what the fuck that meant, but it felt judgy as hell, so he glowered down at Noah. At least the other guy had the sense to look intimidated.

Clare laughed lightly and waved. "Exactly. I'll see you Monday," she said, starting to move forward again.

Noah gave them another look. "You got him okay? He seems heavy," he said. "Do you need help?"

Logan decided to turn down his glower by two notches. Making sure a friend got home safely and wasn't in trouble was a decent thing, so maybe this Noah wasn't a complete piece of shit. Didn't mean Logan had to like him, though.

"We're fine," Clare said cheerfully, shifting so her shoulder was more securely under his armpit. "See you," she said again, and muscled them outside.

It was humid but the air was cooler than it had been in the crush of people inside, at least. Logan took a deep breath, trying and failing to clear his head. He gave up trying to sober up and tucked his nose into the top of her head, breathing her in. He liked how she smelled, like sugar and vanilla and those things she was always baking. Logan couldn't remember the last time he'd done something that could be qualified as *thoughtlessly affectionate*, but there was a first time for everything.

Clare ducked out from under his arm, not commenting on his sudden PDA, and opened the passenger-side door for him. Logan transferred his weight to the door, resting his chin on his folded arms on top of it. His face was almost level with hers, and he impulsively tucked a lock of hair behind her ear. "Hey," he said in a soft, goofy voice that didn't sound anything like him.

"Hey," she replied, sounding a little dazed. He let his fingertips trail down the side of her neck, and her eyes fluttered closed before she stepped back, out of his reach. "Keys?" she asked briskly, and okay, sure, he probably wouldn't have kissed someone as drunk as he was, either.

Clare climbed in and spent a good chunk of time adjusting

his seat, since her feet didn't even touch the pedals how he had it. She was very deliberate, methodical, and her earrings—tiny, dangly silver arrows—swung gently as she checked the mirrors. A streetlight threw a square of light on her face through the window and Logan reclined his seat a little farther to make himself more comfortable. "I fucked this up, didn't I?" he asked before he realized what he was saying.

Oh, well. Just add it to Future Logan's list.

Clare pulled out into traffic, slowing down to let a crowd of guys in button-down shirts and khaki shorts finish jaywalking. "Fucked what up?"

Logan covered his face with his hands. "You hate me and my friends."

"I liked Sam," she countered. A red light flicked to green and she started again.

"She's nicer than she seems, right?"

Clare's lips curved up slightly. "And Brooks?"

"Dumber than he seems. And cheats like hell at basketball."

"Ah," she said, sounding amused.

"*Ah* what? What *ah*?" he asked, well aware this was probably the most pathetic he had ever been in front of a woman, but for some reason it didn't seem to matter as much with Clare.

"Nothing. Just *ah*. It's just a vocalization saying *I heard you*." She shrugged and turned on her signal. "You guys seemed a little tense."

"He's a dick," Logan said. And then, because he just really fucking hated Future Logan, "He was hitting on you, you know."

"Is that what that was," Clare said, like she was fighting a grin.

"Yeah, he's about as subtle as a punch to the face." Clare lost the battle with the grin and Logan leaned his head back.

"You know, for a bit there, I thought you were mad at me," she admitted.

Logan jerked his head up. "What? No, not you. That—no, not you. Just him."

"That's good. I think I like being friends with you, Logan."

Friends. That was not what he wanted, but it was a start. "I think I like being friends with you too, Clare," he said, and let his eyes drift closed.

He hoped he could remember all the problems he had just created for himself tomorrow, and if not, that he would be too hungover to care.

Chapter Thirteen

There was a hint of the river on the breeze as Clare walked Kiki
on their usual circuit. It was quiet on weekend mornings in
downtown, with most of the offices empty and the swarm of
crowds that came for Twins games still out for brunch. She
stopped to let Kiki pee on her second favorite tree, and sighed
to herself.

Last night had not been what she expected at all. She'd been
fairly clear about it not being a date, and thought it might be
good practice for getting out there and experiencing life a little
more. She had initially even harbored vague ideas about finding a new hookup, although she'd quickly decided it was rude
to go home with someone else when you'd recently slept with
the person who invited you. But the charming, suave Logan
she had started to get to know was nowhere to be found once
they arrived, instead replaced by a tense, irritated one who
really didn't seem to like his friend, Brooks, much.

Not that Clare could blame him. Brooks was boring and
way too sure of himself, but from a purely academic standpoint, it was interesting to contrast him with Logan. Logan's
charm was sweet and never overbearing, even when he was

trying to seduce her. There was something safe about him, something that told her she could trust him, even when he was drunk and clearly thinking about kissing her. She got none of those vibes from Brooks, just a lot of blather about Monopoly, which he really seemed to think was the same thing as Sulzuris despite her repeated attempts to set him straight.

Granted, not much of her elevator version of Logan was on display at Pour, either. Things had started out fine, but once Brooks started flirting with her, everything hit a tailspin. She'd gone along with it initially, mostly out of curiosity because she really didn't know many guys like that, but quickly started looking for an escape that Logan had been reluctant to provide. Clare would have also liked to spend more time talking to Sam, who was crude and brash but clearly had a warm heart, given the way she hugged Clare and welcomed her to the *Sisterhood of Logan's Dick.*

That had made Clare snort her gin and tonic out her nose, which was incredibly painful, for the record. But it had shed some light on Logan for her, as Clare was at least the third woman in that one bar whom Logan had slept with, and both of the other women were on good terms with him, too. So Logan was a man who slept with women and then stayed friends with them, which made sense. It was also perfect for her, even if there was a tiny, pointless pang in her heart when she realized she was not a special case for him. It didn't explain why Logan had gotten so annoyed with Brooks for flirting, but maybe there was less behind it than she thought. He really did seem annoyed about the basketball thing, after all.

Clare and Kiki turned north, talking a path along the river that was nicely shaded, if a little busier than the sidewalk. She also hadn't expected to run into Noah last night, much less to have Noah offer to help her with Logan. It was a nice thing for him to have done, and not something she'd expected. She also sort of hoped that he would mention their run-in to Craig and the rest of the team when they played Call of Duty today, since that might get them off her back about *getting more life experience*.

But then there was the fact that when she'd helped Logan to his car, it really had seemed like he was going to kiss her. At the very least, the way he had looked at her had been impossibly soft, and for a few seconds, she had wanted nothing more than to lean into his touch. But in addition to being completely against the spirit of her one-night stand assignment, Logan had been, by that point, completely plastered. Not kissing him had been the right choice. On the slim-to-completely improbable chance Logan had been thinking of something more with her, it was best that she kept things strictly platonic. Not flirting with him was nearly impossible—the man practically oozed flirtation—but kissing him would take things to a place she had to make sure they didn't go.

Kiki started forward, only to stop four feet later to lower her haunches and settle in for a poop. Clare moved off the paved pathway to let the runners past while she waited, tugging a baggie from the purse she had slung over her shoulder.

"Fancy meeting you here," a deep voice said over her shoulder, and Clare turned to find Logan looking way too good for a man who was also absolutely *drenched* in sweat. He appeared to have been out for a run, which Clare found fairly impressive considering how drunk he'd been last night.

Logan bent down and let Kiki, who had now finished pooping, sniff his hand. "Hey there, girl," he said softly, scratching her behind the ears, and wow, there was a lot about this man that was just incredibly unfair.

"How are you feeling?" Clare asked, because if *she'd* been

that drunk, she would be curled up on the couch with Gatorade and only moving if her life depended on it. She scooped the poop into the baggie and tied it off.

Logan shrugged and gestured to a park bench a few feet away, deftly plucking the baggie from her hand and tossing it into the bin. "Like I got hit by a truck this morning, but I rallied." He waited for her to sit, a curiously gentlemanly move, and then sat down and stretched his legs out. She looked at his long legs, dusted with black curly hair, and had a brief memory of what those legs felt like between hers. Clare did her best to master her blush, but there was a gleam in Logan's eyes when he glanced at her that told her she was busted anyway. "I feel like I have some things to apologize for, though," he said, looking out at the path.

"So you had a little too much to drink. I got us home fine."

"More than that. I think—that was your coworker, right?"

"At the end? Noah? Yeah, he's on my team."

Logan nodded slowly. "I think I was a little bit of a dick to him."

Kiki hopped up onto the bench between them and pillowed her head in Logan's lap like *he* was the one who had picked up her shit three minutes ago, not Clare.

"Eh, it's fine," she said. "Noah's—well, he was nicer last night than he usually is, but it's fine. Don't worry about it."

Logan stroked Kiki on the top of her head. "And sorry that my friends are, uh, my friends."

"I meant what I said last night. I liked Sam," Clare said, scratching just above Kiki's butt.

Logan snorted. "I thought you would. I mostly meant Brooks."

"The Monopoly enthusiast."

"Yeah, him."

"You have nothing to apologize for," Clare said breezily.

"I was also kind of a dick," he pointed out. "Just like, in general. Will you at least let me apologize for that?"

Clare smothered a smile. "If you insist. Consider it accepted." She waited to see if he would bring up the moment near the car, and when he didn't she figured that was for the best. It probably didn't even rate for him—he probably did that "soft-hey-and-hair-touch" thing to a lot of women.

A thought occurred to her and she turned to her purse, which was less of a purse and more of a medium-sized tote bag that she almost never remembered to clean out. "And here, to show that there are no hard feelings, have this." She pulled an unopened bottled water out from the bottom. It was a little dented on the top and fairly lukewarm, but Logan was really sweaty. He had to be thirsty.

Logan looked at her bag, frowning in thought. "You just had that? In there?"

"That, probably several hundred receipts, half a dozen tampons, even more receipts, and two bags of dice."

"Dice?"

"Dice," she confirmed.

Logan gulped down the water, his throat working hard, and then crumpled it and tossed it into the recycling bin on the other side of the bench without looking. "I'm going to need to see this," he said, reaching over and plucking her purse off her shoulder before she could do so much as yelp in protest. Affronted at the movement, Kiki jumped to the ground and found a new spot in the shade, her butt pointed toward them both. Logan dug around in her purse until he pulled out a small, velvet pouch the size of his palm. "Is this it? It doesn't feel like tampons, at least."

Clare reached for it and he tugged it out of her grasp,

holding it just out of her range. She lunged and he pulled it farther away, grinning. She was nearly in his lap, and a man that sweaty really had no business smelling that good. She surrendered and moved back to her side of the bench with what remained of her dignity.

Logan opened the drawstring, peering in interestedly. "Explain."

"I dunno. I just—I like having them with me. Like Yaen—my character—is a part of me, or something."

"But you have two bags, you said?"

"One is for when I'm playing Sulzuris as Yaen, and then the other is just all-purpose."

"Just in case an impromptu role-playing game breaks out?" he asked archly. At their feet, Kiki had gotten up and was sniffing at something that took her to the end of her leash.

"It's less weird than you think, once you consider it's literally my job, too."

Logan conceded the point with a nod. "Looks like Kiki is impatient. I should be getting you two back," Logan said, replacing the bag into her tote and offering her a hand up.

And against her better judgment, Clare took it.

Chapter Fourteen

If he sat in just the right spot at his kitchen table, Logan could see the Mississippi River past the Hennepin Avenue Bridge. The sunset tonight was gorgeous, staining the sky pink and orange, highlighting the tops of the tall, billowy clouds that piled up out on the prairies. The clouds were a snowy white, no hint of rain, and blue leached from the rest of the sky as the sun sank toward the horizon. His fingers itched in a way they hadn't in a long time. Aiden had texted again about going out, but Logan was glad he'd passed on it. He wasn't in the mood for a crowded, noisy bar right now. Right now, he almost—almost—felt like sketching, something he hadn't done in years. He wasn't sure if he even had his colored pencils anymore, but was considering digging through his hall closet to see if he'd stashed them there. If they weren't, maybe they were still at his dad's. He could always pick them up next time he went home.

A quiet, almost hesitant knock sounded through his apartment. Logan frowned at the door for a minute—no one ever came to his door without having to buzz up first. Even Sam had to wait for him to let her in, although they had worked out a short–short–long buzz code to save time.

Slowly, he unfurled himself from the table and paused, grabbing the paring knife from near the sink just to be safe. He approached the door like it was a rattlesnake, knife loose in his left hand. "Who is it?" he called.

"Who do you think?" Clare's voice called back, and his stance loosened. He opened the door and her eyes instantly darted to the knife. "Wait, were you going to *stab* me?"

Sheepishly, he dropped it on the counter as she followed him in. "I couldn't figure out who it would be. I got freaked out."

"And naturally, because young white men are prime targets for serial killers, who are also well known for knocking politely, you assumed it was the Golden State Killer?"

"A lot of serial killers get access to their victims by being polite," he grumbled. Sam knew an absolutely terrifying amount about serial killers, information Logan had now absorbed, mostly against his will.

"Fair enough, but wouldn't it be more likely to be like, your neighbor dropping off some mail they got accidentally? Or, you know, your neighbor who you slept with two weeks ago?" She asked it all with a curious tilt of her head, a gesture he was rapidly coming to like.

"Is that what happened? You got my mail?"

She looked away, her cheeks pinking up. "Just thought it'd be nice to hang out, or something."

Interesting. Running into her on the path had been a stroke of luck, and without the haze of alcohol he had managed to return to his usual level of charm. Logan had hoped that would give her enough incentive to want to spend more time together, but she hadn't reached out at all for nearly a week. He had decided to play it cool, waiting for her to come to him. Given how skittish she had seemed about last weekend being a date, he didn't want her to feel pressured. Better that it feel like her idea.

And that way, Logan felt a little bit less like a dick. Win-win, and all that. He tilted his head, echoing her earlier posture. "Depends. Are you secretly a serial killer?"

"How many serial killers do you know of who would admit that up front?"

"You already have a shady habit of dognapping. Is it really such a stretch to think you might also be into serial killing? Now that I'm thinking about it, I really should call the cops on you. You're a menace, Clare Thompson."

"You could do that, or you could live dangerously and go hang out on the roof with me."

"So you can throw me over the edge? Not a chance," he said, grinning.

"You realize I would have to lift you up like, four feet in order to get you over the edge, and that's not even considering that I can at best lift one-third your body weight?"

"Don't sell yourself short. You're little, but I bet you're strong."

"You'd still have to want to go over the edge is all I'm saying."

"I'll bring the knife, just in case."

"Good plan." She flashed him a smile and lifted the tote bag draped over her arm. "I brought some rolls I baked and some fancy cheese. I figured you would want to supply the wine."

"You figured right," he said, already heading to his wine fridge. It was one of the handful of amenities that made his apartment an extra $300 a month, but he felt it was worth it. "Red or white?"

"Don't care," she shrugged, and he shook his head.

"I get not caring what type of grapes. Theoretically. Only a monster doesn't care that Riesling and Sauvignon Blanc are entirely different tastes that go with drastically different foods, but not even caring if it's red or white? That's appalling," he grumbled. She shrugged again, and Logan sighed. "It's warm outside, so we'll go with a Chardonnay," he said, pulling one out.

"I thought wine snobs looked down on Chardonnay."

"There's a season for every type of wine, and sharp cheese on a warm day is definitely Chardonnay season."

"If you say so," she said, jerking her chin toward the door. "Ready?"

Logan grabbed two glasses and a corkscrew and followed her out.

It was surprisingly empty on the rooftop patio, considering how nice the evening was. There was an older couple sitting at the high top table with their own bottle of wine, and two women in their late twenties snuggling on the outdoor sectional, but it was otherwise deserted. He led them to his favorite corner; two loungers with big, thick orange cushions surrounding a small table with a view of the river.

The sunset was still in full glory, the towering clouds scudding across the sky toward the darkening east. A breeze brought a faint whiff of river mixed with the gasoline and baking asphalt of downtown in the summer, and he watched Clare settle into her chair and close her eyes, strain in her neck and shoulders suddenly melting away.

"Rough day at work?" he asked.

She opened her eyes to accept the glass of wine he poured. "Just long. We're working on a new one-shot campaign, and we have to present it to Leadership in about a month. It's a lot of work, and higher stakes than you'd think."

A boyfriend would ask questions here, he thought. He was alarmingly out of practice at this—with Sam and the guys they mostly just made fun of each other. He couldn't remember the last time he asked one of them about their feelings.

"What's a one-shot?"

"Most of our stories are open-ended. It's more about the set-up and the world, and then the players take it from there. But a one-shot is a contained story, or in my case, a world with more specific, directed world-building for players and Game Masters to use, with established characters to help guide new players. Or at least, that's what I'm pitching, although my team wasn't that pumped about it."

"Did you want to talk about it?"

Her silence was contemplative. "I don't always feel like I fit in with my team."

He could tell this wasn't something she would say to just anyone, but he still wanted to tread carefully. "I should have been more of a dick to Noah, you're saying."

She chuckled. "No, it's not that. More just that I'm . . . not quite overlooked, but always half a step behind, you know?"

"Like you're not good enough?" He knew how that felt, although thinking about Peggy and the Schneider account made his stomach twist uncomfortably.

He wasn't using Clare. Not *really*. He was just using the fact that they got along well to solve an unrelated problem he was having. That was all.

"Kind of. Our boss is this really larger-than-life guy, and the rest of the guys on the team just seem to be more what he's looking for. I'm just playing catch-up all the time. And there's this job that might be available, and I want it so badly, you know? But I need to stand out more, I think. I'm easily overlooked."

That felt hard for him to believe, because how could anyone not pay attention to Clare? She was funny, and clever, and seemed to know that Quest game back to front.

"Maybe that isn't the real problem," he said, thinking out loud. "Maybe they just aren't hearing you."

"I need to be more assertive, you mean?"

"In a way. It might not be you at all, honestly. But if it's a lot of guys, they're probably just . . . not hearing you. They're caught up in their own ideas and ignoring yours, which fucking sucks."

Clare sighed, and he hated how frustrated she sounded. "Doesn't sound like something I can fix."

"Not easily," he agreed. "But you need to make yourself hard to ignore. Don't give up, keep bringing up your ideas, over and over again."

"And if they shoot them down?"

"You try again," he said.

She let out another sigh. "I guess it's worth a shot."

He bit into a roll she produced from her bag and almost moaned. "Holy shit, you made this?"

"Last night. Couldn't sleep."

"Damn. When I can't sleep I just watch old episodes of *30 For 30*."

Clare made a face. "Isn't that about sports?"

"Mostly, yeah. Why, not a fan?"

"I think the NCAA is a scam and college athletics is a waste of money. I'm sorry, but when grad students are making sub-poverty wages, teaching is farmed out to adjuncts making even worse money, and tenure lines are being cut left and right, then the indulgence of paying coaches millions of dollars for a stupid game is just insulting."

"Wow, okay."

"You asked."

"What about non-collegiate sports?"

"I like watching gymnastics and ice-skating during the Olympics, but other than that, I can't say I've ever willingly watched a sporting event from start to finish."

Logan laughed. "I take it that means you won't be coming to watch my pick-up games anytime soon."

"Ugh, never. I hate football."

"Good thing I mostly play basketball then."

Clare laughed and reached for another slice of cheese. "Yeah, that's still gonna be a no from me. Besides, that feels rather . . . girlfriend-y." She looked at him out of the corner of her eye, like she was waiting to see how he responded.

Logan hesitated, not sure how to answer. He changed the subject instead. "When did you learn how to bake?"

"Taught myself when I was in college. A character on *Grey's Anatomy* always stress-baked, and I used to watch it when I was in middle school, and I guess that imprinted on me. I figured it'd be a good stress relief, and it turns out, it is. I have to focus on it hard enough that I don't screw up the ingredients, but not so hard that it hurts my head, you know? Keeps me from spinning out when I'm super-stressed or I've given myself a headache from thinking too hard."

Logan did not know what it felt like to think so hard his head hurt, but he nodded anyway. "Well, you're really good at it."

"I know," she said, just a touch smugly. "What about you?"

"I'm a terrible baker, sadly."

She snorted and handed him another roll. "What are your hobbies? Other than sportsball."

"*Basket*ball," he corrected with a grin. "I don't really have any."

"Really?"

He shifted uncomfortably. "I mean, not anymore."

"So you had a hobby but you dropped it?"

"Something like that."

"Let me guess, you wrote fanfic for *The Suite Life of Zack & Cody*."

"What in god's name would that even be?"

"If you have to ask, clearly you're not on my level," Clare chuckled. "But I can totally figure this out." She studied him critically, chewing her lower lip. "Hentai fan art."

"Don't know what that is either."

"Dirty pictures, but you draw them."

"Oh. Well, you're—getting warmer."

Her eyebrows skyrocketed. "The hentai part?"

"No, Jesus. The drawing part."

"You draw?"

"I did. Thought about minoring in art, even, but it didn't seem worth it."

She sat up straight. "Really? That's so cool. The art thing, not that you thought it wasn't worth it. That we'll unpack later."

Her enthusiasm caught him off guard. The sunset had limned her in gold and for a moment, she wasn't just Clare in grey leggings and a navy V-neck T-shirt. She was alive, vibrant, a goddess, lounging on Mount Olympus, sipping wine. She was a flame, and he was a moth.

"It's just sketches," he said, looking away and back out at the sky. He wasn't sure what had come over him and he needed to get a hold of himself.

"When was the last time you drew?"

"A while ago." He had kept it up for a year or two out of college but then stopped, and he couldn't remember why.

"Do you miss it?"

"I was just thinking about drawing tonight, actually," he admitted, surprising even himself. Sam knew he used to draw, but she also knew he hated to talk about it. He'd always felt like that threw off his process, like even admitting he was working on a piece would ruin the entire thing. Part of what he liked about Sam was she never really pushed on stuff like that; she just let him be.

"Hang on," Clare said, turning and rooting through her tote bag. She came up with a pencil and a small notebook. "Here. I would hate to be the reason you didn't try it again."

"You want me to draw?"

"Just a quick sketch. I'll amuse myself."

He took the pencil and notebook, staring at her blankly. "You're serious?"

"Of course I am. Creative pursuits are important, even if they're just hobbies. And if you don't give in when the urge strikes after a long time away from it, it gets harder and harder to start again. So, go. Draw."

"What do you want me to draw? And if you ask me to draw you like one of my French girls, I *will* draw you like a Smurf." Logan had been a goddamn *toddler* when *Titanic* came out, but that line was the bane of his existence.

"As I am legitimately barely three apples high, that would probably be an accurate rendering," she threw back. "Draw whatever you want. The cheese, even."

The colors were slowly fading from the sky and Clare once again looked like a mortal rather than a warm, earthy goddess. For a second, he considered drawing her the way he'd seen her, all softness and light and warmth, but that felt too personal, too real. Too fast. Instead, he focused on her fingers, curving loosely around the stem of the wine glass.

At first, he felt absurdly self-conscious, but Clare was true to her word. She never so much as peeked at him, instead just leaning back and closing her eyes, tilting her chin up to catch the last glimmer of the sun's rays. He wanted to draw that too, the delicate sweep of her jaw, the arch of her neck. *Too personal*, he scolded himself again. He filed it away and concentrated on her hand, now idly twirling the glass back and forth on the table between them. It was rough, and hardly his best work, but it was passable. And more importantly, it felt like something had unlocked inside him, a weight from his shoulders suddenly lifting.

"Done," he announced, and she fluttered her eyes open.

"Did you want to tear it out? I don't have to look," she offered.

It would have been easier to just throw it away. Logan always felt jittery when people looked at his art, like they were seeing something about him he was desperately trying to hide. He had learned to stop babbling at his art professors whenever they checked in on his progress in college, and at least half the reason he never pursued a formal minor in art was because it would involve more people seeing his work.

"It's not much," he said, unable to help himself as he pushed the notebook back. "I haven't drawn in a while, and I wasn't taking my time, and hands are really hard, and—"

Clare reached for the notebook, shaking her head. "I can't draw anything, so you're way ahead of me." She stopped, studying his sketch, and a tiny smile crept across her face. "My hand?"

"It was the nearest thing," he mumbled. The smile stayed and her cheeks turned pink, her teeth sinking into her lower lip. "It's nothing," he said, regretting everything and leaning forward to try and snatch it back. "Like I said, hands are hard and—"

Clare yanked it out of his reach. "Hey, I'm not done looking at this," she scolded. "No one's ever drawn me before." She peered at it closely. "You're very talented, you know."

"I'm okay," Logan said, with uncharacteristic modesty. But he'd always been like that with his art, which was maybe why he'd stopped it in the first place. He liked things that were easier, less personal.

"I work with artists, though, so I know a thing or two. You're really good."

Logan's face felt hot. "You think so?"

"I do," she said, and did that head tilt thing. "And for the record, the fact that you're blushing right now? Super cute." The sky had gone the vivid electric blue of late twilight in the city, her hair shining out against it.

"Cute? That almost feels like an insult."

"I feel like your ego gets fed enough, quite frankly," she said, and he laughed. He couldn't help it—he liked it when she teased him. Usually his flirtations were more charged, layered with innuendo as he danced around the *Do you want to fuck?* question. With Clare, it was more like hanging out with Sam—teasing mixed with genuine friendship. It was easy with her, but challenging, too.

Logan should have thought things through better. He frequently had stupid ideas, as Sam was fond of saying, and he needed to run them by a competent adult before carrying out his plan. But he had dug himself a hole and was just going to have to keep digging until Schneider came back and Clare got bored with him.

Because women always, always did. Logan knew what he was good for, and he also knew what women thought of him: insubstantial and ultimately inconsequential. It didn't hurt, not really, but sometimes it would be made so clear he couldn't avoid it, like with Amber, and that wasn't the most fun. He figured it was inevitable with Clare, so all he had to do was wait.

But the moment he saw her in that dumb unicorn onesie, he should have known it wouldn't be quite so easy. He'd never met anyone as secure as Clare, as sure of herself and uninterested in living up to societal expectations. Sam came close, except he had never once—not even the night they slept together—looked at Sam's face the way he'd been looking at Clare's, like he wanted to memorize it to draw later.

"Besides," Clare continued, still laughing, "as someone who has been called *cute* more times than I can count, often in the context of letting me down 'gently,'" she put air quotes around *gently*, "well, yeah, it can be an insult, but you know when it's meant that way." A pang of guilt skittered through his ribcage. But he reminded himself he actually liked spending time with her, so needing to convince her to show up to a meal with Schneider wasn't the worst thing in the world. It had occurred to him he could just *ask* her to go to the dinner, but with Peggy being both his boss and her aunt, he didn't want her to feel caught in the middle.

No, this route was better. Riskier, maybe, but better in the long run.

Besides, there was absolutely no way a woman like her— smart and put-together and confident—wanted him for anything long term or remotely serious. Getting her to dinner with Schneider was the best he could do.

"Obviously, I didn't mean it that way for you. It's more— endearing, is all," Clare clarified.

"Endearing," he repeated. No one had ever described him that way, he realized.

He liked it.

Chapter Fifteen

Clare still couldn't get over it. Logan, a man with more than a little streak of exhibitionism in him, was blushing. Because he'd drawn a picture of her. Well, her hand. But still. She had been second-guessing herself when she knocked on his door, because what she was *supposed* to be doing was finding more one-night stands and getting more of that specific kind of experience Craig apparently felt she needed. She had tried telling herself this was just a test, making sure that she *could* have a one-night stand and not try and date the guy. If Craig thought she was only capable of being a girlfriend-girl, she would prove him wrong. That was what she had told herself when she left her apartment to ask Logan up to the roof, anyway.

But Logan was . . . irresistible. She suspected he knew that and used it to his full advantage, but she was also powerless against it. And now, with him blushing because of her compliment, she found herself making excuses. She could just fudge it for Craig, maybe learn some more about Logan's life and use those elements in her writing; anything that would let her keep talking to him instead of downloading a dating app and wading through the *Hey, cutie* messages until she found someone she liked even one-tenth as much as she liked spending time with Logan.

"What about you?" he asked. "I need to even the scales. What's something embarrassing about you?"

"You already know all of it," she pointed out. "Also, I refuse to be embarrassed by anything. I like what I like, and you should too. There's nothing embarrassing about drawing, either."

"Come on," he wheedled. "There must be something. I just showed you something I never show anyone."

She thought for a minute. "Okay, it's not a hobby or anything, but it is . . . silly. My friends know about it already, though."

"Silly is good."

"You'll laugh."

"Even better."

"Hey, I didn't laugh at your drawing."

Logan refused to concede the point. "But you did tease me for blushing."

"Fair. Okay, hold on," she said, unlocking her phone. "There's this thing I do. It makes me happy, so I'm not embarrassed necessarily, but it is, as I said, deeply silly." She called up the proper photo album and handed it over.

Logan furrowed his brow. "This is just . . . pictures of you with dogs? Wait, this is a lot of dogs," he added, scrolling down. "Like, a *lot* of dogs."

"If I'm out walking around and I get to pet a dog, I ask the owner to take a picture of me with it," she explained, chewing her lower lip. "And then when I'm feeling sad, I scroll through these pictures. It's hard to be down when there are so many good doggos in the world, you know?"

Logan barely managed to stifle his snort. "That's . . . cute. Endearing-cute, I mean."

"Is it? Or is it an absolutely ridiculous thing to do?"

"It can be both," he said evenly, eyes dancing.

"What if I told you I sometimes make Devi look at them with me, and it's happened so often she has a three-dog limit. So sometimes I look through it and make sure I have my most recent top three ready to go."

Logan handed the phone back to her. "Then I expect to see the current top three."

"There's a tie for third," she warned. "Three ways."

"Isn't that cheating?"

"Devi is a very indulgent best friend."

"Then let's see the top five."

"Okay, here are the three third-place finishers," she said, finding the photos of a chihuahua in a sweater from last March, a pitbull mix she had seen by the path around Bde Maka Ska last week, and a Frenchie bulldog an administrative assistant brought to work one day.

Logan looked at them all seriously, nodding. "Very cute. I especially like the Norwegian sweater on the little one."

"Right? I love puppers in clothes. The more human-looking, the better."

He handed her phone back. "Who's the second-place finisher?"

"This corgi. Saw her two weeks ago waiting at a bus stop with her human."

"They do have hilariously tiny legs," Logan agreed.

"I know, I love their hurried little waddle," Clare said. "Okay, and then this beast is my current number one. Saw him on the patio at Arbeiter Brewing. He's a malamute, which means he's roughly the size of a house, but fluffier than a fluffy kitty."

"*Fluffier than a fluffy kitty.* You really have a way with words."

"Shut up," she said, laughing. "He was very soft."

"I can tell by the way you've got your face buried in his neck. He must have very patient owners."

"They couldn't stop laughing at me," she explained. "Most people think it's either funny or weird, but whatever. Like I said, it makes me happy."

Logan put her phone on the table between them and poured himself another glass of wine, topping her off when she held out her glass. "We've established that you love dogs, but I can't help but notice you don't have one yourself. Why not?"

"My schedule, mostly. Dogs need routine, and sometimes I end up working long hours to finish up a project and I can't get home to walk one. They're not like cats, who are mostly self-sufficient. I could hire a dog-walker, I suppose, but I want to be there to play with it, you know? I'd just feel too guilty right now, so I spend a lot of time spoiling Kiki and weirding-out strangers."

"What about a cat?"

"I like cats, but not enough to own one," Clare replied. Logan nodded thoughtfully, sipping at his wine.

"I have a question for you."

"Shoot."

Clare folded her legs under her. "How did you know my last name? In your apartment, you called me Clare Thompson, but I don't think I ever told you my last name."

It seemed like Logan was carefully considering his words. "Mailboxes. Yours isn't too far from mine."

It was plausible, but still surprising. He turned to look at her. "Okay, so once and for all, explain Quest for Sulzuris to me. You've explained the basics of what it's about, but how do you play?"

Night had fully fallen and the solar-powered lanterns

scattered around the rooftop deck kindled to life by the time she finished explaining. To her surprise, Logan had listened.

And asked questions. And seemed interested.

They had next to nothing in common, but as the night wore on, Clare found herself still talking to him. And talking.

And talking.

She listened to him explain why he loved sports so much, and how he'd decided that business was a better major for him than art. He patiently explained the stock market to her twice—something she'd always been afraid to ask Aunt Peggy about—before she nodded, pretending that it made sense and wasn't just a figment of the world's collective financial imagination.

Clare had stopped by his place earlier with this idea to prove to herself they really were just friends, but she was quickly realizing that was stupid. She had thought this would clarify where they stood, but instead she was just sinking deeper into confusion. It didn't help that she couldn't seem to stop flirting with him, like there was a disconnect between her brain and her mouth.

The rest of the residents had long since abandoned the roof and the moon was tracking across the sky when a comfortable silence fell between them. The wine was long gone, as were the rolls, and only a few bites of cheese remained. Clare genuinely liked spending time with Logan, and she got the sense he wasn't like this with many people. To be perfectly honest, that felt good.

Clare rolled onto her side to get more comfortable, resting her cheek on her pressed-together hands. "You mentioned that your dad is retired, but not anything about your mom," she observed. Her voice was rough from overuse, threatening to crack on her second-to-last syllable.

Logan rolled over to face her. "That's because she died when I was three," he said softly.

"Oh," she said, equally quiet. "I'm sorry I asked like that."

"There's no way you'd have known. I don't really remember her much. It was a freak thing, an aneurysm in her sleep. Dad has lots of pictures though, and he talks about her sometimes. Less now, but a lot when I was little. Made me feel like I knew her."

Clare's heart softened and ached. She could picture him, a little boy with big blue eyes and dimpled elbows, sitting on his dad's lap listening to stories about his mother. "I'm really sorry you went through that," she said. "Even if you don't remember it, it must have been traumatic."

"Yeah." He didn't say anything else and she didn't press.

"What about you? I told you my foundational trauma. Your turn. What's a thing that made you who you are?"

"You're really into even-stevens, aren't you?" Clare said with a jaw-cracking yawn. "Mine's not nearly on the same level as yours."

"Try me."

She thought for a bit. "Okay, I've got one. But I feel bad comparing it to yours."

"It's not about comparison," Logan argued. "It's about me learning who you really are."

Clare had never thought Logan would want to know *who she really was*, but it wasn't like she had the willpower to refuse. "When I was fourteen, the hottest guy in school asked me to Homecoming, saying he wanted to meet me there. Or so I thought. I got a note in my locker from him, and I just assumed it was real. Even though we'd never spoken outside of the time he asked for my help during geometry. But I was stupid, and naive, and thought I'd really made an impression on him. So, I got dolled up and went."

Logan sucked in a breath. "I think I know where this is going."

"You probably don't. It was a prank, yeah, but not by Ryan. He had nothing to do with it. Even danced with me when he found out about it, but it was out of pity, so it was pretty awkward all around."

"Who was it?"

Clare turned to her back, her cheeks heating at the memory even if the sting of it was mostly gone. "Some guys I played Sulzuris with and thought were my friends. Turns out, they were assholes who wanted to teach me a lesson."

"What the fuck were you supposed to learn from that?"

"Unclear. Part of it was that one of them had asked me to Homecoming, but I just didn't think of him like that, so I said no. But for the rest of them, I think it was half *girls shouldn't be comfortable in gaming spaces* and half *don't forget nerd girls are below nerd guys in the social hierarchy*. Mostly just your garden-variety misogyny."

"Jesus, I'm sorry."

"I mean—I did feel a little bad for Kyle. I probably was sort of flirty with him, and it does suck to be rejected."

Logan made a face. "Everyone gets rejected; you don't set up an elaborate revenge plot just because someone doesn't like you the same way. But that sucks, I'm really sorry."

"Like I said, nowhere near the level of yours. But it is why I originally thought maybe you were pretending to be interested in me as like, a joke or something."

"What?" Logan half sat up, looking appalled. "You thought I'd do that?"

"Not now that I know you, no. But—I mean, come on. Look at us. We're not exactly in the same league."

Logan rolled to his back then, steadfastly refusing to meet

her eyes. She shifted uncomfortably, but he shook his head. "Did it ever occur to you that you might be out of *my* league?" he said, with unexpected heat.

"Please, I've seen the women you bring home. And you look like an underwear model, whereas I look like, well, someone who plays a tabletop RPG and owns a lot of sweaters with dogs on them."

"You've seen the women I bring home?" he asked with an arch of his eyebrow.

"In the elevator," she muttered, grateful that the darkness would mask the rising heat in her neck.

"Mmmm," he said, and she got the distinct impression he didn't believe her. "You realize that attractiveness is not just about physical looks?"

"It's easy to be philosophical when you look like *that*," she said, flapping her hand in his general direction.

"First of all, stop acting like you look like Chewbacca. Second of all, Chewbacca probably has his takers, so maybe that was a bad example, and also you're cute in a good way and I think you know it. Third of all—Jesus, Clare, do you know how intimidating you are?"

"Um, what?" she asked, dumbfounded. "I'm a short nerd with a baking fetish; that hardly qualifies as intimidating. And you were just telling me I need to be more assertive at work."

"Don't be like that," he scolded with a new edge of roughness in his voice that sent a frisson of sparks down her spine. "That work shit is on them, not you. Don't sell yourself short. You're what, twenty-seven?"

"Twenty-six," she corrected.

"You're only twenty-six, but you already know who you are. You just—embrace it. Your whole self. I'm cocky, but you're confident. And that? That's intimidating as *shit*."

Clare swallowed hard. "Oh."

"Yeah, *oh*. I'm hot, but looks aren't guaranteed for ever. Your sort of confidence isn't going anywhere."

"Now I think you're selling yourself short there," she countered. "And way overstating how sure of myself I am." She was hardly that confident at work, a fact Craig was constantly pointing out, and that she herself had admitted on several occasions.

"I'm not," he said fiercely.

"What are you saying?"

"I'm just saying—actually, I don't know what I'm saying. But I do know that long term, someone like you would get bored with a guy like me."

Clare wasn't sure how to respond to that. "Oh," she said again, still trying to parse what he'd said. *Does that mean he wants something long term, or he doesn't?* "You don't seem boring to me," she said, deciding it was best to not address the elephant in the room at all. Maybe it would disappear that way.

Logan's smile didn't quite reach his eyes. "Anyway, did you get revenge on those assholes? The ones who set you up?"

He was changing the subject, something she was noticing he did when things got too personal, even if he'd been the one to take it there in the first place. But she was a little too thrown by his description of her to put up much of a fight.

"Of a sort. I was the Game Master, so I sabotaged the game the next time we played. They thought I'd just keep playing with them, I guess. But I killed off all their characters and then blew up the universe we were in, so they'd have to start all over with someone else as GM."

Logan grinned. "Good. Serves those dickbags right."

"It did feel good," she agreed. "Your turn. Best revenge story."

"Oh, I've got a good one," he said, and the heaviness of a few moments ago melted away into the night. Logan told a long story about a roommate who refused to honor house rules about not eating each other's food, some laxatives, a house with one bathroom, and the risks of toilet-based revenge.

At some point, she must have drifted off to sleep, because when she opened her eyes, the sun was rising behind them, and Logan's thin plaid shirt was draped over her like a blanket. She didn't remember him giving it to her, and even though he was sound asleep in the chair next to her, she could see goosebumps prickling his skin.

It was a shame he wasn't interested in anything more, and neither was she, because Logan Walsh would be an excellent boyfriend.

The campaign was not going well. The Dragon Army had them on the ropes, and it turned out an un-cursed Ildash was significantly less powerful than he had been. Toni's elf paladin—Degar, an expert swordsman who still didn't trust Ildash—had taken heavy damage. Vaildra, Annie's demon rogue, had been caught behind enemy lines and was trying to talk her way out of execution for espionage, while Yaen was bogged down with Ildash, who had been overcome by guilt for his previous actions and was refusing to join the battle for fear he would accidentally hurt someone on their side.

"Does Ildash have to have so many feelings?" Toni grumbled. "I'm basically fighting this war on my own right now."

"As this game is our chance to escape from toxic masculinity and have men take responsibility for their actions for once, yes, the feelings are necessary. What's your move, Degar? Healing potion or keep fighting?" Devi prompted.

"Healing potion, do you think?" Toni asked the group. "I

feel like that has better odds, and I've been getting my ass kicked over here."

Annie nodded sagely. "I agree. Healing potion."

"Healing potion," Toni repeated, rolling the dice.

"It works, but you have to retreat from the front lines while it takes effect. The Dragon Army is pressing in on your left flank, and the vanguard is taking heavy losses. And then suddenly, time stops. The armies freeze where they are, stalled mid-charge. A lone butterfly is suspended in the air in front of Vaildra between her and her interrogators."

"Wait, are we about to meet—" Annie started.

"Shush. Patience," Devi said. "A column of purple flame appears in the center of camp and Ildash leaves Yaen's tent, approaching it cautiously. The flames solidify into the form of a woman, ethereally beautiful with glowing brown skin and thick, curly black hair. Finally, Ildash speaks. '. . . Your Majesty?'"

An explosion rocketed around Toni's table. "The Amethyst Queen?" Annie screeched. "She came to help us?"

"She came to see you," Devi qualified. "Help . . . that depends on next week."

Clare pumped her fist, and Toni and Annie high-fived.

"Cannot believe we're finally meeting her," Clare said, sweeping up the crumbs of her seven-layer bars and dumping them onto her plate. "How was work this week, Devi? Any more run-ins with that lady?" she added.

Devi reached for the chips and guac Toni had brought. "You mean the professor who wants me to find that book that might be blue and maybe was published in the last ten years? And who thinks I'm incompetent for not producing it immediately? Now she says the cover was 'maybe periwinkle,' like that is at all helpful. What about you? You still pretending you aren't into that dreamboat you banged?"

"I'm not," Clare said with a casual shrug.

It wasn't really the truth—Logan was quickly getting under her skin—but she couldn't explain why she was holding back without having to explain the situation at work, and she knew how the girls would react to that.

What they didn't know couldn't hurt them. Devi and Annie especially still had a grudge about the time Craig had her try kayaking, and admitting this would probably end up with them trying to convince her to quit, and Clare couldn't face that. This was her dream job and Craig was just trying to make her a better writer; she just had to prove herself, that's all. Once she did that, he would back off. She was sure of it.

"You haven't seen him at all?" Annie asked.

Once again, Clare shrugged. "I have, a bit. We hung out on the roof last night, but that's it. It was all totally casual, no romance." Admitting *we stayed up there all night talking* would have raised way too many questions she didn't want to answer.

Devi narrowed her eyes. "Are you sure?"

"Positive. He's been clear he doesn't want anything serious and anyway, we have like, nothing in common. He likes *basketball*, for Christ's sake."

"Ew," agreed Toni.

"Exactly. Which is why we're just friends."

"Okay, but you should know I've totally read this fanfic, and it ends with an epilogue where you've got a baby and another on the way," Annie said.

"I guarantee that's not what's happening," Clare said, just vehemently enough to make the rest of the group exchange looks. Clare decided it was time to change the subject. She asked Toni about her horses—Wayne and Garth—and fortunately, once Toni got going on her boys, literally nothing on earth could stop her.

But while Toni launched into a long story about the barn where she boards them and the owner's insistence on being called Mama Horse, which was very unsettling, Clare let her mind wander back to Logan.

Saying that there weren't feelings involved wasn't exactly true, but it was the safest thing for her to tell herself. She was determined not to repeat old patterns, and her old self would have already been practicing signing her name as *Clare Walsh*. Well, she probably wasn't that bad, but she was, by definition, a girlfriend-girl.

The smartest thing to do would be to slowly disengage with Logan; let their bond gradually wither into nothing more than friendly elevator banter. It would suck, but it was necessary.

Chapter Sixteen

It was Saturday morning, which meant Clare should be baking soon. Logan sat down in the armchair that looked straight out his side window and into Clare's apartment, peering into her kitchen. He felt weird—jittery, almost—and had since the other night on the rooftop. She had fallen asleep before him, hands pillowed under her cheek, and Logan had drifted off while watching her. The next morning, safe in his apartment, he had quickly sketched out what her face looked like while she was sleeping, and then immediately tore it up and threw it away. He still couldn't decide if he'd done so because the sketch looked wrong, or if he'd thrown it away because it was just a little too right.

But right now, he couldn't see her, and it was her usual baking time. He also had to make his lie real for Schneider, although he detested thinking of it that way. They were friends now, sure, but she still kept making jokes about how he wasn't her boyfriend and he needed to change that. He pulled out his phone, determined not to think about the fact that he felt almost nervous.

Logan
Don't you have baking to do this morning?

Clare
Stalker.

Logan
Want an assistant?

There was a slight pause before she replied.

Clare
If you're offering.

Logan bit back a smile and looked up to find Clare standing at her kitchen window with her arms crossed. She made an exaggerated glance at her wrist, like she was checking the time, and then tapped it.

Logan
Be right there.

Clare had the ingredients spread out on the counter by the time he got to her place, and she jumped right in without preamble. "Have you ever baked before?" She was wearing a bright yellow T-shirt and jeans, looking for all the world like a ray of sunshine.

God, he was getting cheesy.

"No," he admitted, washing his hands and coming to stand next to her.

"Have you at least watched someone bake before?"

"My dad made me cakes from box mixes for my birthday, yeah."

"Okay, that's a start. But we're doing this from scratch, so keep up," she said playfully. She started giving him instructions, showing him how to melt the chocolate in the microwave without burning it and explaining in far more detail than he personally thought was necessary why it was important to add the eggs last to the cheesecake batter.

"You'd think because it all gets mixed together you could just dump it all in at once," he observed, stirring the sticky mixture under her careful observation.

"You'd think, but you'd be wrong. Baking chemistry isn't just about combining things, it's about combining them in the right order."

"Like sex," Logan said without thinking.

Clare's eyebrows lifted. "Oh?"

His ears burned—it was a stupid analogy, and she would think he was stupid for making it. But he couldn't just say something like that and not explain. "You know, order matters. Chemistry matters."

Clare motioned for him to pour the batter into the dish on top of the crust. "I'm listening," she prompted.

Logan watched as she slid the dish into the oven, momentarily distracted by the shape of her ass. He caught himself just in time and leaned back against the sink as she turned. "Well, like with us and the elevator the other day. You never go straight from, 'Hello, nice to meet you,' to full-on fucking. Even if it's just a hookup, there are other steps."

"Such as?" she asked, glimmers of a smirk playing across her lips.

"Well, you start with hello, obviously," he replied. "Even if it's just casual, there's a prelude. Flirtation, either verbal or physical."

"Can't say I've ever *physically* flirted with someone without at least some verbal flirtation first," Clare said.

"Never met someone on the dance floor?"

"Um, no."

"Oh, well, it's not that different from meeting them elsewhere, except you let your bodies do the talking first."

Clare nodded absently, eyes dropping to his forearms. He had rolled his sleeves up to bake and now it seemed like she couldn't tear her eyes away from them and the fine dusting of flour over them. She licked her lips and nodded again.

Logan managed to wipe the smile from his face before she looked back at him. "Right, but like I was saying, there has to be a first step of some kind, even if it's brief. An exchange of intentions, if you will."

"And then?"

"Then, if you're on the same page, you move somewhere more private."

"Or not," she pointed out, and this time he didn't hide his smile.

"Or not," he agreed. "And then, well, you know."

"Enlighten me," Clare said, fidgeting. He watched her awkwardly cross and uncross her arms, letting his grin deepen.

"Come on, you've had hookups outside of me."

"I haven't, actually."

"Really?" he asked.

"Really."

He processed that information. He had figured she was more into relationships than he was, but not to this extent. "So casual isn't your usual thing, then."

"Call it expanding my horizons," she said, boosting herself up onto the counter. Her feet thumped against the thin wooden door of the cabinets and she drummed her fingertips on the work surface.

Right. Logan knew what he was good for, but that didn't mean he was going to back down from a challenge. "Okay then. Where we were?"

"Privacy."

"Right, privacy." Logan pushed off the sink and took a step toward her. "You've met each other, you're on the same page. There are sparks. This is when the seduction truly begins."

Clare made a slightly choked noise in response, but she was watching him avidly, movements suddenly stilled.

He let his grin get a little darker, more potent. He was treading on thin ice, a mere translucent veneer between him and dark, dangerous depths. But Logan wasn't much for thinking. He felt, and he did, that's all. "A lot of people think seduction is about getting what you want, but it isn't. It isn't about getting someone to give you what you want, it's about convincing someone to *take* what *they* want." Another step forward, another hard swallow that he tracked down the column of her throat. A voice in his head whispered *hit the brakes* but the train had long since jumped the tracks. This was something he knew, something he was good at.

This was something he *wanted*.

Clare cleared her throat, but her voice still came out breathy and shaky. "And how does that work?"

Logan fitted himself between her knees, hands pinned flat to the counter on either side of her thighs. "Convincing someone to take what they want?" he said, acutely aware that this close, the light brown flecks in her eyes looked golden. The freckles on her nose came into sharp focus, along with the pinkish tint staining her cheeks. There was an eyelash that had fallen to her cheekbone and he brushed it away with his thumb, dragging his gaze back to hers. *Slow down*, his brain hissed, but a deeper part urged him *keep going*.

He trailed his finger along the curve of her jaw, tilting it up. He watched the flush on her skin deepen, her pupils dilate. "Well, first . . . you make it clear you want the same thing."

He put his hands back on the counter, fingers splayed to overlap hers. "You give them an opening," he said, his own voice going hoarse. He leaned forward until the tips of their noses touched, but no further.

Clare reached out and grabbed him by his belt loops, tugging his hips flush with the counter. "You mean like that?" she said, grinning up at him.

Logan's heart did an odd stutter-step. "I did, yeah," he said, chuckling. He threaded his fingers into her hair, cupping his palm around her jaw and resting his thumb on her lower lip. He pressed down lightly, parting her lips, wondering idly why it felt like his heart was pounding harder than it ever had. He had kissed dozens of women, probably hundreds, and never once did it feel like his nerves were this overloaded, sending jittery, shaky signals through his body even as he laughed and pressed their foreheads together.

It has to be her call. That was his one coherent thought: Clare needed to start this kiss. He needed to be certain this was what she wanted, because then maybe it wasn't so bad, what he was doing.

Chapter Seventeen

Clare was having an out-of-body experience. She could have sworn she was floating above herself, watching Logan slowly prowl toward her. Watching her own arms reach out and tow him closer, giggling confidently. Watching his hand span her jaw, his other hand skating up the outside of her thigh to rest at the hollow of her waist. Their breath mingled and his nose brushed along the length of hers, nuzzling into her but not letting their mouths touch.

She licked her lips, flicking her tongue against the pad of his thumb where it rested on her lower lip and listened to him inhale sharply, like he'd been stung. *You give them the opening*, he'd said, and she knew she was in control, even as his touch kept her pinned in place.

Clare curled her fingers more securely into his waistband and this time it was a surprised huff of air that fanned her neck. She pulled back, just far enough to look into his eyes, and watched the corner of his lips tug upwards. "You're really making me work for this, aren't you?" he murmured.

Work. The word shouldn't have given her pause, especially since he was using it as a verb, not a noun, but suddenly she was thinking of Craig's challenge, and the job, and the way her teammates all laughed at her. *Old Clare would have fallen for Logan immediately; new Clare needs to be stronger than that.* Her reply had been on the tip of her tongue—something flirty, seductive, teasing—but she pulled back. "Wait," she said.

Logan froze. "What's wrong?" he asked, his hands falling away.

The loss of his touch made the air feel cold, her skin still tingling where his hands had been. Logan stepped back to give her more space. "Nothing, it's just—sorry, I wasn't expecting things to go that direction today," she said, pushing herself down from the counter in an effort to get a hold of herself. It was harder than killing a tentacle monster with a butter knife, quite frankly.

Logan stayed behind the counter as Clare moved away. Distance was good; having a faux-granite countertop between them was even better. She'd gotten carried away, that was all. Logan was too good at this and way too handsome for her, and just about anyone would have fallen under his spell. But she couldn't go there, not with him. Her little experiment on the rooftop had been more of a failure than a success—no, she hadn't slept with him, yes, she had discovered she definitely *wanted* to sleep with him again—but as long as she kept things on this side of physical, she was still doing what she needed to do. New life experiences were hookups and flings and that sort of thing, and falling for a guy she hooked up with was exactly what her coworkers thought she would do.

Craig had challenged her to change things up. And Noah had seen her with Logan, and she wasn't sure she could count on him not to bust her if she started dating Logan. Craig was chatty, and Noah was his favorite. The odds were just too high.

This wasn't about her personal life; this was about her job.

And Clare had worked too hard to get where she was, and had wanted it so badly for so long, that she couldn't afford to let Logan's muscly forearms distract her from it.

Logan seemed to be waiting for her to explain herself further. "It's not you, it's me," she said, and then immediately winced at the cliché. "I mean—I just thought this was a one-time thing. I wasn't expecting, um, you know."

"For me to want to kiss you again," Logan supplied.

Clare laughed weakly. "Yeah, that."

"Why not?" he said, and Clare had to swallow hard because Logan was a man who knew how to pitch his voice in the most devastating register possible. He took a small step toward her. "Why wouldn't I want to kiss you again?"

She hadn't counted on him arguing the point. "I mean, no offense, but like—that's your thing, right?"

There was a flash of something in his eyes and for a moment, she wondered if she'd gone too far. But then he laughed, no trace of hurt feelings to be seen. "That is me, yeah. But I have hooked up with people more than once, you know."

"I know, but—"

"Oh, you do?" he interrupted, arching an eyebrow.

Clare's traitorous cheeks blushed. "I just meant I wasn't expecting this, that's all."

Logan leaned forward, forearms resting on the counter. "What were you expecting?"

"For us to be . . . friends?"

"Friends," he repeated, and then he grinned dangerously. "I would have thought you were smarter than that, Thompson."

Chapter Eighteen

Logan's phone buzzed on the counter and he set down the bottle of wine he was in the process of opening. Sam was coming over with pizza to watch the Timberwolves play the Lakers, and he figured this was her standard "sorry, running late" text. Little did Sam know, he had never once, in their ten years of friendship, expected her to be on time. He unlocked his phone and blinked at the name at the top of the text.

Clare
Very big, very awkward favor to ask.
As a FRIEND
I have the stomach flu and desperately need provisions, but everyone is either out of town or stuck at work
And the last time I ordered from QuickEats, they just gave it to some random person who was in the lobby so now I have trust issues
Could you run to the store and get me a couple bottles of Gatorade and packets of instant ramen? You can just leave them outside my door and I'll pay you back later

Logan
Define "everyone"
And "FRIEND"

Clare
I would except I have to go puke now

He smiled softly, glad she wasn't so sick she couldn't dish it back. He hadn't heard from Clare since their almost-kiss, and he wasn't sure how to navigate things now. He had gotten carried away and spooked her, if her whole "don't you just sleep around a lot?" speech had been any indication. But if Clare was asking him a favor—even if he was the last person on her list and she was being not subtle about not wanting to date him—maybe there was hope for them after all.

Logan
What flavor Gatorade? Blue?

Clare
What are you, a monster? Yellow or gtfo

Logan glanced at the clock on his microwave to confirm that Sam was supposed to arrive in ten minutes, which meant he really had at least twenty-five. He grabbed his keys and his wallet, sliding on the sandals he left near the door, and headed out. He was still in an old pair of basketball shorts and a sleeveless shirt from a charity tournament he and Vince had played in a few years ago, but the store was just around the corner from their building anyway.

He had at least ten minutes to spare before Sam's true arrival time when he reached Clare's door. He knocked and waited long enough that he was about to pull out his phone to make sure she was still conscious when he heard slow shuffling on the other side of the door.

"Logan?"

"You were expecting someone else?"

She sighed and he bit back a grin. "Just leave it at the door. I don't want to get you sick. Oh, and here." She slid a ten-dollar bill under the crack in the door and Logan rolled his eyes, crouching down to shove it back.

"I'm not taking your money, just consider this being neigh-borly," he called.

Another sigh. "Okay, but I'm waiting until you leave to come out and get it. You really don't want this; it's nasty."

"Understood," he said, setting down the plastic bag. He took a couple of unnecessarily loud steps away before tiptoeing back to her door, careful to stay close to the wall.

Ten seconds later, the door unlocked and Clare crawled out.

Literally crawled. On all fours.

She grabbed the bag and turned around, freezing when her gaze met his feet. She raised her eyes slowly, like she was hop-ing against hope it would be someone other than him. Logan leaned his shoulder against the edge of her door and crossed his arms. "Whatcha doing down there?" He probably shouldn't tease her when she was sick, but he couldn't help himself. She was just too damn cute.

Clare rested her forehead on the grey industrial carpet lin-ing the hallway. "Hoping you wouldn't see me like this?" She pushed herself up heavily, wincing until she was settled with her back against the other side of the door jamb. She was in a white T-shirt several sizes too big for her and for a moment, Logan was seized with irrational jealousy at the idea that per-haps it belonged to another man. But then he saw that it said

Galadriel for President in a faux-political ad font and the need to punch someone eased. She crossed her arms over her stomach and he took in the grey, clammy pallor of her skin and the sweat darkening the wisps of hair on her forehead.

He frowned, his retort dying on his tongue. "How long have you been sick?"

"I dunno, woke up early this morning feeling like shit." She hissed, crossing her arms tighter, and Logan crouched down to her level. "Maybe food poisoning, although I can't figure out what it would have been, which leaves stomach flu, I guess."

"Stomach pain?"

"When you've been puking your guts out for twelve hours your stomach is probably going to hurt, yes," she said, face tightening again. Clare flinched away when he lifted his hand. "Seriously, don't touch me. You probably shouldn't even be standing this close."

Logan ignored her and touched the back of his hand to her forehead. Her skin was scalding. He trailed his knuckles down the side of her face, watching her eyes flutter closed at his touch. "Where does it hurt?"

"My stomach, I told you."

"No, I mean—is it your whole stomach? Or just one side?"

She shook her head, stopped, and her eyes went big. "Shit, do you think it's appendicitis?"

Logan gently pried her hand away from her midsection. "I'm going to push and when I let go, tell me how it feels," he said and very lightly pressed down on her right side. She grimaced, and when he lifted his hand, she let out a pitiful squeak.

"That hurt," she whimpered. "A lot."

Logan stood. "Where's your purse?"

"It might not be appen—"

"I'm not going to let you sit here by yourself and find out," he said curtly. "By then it might be too late. Purse, phone, and shoes. And keys. Where are they?"

"Uh . . . right inside the door for purse and shoes and keys, phone—" she broke off, curling into a fetal position. "Phone is . . . maybe by my bed?"

Logan shouldered into her apartment and found her phone hidden under a tangle of blankets in her bed. He grabbed her purse and shoes and walked back to her, once more crouching down. "Wait, you've got—shorts or something on, right?" he said, realizing her shirt was long enough that she might not.

"Yeah," she said through gritted teeth. "I didn't come out into the hallway pantsless."

"That's a shame," he teased, even though his heart was racing. He was glad the shoes he'd found for her slipped on; his hands were shaking so badly he wasn't sure he could tie them.

Clare laughed weakly and let him ease the shoes onto her feet. Logan handed her her purse, phone safely tucked inside, and emptied the Gatorade and ramen out of the bag and onto the floor inside her door. He pressed the plastic bag into her hands. "For puking," he said solemnly, and helped her up.

He let her lean on him for two steps and then stopped, carefully swooping her up against his chest, legs dangling over his other arm. "This okay?" he asked. She smelled like sick, overly sweet with a tang of sweat, and she nodded. Logan took a step toward the elevator and then paused. "I'm—"

"Going to have to take the stairs, yeah. Can't risk getting stuck," she finished.

"It might hurt. I'll try not to jostle you," he murmured, silently cursing the building's management, and she nodded again.

She was trying not to make a sound, he could tell. But even though he was doing his best to insulate her from any jarring movements, being carried down five flights of stairs was going to be bumpy. Every whimper and moan she let escape felt like a dagger in his chest, and by the time Logan made it to his car in the underground garage he wasn't sure if the sweat making his shirt stick to his chest was from her or him. Clare lumbered over to a trash can and threw up several times while he waited, rubbing her back until she straightened. "Ready?" he asked.

Clare could only manage a nod.

The hospital was just on the other side of downtown, but it felt like it was in another state. Every red light had him screaming inside, glancing at Clare out of the corner of his eye. She was resting her face against the window, eyes shut, breathing ragged. He pulled into the emergency room parking lot and jumped out, not even letting her try to walk. "I've got you," he said as soothingly as he could past the lump in his throat. She whispered something he didn't catch in response.

The doors hissed open and a blast of cool air and bright fluorescent light hit them both. Maybe it was his imagination, but Clare seemed to have gotten paler since their hallway, dark circles blooming under her eyes. A nurse hurried over with a wheelchair and Logan set her down as carefully as he could. The triage nurse began asking questions that Clare did her best to answer, eyes darting between the nurse and him.

"Let's get you to a room," the nurse said kindly, once Clare had explained her symptoms.

Clare looked at Logan again. "Are—"

"Your boyfriend can come too, it's fine," the nurse replied.

"He's not—"

"Great," Logan interrupted. "Lead the way."

"You don't have to, I'm fine," Clare said as he followed them around a corner and through a set of doors.

"You are not fine," he corrected. "I'm staying."

The nurse took them to a hallway of curtained-off rooms. "You'll be here until we admit you. If you can, put the gown on, ties go in the back. Someone will be with you shortly," she said, swishing the curtain closed.

Clare moved gingerly from the wheelchair to the bed. "You really don't have to stay. Devi should be almost done with her shift at the library, and if she can't come, I can call someone else."

"I'm not leaving you here alone," Logan said firmly. His heart was still in his throat and privately, he marveled that he hadn't yelled for a goddamn doctor already. *Can't you see she's in pain?* He didn't understand why they couldn't give her pain-killers first, then make her wait around. "Need help with the gown?"

"I can manage," she said. "Do you mind turning around?"

Logan faced the curtain between them and the next compartment, which was currently empty. There was the rustle of cloth and a few whimpers of pain, but soon enough she cleared her throat. "Okay, I'm decent," she announced.

Logan turned back and watched her struggle with the sheets, stepping forward to lift them up to her waist. It was easier to focus on the rough cotton than meet her eyes. "You ready in there?" someone called from the hallway.

Logan took her upturned hand in both of his and sat down. "Ready," she replied.

Chapter Nineteen

Clare's eyelids were heavy. Heavier than heavy. It was like gravity had conspired with the universe to become unnaturally powerful, specifically on her eyelids. A quiet whirring sound hummed in the distance, emitting the occasional tiny beep. She considered giving up the fight and letting gravity win, keeping her eyes closed, when she heard the squeak of someone shifting in a vinyl chair.

She pried her eyes open to discover she was looking at the top of Logan's head. His forearms were resting on his knees, gaze fixed on his phone just below the level of her bed. He was texting, letting out a vaguely annoyed *harrumph* every so often. The world slowly coalesced into something understandable around her, the edges of the hospital room coming into sharp focus and the events of earlier crowding into her brain.

The trip to radiology, followed by a hurried consultation with a surgeon. Then the anesthesiologist, patiently telling her to start counting backwards and chuckling when she asked if she could do it in Elvish. It probably seemed silly to him, but the bravado was the only way she could get through this without crying. She had hazy, formless memories of the recovery room, a nurse telling her that her boyfriend would be waiting in her room and Clare trying in vain to explain that Logan was just a neighbor.

Or maybe that happened in this room, another indistinct memory of him standing off to the side as she made her thick, clumsy tongue explain that they *weren't really anything, you see, not like that.* She cringed, hoping that memory was wrong.

Logan ran his hand through his hair, back and forth until it was standing on end, eyes still on his phone. She lifted her hand to get his attention, but instead of waving she found herself reaching out and smoothing down an errant lock of his hair. It was thick and soft to the touch and suddenly there was nothing she wanted more than to run her hands through it.

Logan's head snapped up. "You're awake," he said, scanning her from head to foot like he was trying to catalogue any missing parts.

"Awake and appendix-less," she said.

Logan frowned thoughtfully. "There's something you should know," he said, leaning forward. "Something . . . went wrong. In surgery."

"What?" She sat up as best she could, quickly scanning her body. Two arms, two legs, all seemingly intact. There was that, at least.

He tucked a wisp of hair behind her ear, looking mournful, biting the thumb of his other hand. "They—they ended up having to do an experimental procedure. You now have Nicolas Cage's face and John Travolta has yours."

His face split into a grin and she snorted, followed immediately by a whine of pain. "You dick," she said, clutching her still-tender stomach as she cackled. "Laughing hurts."

"Oh shit, sorry," he said, but his eyes were dancing, and she decided the pain was worth it, if it meant he looked at her like that. "It is weird though, seeing you with Nicolas Cage's face. Doesn't look right," he said.

Clare grabbed the nearest thing to her—a giant remote with a cable attaching it to the bed—and smacked his shoulder.

Logan plucked it from her hand before she could hit him again. "Seriously, how are you feeling? Do you need me to get the nurse?"

Clare felt wrung out, quite frankly. But she smiled wanly anyway. "I'm fine. Could feel better, but I felt worse earlier."

Maybe it was just her imagination, but it seemed like he let out a long, slow breath. "Good. Good good good," he said.

"How did you know, by the way? That it was appendicitis? You might have saved my life."

Logan looked toward the door and ruffled his hair again. "You would have gone to the doctor eventually," he said.

"Not necessarily. Several years with shitty health insurance means I got very good at putting off basic necessities and ignoring problems. But how did you know? You were so certain it wasn't just the stomach flu."

For a long moment, he didn't answer and when he spoke, he kept his eyes on the ground. "I used to look stuff up. Ways people died suddenly, how to know they were sick, when to go to the hospital. That sort of thing."

Clare's insides had already taken a beating, but it was nothing compared to the blow he just landed on her chest. "Oh Logan," she said quietly, but then a nurse walked through the door with the surgeon in her wake.

"Oh good, you're up," Dr. Drew said, pulling out a stool from the nurse's station near her bed and clasping her hands between her knees. "How are you feeling?"

"Okay, I guess," Clare said, trying to peel her eyes away from Logan. She wasn't sure how to respond to his revelation, or if he even wanted her to. Dr. Drew ran through how her surgery went (smoothly, no complications, no spur-of-the-moment face transplants), and the restrictions she would have for the next few days (take it easy, mostly, and no heavy lifting, which Clare didn't really do anyway.) She finished up with an indulgent smile at Logan. "Any questions? No? Well, I'm glad he talked you into coming here," she said, and Logan ducked his head in uncharacteristic embarrassment. "Things could have gotten very bad, but we were able to intervene in time. You'll be able to go home tomorrow, assuming nothing changes."

She left, and the nurse, Jamie, took Clare's vitals while Logan fidgeted; rubbing his palms on his thighs and then through his hair, standing up to move out of the nurse's way and then sitting down just a little too fast. Jamie left and Clare opened her mouth to ask him something—about his admission earlier, or maybe about why he even bothered to stay when she told him he didn't have to—but Logan stood up again. "I'll give you a minute to get settled," he said, striding out like he wanted to be anywhere else.

Clare looked around the room, wondering what exactly she was supposed to do to *get settled*. She ended up raising the back of the bed so she was sitting up straighter and moving the blankets around her legs, just for something to do.

He was gone long enough she started to worry, but then Logan came back with something small clutched in his hands. "Sorry, there's not much to do here and there's nothing on TV, at least nothing that isn't sports or home improvement stuff. And I know how you feel about sports, at least. Not sure how you feel about shows that overuse the term *man cave* but I'm taking a guess that you don't love them." He held out his hand. "I figure this would kill, like, maybe ten minutes?"

Clare squinted, wishing she had thought to bring her glasses. "Is that . . . nail polish?"

"Yeah. Jamie, um, loaned it to me. She said we can't do your fingers because they have to, like, see them? I didn't totally follow, although I guess it has to do with circulation or something. But she said your toes would be fine."

"Really?" she asked, cocking her head. Now that she was looking at him without the immediate haze of anesthesia hanging over her, she realized he was not wearing the workout clothes he had been in before. He was in blue scrubs that were too tight across the shoulders and around his biceps and baggy around his waist. "Wait, did they give you *clothes* too?"

"Just temporarily," he said, the awkwardness that surrounded him coming at her in waves. "I was a little cold, and one of the other nurses said they have extras."

"That sounds fake."

He sat down, sighing. "There's not really a not-conceited way to say this, but women—and some men—um, they have a certain reaction to me."

"They give you things," Clare filled in.

"They give me things," he confirmed. "It's, you know," he said, gesturing at his face and then his torso, "this."

Clare snorted and the tension in the room shattered. She took pity on him, as his ears were burning, and changed the subject. "Who were you texting just now?"

Okay, maybe not that much pity.

"Sam. We were supposed to watch a game together, but I bailed. Don't worry about it, she's fine."

"She wasn't mad that you stood her up?"

"Honestly, yes, she was, but it's whatever. It's Sam."

"She's fine now?"

"She'll get over it," he clarified. "She's always, like, fifteen minutes late to anything we plan anyway. Considering how long I've known her, I've probably spent two whole days waiting for her procrastinating ass. I've earned a freebie." There was a note of fond annoyance as he talked about Sam that always made Clare want to smile.

Logan held up the nail polish. "Did you want to use this? I can go give it back to Jamie, if you don't."

Clare almost never painted her fingernails, although not for any real reason. She liked dressing up and being cute, but nail polish was just one extra thing she never really got into. But the color was a pretty turquoise and Logan seemed to want to hang around, so she nodded. "Sure, why not. Not sure I can bend to reach my feet, though."

Logan cracked open the top. "I'll do it," he offered.

"Have you ever done someone's nails before?"

"How hard can it be? It's like painting a very tiny wall."

"The difficulty is in the tininess, not the skill level."

"Whatever, I've got this," he said, deftly flipping up the blanket and carefully sliding off the grey, fluffy socks they had given her before surgery. He picked up her left foot delicately, lifting it slightly closer to him.

Clare bit back the sharp inhale she wanted to take. Even post-op, full of painkillers that dulled her senses to a grey, formless blob, his light touch sent sparks across her skin. A tiny, cool brushstroke tickled her cuticle, and she made herself tease him instead. "Oops, looks like you already screwed up," she said.

He looked up at her, eyes dark, and she realized she had made a grave miscalculation. Now, he wasn't just holding her foot, he was holding her foot and gazing at her and all she wanted to do was kiss him. But she had been dry-heaving in his car just a few hours ago, and she was currently in a hospital gown that resembled a tent. Meanwhile, Logan looked like he was auditioning for the role of McDreamy's younger, hotter brother. He would be a perfect character on one of those shows, breaking hearts and saving lives, and—

"Clare?" he said, with a slight air of impatience.

"Hmm?"

"I said, since you're here overnight, did you want me to run back to your place and get you anything? Or I could call a friend; have them do it."

"Peggy is the only one with a key, but she's at her friend's cabin this weekend with Kiki. But I could call Devi, and she would meet you there and bring it here for me, I'm sure."

"I assume Devi was the *stuck at work* portion of your friends?"

"She's a reference librarian at the U. Pulled the evening shift this week, which sucks. She's done by eight-ish, and she's usually so exhausted she goes straight to bed when she gets home."

"So probably not awake this late."

"No, she's asleep for sure, but she'd understand. If you wanted to get going, you can. I'm seriously fine, you don't need to babysit me if you don't want to. I'm sure you'd rather be home."

Logan lowered his gaze to her foot, moving to her next toe as he delicately skimmed the brush down her nail. "Who said anything about me wanting to go? I just thought you might be more comfortable with a friend here."

"Aren't you a friend?" The words were out of her mouth before she could second-guess them.

He paused. "A friend, yeah."

"Logan—"

"No, I get it," he said. "You've been pretty clear I'm *just a friend.*"

The hint of bitterness in his voice took her aback. She had thought it was just banter; that when he teased her about wanting to date she never thought he *meant* it. That was just how Logan was, flirtatious and charming and always trying to win. Clare hadn't ever thought a guy like Logan would want to date her, simply because he didn't really date.

She still couldn't picture a world where Logan really did want to be her boyfriend. He was him, and she was her. But maybe it wasn't that; maybe it was that she'd wounded his ego. It probably had been embarrassing to listen to her insist to any-one who would listen that he wasn't her boyfriend, even if it was the truth. Clare bit her lip, considering her words carefully. "Friend is a good word, though," she said, her eyes on the top of his head as he pulled the brush down the nail on her middle toe. "I care about my friends." When he didn't look up, she kept going. "I'm sorry if I hurt you."

"You didn't hurt me," he said flatly, moving to the next toe. "I get it." Clare didn't think he did get it, actually, but his tone was final. Logan looked up, his face clearing. "Let me finish your other foot, then I can run back and get your stuff. I assume you need your glasses?"

"How did you know I wear glasses?" she asked, deciding to follow his lead and act like the previous two minutes hadn't happened.

Logan feigned an exaggerated squint. "How did you know?" he mimicked. He ducked the light kick she sent his way and clicked his tongue in disappointment. "Don't go messing up my hard work," he scolded. He caught her ankle firmly, giving her a brief, hooded look. "Behave," he said sternly.

Clare stilled and a frisson went down her spine. She licked her lips, nodding. "Proceed," she said, and he returned to his work, heedless of the storm he had started in her veins.

Chapter Twenty

"Easy there," Logan said, hovering a few steps behind Clare. She insisted on walking into her apartment—they risked the elevator this time—but she was still too slow and shaky for his comfort. She kept telling him she was fine, but Logan would have preferred she stay in the hospital another night. Jamie had flatly told him there was no need, but Logan personally felt it was better to be safe than sorry.

Besides, once she was out of mortal danger, hanging out in the hospital room with Clare was kind of . . . fun. He had grabbed her e-reader from her bedside when he came back to get her things, and she spent most of the next day reading while he watched highlights of the game he'd missed. She napped on and off, and Logan was surprised by how much his chest ached to watch her sleep. She had regained most of her color by then, but the memory of her, grey-faced and shaky on the hallway floor, would not easily leave him. He had never been good with illness, but something about Clare overrode his usual run-far-away instincts, replacing them with a need to be by her side at every moment.

Clare sat down heavily on her couch and looked at her

phone. She squinted through her glasses—they must have been dirty—and leaned her head back. "Devi'll be here soon. You can head home."

"I'd rather not leave you alone," Logan said, taking a seat in her cozy armchair. "You seem to be prone to exploding organs and I'd rather not risk it."

"As the only organ that would explode has now been removed, I think I'm safe. And like I said, Devi will be here any minute now."

"Then it's not much trouble for me to wait. Unless you don't want me here?" He was kidding, but only sort of. After that moment in the hospital when he'd snapped about being *friends* he knew he needed to tread carefully. He wanted her friends to like him and if they didn't, well, that would really suck. And if Clare straight up didn't want him to meet them at all? Well, that would suck the most.

No, he was not going to examine that any further.

"Yes, I want to keep your hideous visage from scaring her," Clare deadpanned. "No, I just meant—you already spent all last night and today with me. You don't have to hang around if you don't want to."

What if I want to? Logan couldn't bring himself to ask that. It felt too real, too vulnerable, and anyway, Clare clearly didn't want anything like a relationship with him. If he wanted to be able to pull this off with Schneider, he needed her to be more comfortable with the idea of them dating. There was a part of him that wanted to prove to himself, not just Schneider, that he could do this—he could be a good boyfriend, that he could find a woman who liked him and wanted to stick around. It was stupid, but Logan had never pretended to be smart.

And then there was the part of him that wanted it to be real, but he didn't know how to handle that.

Devi chose that moment to push in through the door in a whirlwind of energy and disapproving looks. "What the fuck, Clare," she said the moment she arrived. "Seriously, what the fuck."

Clare had her head back with her eyes closed, and she didn't even bother to open them. "Hey, Devi."

"You were in the *hospital* and you didn't call me until *now*?"

"I was fine; Logan was there." Clare accompanied this with a vague wave of her hand in his general direction.

She seemed to notice him for the first time, whipping her head to him so fast her hair swung into her face. "You must be Logan. Devi," she said, holding out her hand for a firm, business-like shake. "Thanks for taking care of her."

"Not a problem," Logan said, surprised to find he meant it. He hadn't showered in two days and would be smelling that hospital antiseptic scent for at least another week, but he would do it all again in a heartbeat.

Probably best not to examine that either.

Devi was looking curiously between them, and Logan decided it was probably time for him to leave, before Clare announced once more that he was not, in any way, shape, or form, her boyfriend. His ego could only take so much. He pushed up to standing and tucked his hands in his pockets. "Now that you're in good hands, I'll be on my way," he said.

He had turned to go when Devi spoke up. "We should thank you properly," she said in a voice that told him he would do best to immediately agree to whatever she offered. "Would you want to join us on a Quest for Sulzuris campaign? I could pull a special one-shot together for us next weekend."

Logan looked at Clare to make sure this was a welcome suggestion, and was surprised to find her eyes lit up. "Oh my god, would you want to?" she said enthusiastically. "That would be fun."

"You sure?"

"Of course. I'll help you get a character together this week."

The knot of pressure in his chest eased, and he grinned. "Then count me in."

"Is there something going on out there?" Sam asked sharply.

Logan jerked his head away from where he had been peering toward Clare's apartment. Devi had left a few hours ago and now someone else was there, a woman with platinum blonde hair who was curled up on the couch watching TV with Clare.

"Hmm?"

"You've barely watched the game."

"I'm watching."

"Uh huh. What's going on?"

"We're losing."

"Lucky guess. By how much?"

On the TV, the game cut to commercial before he could check the score and Logan flopped back on his couch, sighing heavily. He covered his face with his hands so he didn't have to see Sam's sharp look. "I'm an idiot."

"Yeah, I know."

"No, I mean, I really, really am."

"No argument here."

He dropped his hands and glared. "You're going to make me tell you everything, aren't you?"

Sam's eyes lit up and she folded her legs under her. "Oh, this is going to be good, isn't it?"

"No, it's bad."

"Bad as in embarrassing, or just bad?"

"Just bad. Don't look so thrilled, Jesus."

"Let me have this." She tossed her ponytail over her shoulder and straightened. "Okay, shoot."

"I took Clare to the hospital."

"Yeah, I know, because I was left standing like an *asshole* outside this very building for *forty minutes* until you deigned to respond to my texts and calls."

"I know. But I stayed with her." Sam had been texting him while he was in the hospital with Clare, but he had let her believe he left after he drove her there, not willing to handle the avalanche of shit he was going to get from her then. Logan had refused to drive Sam to the airport once three years ago, and he still hadn't heard the end of it. Sam knowing he spent the night in the hospital with Clare was going to give Sam way more information that he was willing to hand out. But the avalanche was coming, so he might as well trigger it now.

". . . in the hospital?"

"Yeah."

"Overnight?"

"Yeah. And the whole next day."

"Like you were a couple. But you're not."

"No, of course we aren't. Or, I mean, she doesn't want to be."

"You're sure of that?"

"Positive."

"But do you want more?"

"I—don't know," he admitted. If he told Sam about Schneider and his original plan, she would punch him in the face.

"Okay, first of all, I fucking called it. Second of all, close your eyes."

"I don't trust you enough to do that. You're going to write *loser* on my forehead with permanent marker again."

Sam rolled her eyes. "That was one time, and you deserved it. Close them and trust me, okay?"

With one last suspicious look at her, Logan closed his eyes. "Fine, now what?"

"Think about the future."

"Like flying cars and shit?"

"How are you this handsome and yet this dumb?"

"Practice," he said, and cracked one eye open. "I'm still waiting."

Sam made an annoyed noise in the back of her throat. "Think about the future. Your future, specifically. Not tomorrow, but like, a year from now. Picture a perfect day."

At first, Logan couldn't think of anything. His life would probably be exactly the same as it was now; but then something shifted into focus. Lazy Saturday mornings in bed, followed by pancakes and laughter. There was a dog, jumping on the bed with them and demanding walks even before they had their coffee. Everything was bathed in a warm, yellow light that reminded him of Clare, who was with him for all of it.

Logan's eyes flew open and he stared at Sam in horror, everything sinking in. The pieces had all been there before, but he hadn't quite managed to put it all together. He was terrified the whole time Clare was sick, and liked spending time with her with no plan or agenda or even reason. He had been trying all damn day not to think about what that meant. And now— now he couldn't *not* think about it.

Oh.

Fuck.

Sam scrunched up her nose. "You doing okay there, buddy?"

Logan tipped his head back against the couch, groaning. "No."

"You like her, don't you?"

"I do."

"Awww, Logan's first feelings. This is so cute, like watching a baby goat walk for the first time."

"Fuck you, I'm way more coordinated than that," Logan said, even as his heart was racing.

"If that's what you need to tell yourself," Sam said, pushing herself up on her knees and patting the top of his head. "Cheer up, feelings are rarely fatal."

He was so, so fucked.

Chapter Twenty-one

"Hey, Clare, got a minute?" Noah called across the office. She deleted the sentence she'd just written—Captain Ellis should have seduced the prince, not the king, she decided—and hit save.

"Yeah?" she said, standing and walking over to where Craig and the rest of the team were huddled. She had been thinking about Logan's advice from the roof: she needed to be more assertive, more determined. And not in the roundabout way she'd been doing it before. She needed to be bold and blunt. Unforgettable.

"Settle something for us," Noah said, sharing a conspiratorial grin with Craig. "If you and your party were stuck in a barren wasteland with thousands of reanimated orcling corpses between you and your destination, would you rather they retain the ability to fight with a limited number of ranged weapons, or have their teeth and claws be instantly fatal?"

"Zombie orclings with limited bow and arrow range, but you survive their bite; or zombie orclings that operate under the usual zombie rules, you're asking?" She leaned her hip against one of the tables while Craig watched her closely.

She could feel that this was some sort of test, but she wasn't sure how to pass it. She would just have to go with her gut. "Ranged weapons," she decided. "It's different from other zombie universes and would set it apart."

There was a beat of silence, and then Noah beamed at Craig. "See? Even Clare agrees with me."

She disliked that *even Clare* phrasing, and she disliked the look on Craig's face even more. He looked annoyed, and Craig, like a lot of sensitive writer-types, tended to lash out when irritated. Clare wasn't like that, but plenty of the men at Quest Gaming were. She was about to do a U-turn and argue for what had clearly been Craig's idea, before she decided against it. If she wanted her team to listen to her opinions, she couldn't be wishy-washy. Maybe Craig might even be impressed with her for standing her ground, once he got over the sting of her siding with Noah. That was how a Senior Designer would act, after all. "It's just so much more unusual, you know?" she said in as friendly of a tone as possible to show Craig there were no hard feelings. "There'd probably be some marketing value in that. Disintegrating orclings throwing spears, that sort of thing."

Noah gave Craig another smug look, and Craig straightened. "How's that project of yours working out, Clare?" he asked, just a little too loudly.

She kept her smile placid. "Captain Ellis is great, thanks. Right now I'm working on a kingdom where—"

"And your assignment?" he asked bluntly. "You really do need more of that *life experience* we talked about. Especially if you think you should be put up for Senior Game Designer."

Clare blinked, surprised he was being so blunt. "I'm, um, working on it." Okay, so she'd had one one-night stand, and now she was sort of developing feelings for Logan, but the longer she thought about it the grosser it all felt and the more she just wanted out. "Noah, uh, ran into me when I was out the other week," she added, praying that Noah would show one of his occasional flashes of decency.

"Is that what that was," Noah said drily. "Then yes, I can confirm that."

"Keep it up then," Craig said, face still stern. The team started to disperse, drifting back to their computers, and Clare pulled out her phone when she sat back down. For a minute she wanted to text Logan, but she felt weird about that all of a sudden.

Clare
Work question
How involved is too involved for a boss to be in your personal life?

Devi
Involved at ALL is too much
What did Craig do?

Clare frowned to herself. Her friends had never really liked Craig, and didn't understand why she followed his advice. But that was because none of them really understood what this job meant to her. Sure, they all loved Quest for Sulzuris unreservedly, but for the rest of the group, it was just a game they did on the weekends. For Clare, it was everything. Writing for it was all she had wanted since she was a kid first discovering how exhilarating it could be to pretend you were freeing imaginary lands from dragons and cursed kings and evil sorcerers. If she told Devi what Craig had suggested, Devi would tell her to quit, and that simply wasn't an option, not when she might be able to move up. She decided to backtrack.

Clare
Nothing
Just watching him interact with the guys, is all

Devi
You know the way they don't include you in shit is bad, right?

Clare
I know, I know
But it's my choice
I hate Call of Duty and laser tag and camping

Devi
Weird how your boss only does group activities you don't like

Clare
Forget I asked

Devi
Seriously, is everything okay?

Clare
Everything's great, I promise

Clare put her phone away, feeling somehow worse than before.

Chapter Twenty-two

"Explain the part about spell slots to me again," Logan said as they approached Devi's front door.

"You don't have to have this stuff memorized," Clare said, but he did not feel nearly as chill as Clare wanted him to be. He was normally all confidence when it came to meeting new people, but he was now seized with an unfamiliar bout of nervousness. He wanted Clare's friends to like him, and he wasn't used to needing that sort of approval.

Also, he liked Clare. Everything was terrible.

"There's no time limit on this," Clare continued. "And we'll all talk you through any questions you have. We were all newbies, once. And the goal of every Sulzurian is to get other people to love the game as much as we do."

"They won't get annoyed? I could still fuck this up, you know," he said, taking the tote bag of brownies from her hands as she opened the door.

"There's no real way to fuck it up, that's the whole point of this game," Clare replied reassuringly. "Hey, we're here!" she called into Devi's kitchen.

"Bitch better have my brownies," Devi called back as she emerged. "Oh, hey Logan, you ready?"

Logan held up his character sheet with what he hoped was a charming smile. "As ready as I can be. Clare keeps promising I can't like, lose this for you guys, but there's a *lot* of rules."

"So many rules," Devi agreed. "But Clare's right, we'll help you out. And I'm the Game Master, so a lot of it is on me. I promise not to kill you."

"What if I accidentally die?"

Devi grinned and handed him a bowl of chips. "We'll figure something out," she promised. "This is a universe with magic. You might end up a zombie, but we'll make it work."

Clare had told him roughly the same thing, but it helped to have Devi repeat it.

Toni, Chase, and Annie arrived at the same time in a cacophony of noise. Toni had beer that needed to go in the fridge, Chase was busy telling Annie some story from work, and Annie kept tripping on the shoes by the door and swearing loudly.

Annie noticed Logan first. "Oh, you must be—the neighbor," she said, awkwardly catching herself when Clare bugged her eyes out at her.

Neighbor was definitely not *boyfriend*, so clearly he had his work cut out for him. "I'm Logan, yeah. And you are—?"

Annie introduced herself, followed by Toni, and then Chase took his seat across from Logan with a nod. Logan shifted a little and sat up straighter just as Devi sat down at the head. "As we all know, this is a special one-shot campaign, as a thank you to Logan for taking care of our Clare," Devi started, and Logan's stomach bloomed with warmth. *Our* Clare. Like he was included in that group.

Devi called up his character sheet that he and Clare had

created. They had worked on it for two solid evenings to figure out his character because he was leaving nothing to chance. He was taking this very seriously. They were doing a whole special one-off storyline just for him, with everyone playing their regular characters but on a hiatus from the main story. That way, he could join in for the day without derailing their current campaign.

Devi looked up at the group, eyes dancing. "Everyone, please welcome Keith the Ogre."

Well, maybe not *that* seriously.

Annie broke first and snorted. "Keith?"

"It's not a name you hear often," Logan countered with a grin.

Toni laughed and Chase smiled, shaking his head. Devi launched into more of Keith's backstory, and introduced their event for the day. The party had wandered into a tavern while Ildash was off consulting with some sorcerers, and an old woman told them there was treasure buried under the mountain above the village, and offered to split it with them if they'd go retrieve it. From what he could tell it was much more low key than their current storyline, featuring wars and the end of the world and all that, but Clare assured him they all loved these sorts of silly one-shots just as much as the big ones. It gave them a chance to explore the world and goof around, she said, and it would be a good introduction for him.

Devi turned to Logan. "Keith, it's up to you. Do you accept the quest on behalf of the group?"

Logan looked around. "Yes?" he asked everyone. "Is that— that's the point, right? We want to do this?"

"We do," Clare assured him.

"Then yes, I accept," he said, and the campaign began in earnest.

It took him a little while to get into the swing of things—he kept asking everyone's opinion on each of his turns, which was clearly annoying Annie—but Clare was right, Quest for Sulzuris was a lot of fun.

"Okay, Keith. You approach the dragon in front of the treasure chest, and he gives you a choice: a fight, or answer a riddle. Beat him or answer the riddle correctly, and the treasure is yours."

Logan knew what they expected him to choose. Keith's character strengths were all in the fighting category, and Devi was probably trying to make it an easy choice. Keith had already gotten into—and won—three separate brawls during the two-hour adventure, including one where he'd rolled an unbelievably exciting natural twenty, which was just "rolling a twenty on a twenty-sided die" but felt as momentous as making a half-court shot. Obviously, he was supposed to pick *fight the dragon*. But Logan was feeling adventurous. "The riddle."

Devi subtly arched a brow but didn't comment on his choice. "The dragon stretches her wings, settling down in front of the chest more comfortably. 'What has one eye, but can't see?'"

Logan wrinkled his brow. "One eye, but can't see?" *Fuck.* He shouldn't have picked this, because there was clearly an obvious answer, but he was stumped.

Next to him, Clare made a motion for Devi's attention. "The rest of us are just outside of the cave, right? Can we help him answer?"

Devi thought for a moment. "The dragon will let you show him things, but not speak."

"Oh, I've got this," Toni said confidently. She stood up and started wiggling her hand up and down.

". . . Swimming?" Logan guessed.

"No," she replied, trying again, this time bugging out her eyes like that might be helpful.

"Oh my god, you are so bad at this," Annie grumbled, proceeding to make more or less the same hand motion at him.

"Still swimming," he said, grinning and wondering how in the hell playing a game of fake charades could be this fun. Chase was miming something that looked like throwing darts, which was not at all helpful either.

Clare poked him in the shoulder, holding up one finger and stabbing it against her palm, then making a tugging motion like she was pulling on a thread. "Sewing?" he guessed, and she nodded and then shook her head, holding her finger up and shaking it. "A . . . needle?" Clare grinned, nodding, and a pack of butterflies exploded in his stomach.

He turned back to Devi, who was beaming. "A needle," he said confidently.

"The dragon spreads her wings and flies away, leaving the treasure chest behind. Do you want to share the spoils with the group, or—"

"I share them," he said, and the rest of the group started cheering.

"Drinks on Keith!" Annie cheered, and Toni and Chase high-fived each other. But Logan only had eyes for Clare, who was glowing with pride.

He still had to broach the subject of dinner with Schneider with Clare, and he needed to untangle this mess of feelings that had caught him completely off guard. Knowing that he was having this much fun with all of them should have sent him into a tailspin.

But instead, it just felt right.

Chapter Twenty-three

Clare's phone buzzed with a text and she picked it up, her pulse spiking when she saw it was from Logan. Their interactions had felt charged since game day, like things had shifted ever so slightly in a particular direction.

Logan
I know this is weird, but I have to take some stuff down to my dad in Northfield.
Would you want to come? Just for the afternoon.
Idk I feel like you'd get along well with Burt.

He was asking her to *meet his dad*? They were, at best, a one-night-stand-turned-friends-turned-maybe-something-more, but the maybe-something-more part was still largely unsaid and against her better judgment. Meeting his dad felt like a huge, momentous step, considering they hadn't so much as kissed since the night they slept together. There was a now familiar twist in her stomach whenever she thought about how it all started, but she wasn't sure how to explain it without making Logan sound like a research project, and she was learning that even his adamantium ego had limits. Part of her felt like she should push to talk to him about it, clarify where they stood a bit more, but whatever. Clare had always found she'd had a tenuous relationship with her dignity anyway. More often than not, pride seemed like an excuse people used to keep themselves from doing what they really wanted to do but were embarrassed to admit it.

Clare
Sure. When are we leaving?

An hour later, Clare was waiting just outside the underground parking garage for Logan's car to pull up. He seemed a little strained as she climbed into the passenger seat, giving tight, one-word answers until they were out of the city, flying down the interstate. There was a storm brewing to the west, clouds stacking up across the farm fields like ominous soldiers, but for the moment, the sun was still shining. "So, Northfield?" she said, more to break the tense silence than anything else. "You grew up there?"

Logan rested his elbow on the ledge near the window and rubbed his hand back and forth through his hair. "I did, yeah. My dad grew up there, so we had family around after—well, after."

"And what are we bringing him?" she looked around the car but didn't see any sign of anything that looked like a delivery.

"Stuff from Smorgasbord. He loves their frozen meals, but they don't have one near him, and he hates driving in the Cities. Once a month or so I stock up for him and bring it down."

"That's really sweet of you."

Logan shrugged awkwardly and signaled, moving toward an off ramp. It was now or never, so Clare screwed up her courage.

"Can I ask you something?" she started. He nodded, eyes on the road. "Why did you ask me to come along? I mean, obviously I'm happy to, but—we're not like, dating or anything, and meeting your dad feels, I dunno, formal? Big? Something like that, you know?"

Logan stayed silent for so long she considered opening the door and rolling out of the car.

"Because I wanted you to see me," he said finally.

Clare wondered if Logan did this sort of gut-punch-admission thing with anyone else, or if he reserved them for her. "See you?" she echoed.

"Who I am with my dad—only Sam ever comes down, and not often. I just—I wanted you to get to know me, I guess." He turned up a long gravel driveway and by the time Clare had found her voice they had come to a stop in front of a small yellow farmhouse. "Here we are," he said with forced brightness.

A man about Logan's height emerged from behind the house. He had Logan's frame, tall and lean, but his nose was longer and his smile lacked Logan's dimples. "About time, lunch is almost ready," he said genially. "You must be Clare. I'm Burt," he said, holding up a hand that was nearly black with dirt. "You'll forgive me for not shaking your hand." He looked at Logan, who was pulling several tote bags from his trunk. "Did they have the chocolate-covered cranberries this time?"

"They didn't, but they did have more of that tikka paneer so I got you a bunch," Logan said.

Clare took a bag from his hand and followed them inside, toeing off her flats and setting the bag down on the floor of the tiny, immaculately clean, if somewhat old-fashioned, kitchen. Burt liked chickens, it would seem. There was a chicken-shaped flour canister on the countertop, and an old-fashioned wall-paper border around the top of the walls had a series of repeating chickens, roosters, and chicks hatching out of eggs. The smell of something savory was wafting out of the oven and her stomach rumbled.

"Hope you like quiche," Burt said, washing his hands.

"Dad's a vegetarian," Logan supplied, stocking the freezer with what appeared to be enough organic frozen dinners for an army.

Clare couldn't help smiling. "Quiche sounds delicious, thank you."

"Clare's a baker," Logan said, head now in the fridge.

"Not professionally, or anything. Just for fun."

"Well, it's a store-bought crust so I hope you won't judge me for that," Burt said from the sink.

"No judgment, I swear," she said. Her smile might be permanently etched into her face at this point.

Burt jerked his chin back toward the front door, wiping his hands with a towel, when Logan emerged from the fridge. "Why don't you give your friend a tour? I'll let you know when it's ready."

Outside the sun dimmed as the clouds reached them and a quiet rumble of thunder rolled through. Clare obediently followed Logan into the living room, nodding absently at his explanation that *this* was the living room and *that over there with the duck and fish paintings* was the study, and up the stairs, where the walls were lined with school photos of him in ascending order. She stopped to examine each one, biting back a grin at his gap-toothed third-grade photo and the seventh-grade one where he had braces and a haircut that shouted *cool kid*. Logan was waiting impatiently at the top of the stairs, but she paused on the last step. The only image of someone other than Logan was a portrait, done with what appeared to be colored pencils. It was a woman, young—very young—with Logan's dark brown hair and light blue eyes, two dimples framing her smile. She was stunning. "Your mom?" Clare whispered.

"Yeah."

"You drew this?"

"Senior year project, yeah. Dad was the one who had it framed."

"She's beautiful, Logan." Clare whispered like she was in church. It felt like they were talking about something holy, sacred. Maybe they were.

He gave a small, sad smile. "Dad always says I got my looks from her and my brains from him, but only one of those is a compliment. My bedroom's over here," he added, steering her into a small room that overlooked the front yard. Thunder cracked, closer, and Logan startled.

Clare looked at him thoughtfully. "Are you . . . scared of thunderstorms?"

"What? No."

"I'm not teasing," she said. "And you just jumped about a mile."

"Am I that easy to read?"

"Honestly? No, I don't think so. But you are, aren't you— scared of thunder?"

He sighed and sat down on the end of the narrow twin bed. "I'm not scared. I just don't like loud noises. Or sudden things."

"So, you hate fireworks, I take it."

"Loathe them," he said, a small smile returning to his face. "Anyway, this is, um, my childhood bedroom."

Clare nodded, turning slowly. "I assume you spent all of high school sneaking girlfriends up here."

He smirked and she felt better seeing that. Confident Logan was a lot easier for her to handle than the nervous man she had spent the last forty minutes with. She spotted a book on his low bookshelf and pulled it off, crowing with delight. "Please tell me this is your high school yearbook."

"Oh god, no, don't look at that."

"Well, now I have to," she said, sinking into his desk chair. She flipped through it, stopping at a page that had half a dozen candids, several of them featuring Logan in a band T-shirt. "John Mayer, huh?"

"Shut up," he muttered, and when she met his gaze across the room, they both grinned.

She narrowed her eyes. "Hold on. Why do I get the sense you were prom king?"

A smug look spread across his face. "Because I was."

"I would have hated you in high school, you know."

"And I would have ignored you, and we both would have been wrong, wouldn't we?" he retorted. He shrugged, a little abashed. "And anyway, it wasn't like I campaigned for it or anything. Just happened."

"That's worse. You know that, right? *I was so popular it just happened*, is not something normal people get to *say*. Good lord, who even are you?" she grumbled. She closed the yearbook and swiveled the chair, eyes landing on a framed photo tucked away on the gable windowsill. It was of a child's chubby hand, pressed against a white, feathery wing like they were clumsily picking the chicken up. Clare cocked her head to the side. "Is that you?" she asked, pointing.

Logan followed her gaze and walked over, picking it up thoughtfully. "Yeah, that's me. My mom took it. She was self-taught, but some of her stuff was really good."

"So that's where you get your talent from?"

Logan sat on the edge of his bed, still examining the picture. "I guess. Dad said she loved any and all art and tried every medium at least once. Apparently, she was best at photography and worst at pottery."

Clare smiled softly. "She sounds like fun."

"That's what everyone says." He shrugged, a shadow crossing his face. "I wouldn't know personally, though."

Clare nodded and hesitantly pushed herself out of the chair to perch next to him on the bed. "That must be really hard," she said, resting her hand on his forearm. "I have no idea what it's like, but I'm sure it's hard."

He lifted and dropped one shoulder, eyes still on the photo. "I just—I don't have much of her. Some photos of us as a family, and then the stuff she made herself, like this. That's all."

A piece of the Logan puzzle fell into place for Clare. "Is that why you don't like sharing your art with people? Because it's what you share with her?"

He was silent for a long time. The rumble of thunder drew nearer, but he didn't flinch. If anything, he seemed to shift closer to her. "Yeah, I think—yeah," he said, closing his eyes and letting his head droop between his shoulders. "I never really thought about it like that, but you're right."

Clare lifted her hand from his arm and placed it on his back, rubbing in a small circle. "Forgive me if I'm overstepping, but—would she want you to? Keep it secret like this?"

"It's not a secret, I just don't tell anyone about it," he said wryly.

Clare bit back a grin. "But for real, wouldn't she want you to show the world what you can do?"

"It's not like I'm going to be in the MoMa," he protested. "Or even the Walker."

"Being in Minnesota's premier art museum would be awesome, but something doesn't have to be internationally renowned to be worth it. It could just be a hobby. For fun, not profit."

Logan leaned into her, his body long and warm next to hers. Warmth blossomed in her veins, and he leaned his temple against hers, his hand coming to rest on her thigh.

"You do things to me, Thompson," he said in a low voice.

"Good things?" she said, trying to keep the quaver out of her voice.

He lifted his head to look at her, his eyes dark and hooded. "Things I never knew I wanted."

"Quiche is ready!" Burt called from downstairs, but they stayed looking at each other for another few seconds.

Clare got herself together first and stood. "Come on," she said, holding out her hand. "Your dad's waiting."

And to her everlasting surprise and delight, he took her hand as she led him back downstairs.

Chapter Twenty-four

Logan was surprised by how easy lunch was. He had warned Clare his dad liked to talk about World War Two, and while it turned out she unsurprisingly knew nothing about the strategies employed at the Battle of Midway, she did know an awful lot about how to make various things explode, a fact that utterly delighted Burt. Logan ate his dad's spinach and mushroom quiche and watched them talk, somehow both relaxed and terrified out of his wits.

Logan was in so far over his head. Getting Clare to date him was just supposed to solve a work mess he'd gotten himself into, but now she was shaking him in ways he didn't think possible. Like with most things Logan did, he hadn't given much thought to inviting Clare to meet his dad. He had been honest in the car when he said it was because he wanted her to see him, but now she *saw* him, and he wasn't entirely sure he could handle it. He wasn't thinking straight and what's worse, the longer he looked at her, the less he was thinking at all.

Because Clare really did see him. It wasn't that he wasn't open with Sam, but there was always an edge of cynicism to their interactions. Sam got along well with Burt, but she didn't seem to thoroughly enjoy herself the way Clare was right now, as she was explaining in depth how she had once learned how to handle a crossbow.

And Sam had never once put together that he refused to share his art because of his mom. Hell, he had never really put it together; he just knew it was something private, something connected to her.

And now he was stuck with the irrevocable knowledge that he cared about Clare more than he had ever cared about any- one, and it was a supremely stupid choice on his part because he couldn't tell if she felt the same way. She might care about him, but it wasn't the same. He knew it in his bones. There was no way someone like her would feel the same way about some- one like him, and he was just going to have to figure out a way to deal with that. He tried to tell himself that as long as she agreed to the dinner with Schneider he could handle her walk- ing away—because at least then he would still have his job—but it was a thin, flimsy lie.

Burt scraped his plate clean and slapped his hand lightly on the table. "Looks like the rain's stopped," he observed, and sure enough, the sun was out again, setting everything shimmer- ing. "Would you kids want to let the chickens back out?"

If Logan thought Clare would object to being put to work, he would've been wrong.

"Chickens?" Clare said brightly. "You have chickens? Like, real live ones?"

"Where do you think the eggs come from?" Burt grinned.

Out in the back yard, Logan unhooked the door to the chicken coop and let the girls come clattering out with their hurried, awkward gait. Clare had an enormous grin on her face, like this was the best thing she had ever seen. "You didn't tell me your dad was a farmer," she chided, crouching down and then springing back when one of the chickens *bawked* loudly.

Logan nudged the offending chicken away from her with his foot. "He's not. His parents were, but he got a job at a hardware store instead. He just keeps some chickens, and every few years he goes through a bee phase and gets a hive or two."

"This is amazing; I'm *furious* you didn't tell me this," Clare said. "What happens when the chickens are too old for laying?"

"Well, for most people, that's what we'd call dinner. But Dad's a softie, so they just slide into a happy retirement here."

"I'm surprised he doesn't have a dog."

"A dog would scare the chickens," Logan shrugged.

Clare surveyed the expansive lawn and started trudging through the wet grass toward his old swing set. The hems of her jeans were soaked by the time she reached it, and clouds were once again rolling in and blotting out the sun. The light was weak, but it turned the grass a brilliant emerald green, and Logan hung back a little, watching the way her hips swayed as she walked, her red and white gingham shirt standing out against the lawn.

She sat down on one of the swings, heedless of the water that was beading up on the seat, and started swinging. He sat down on the swing next to her, wiping his palms against his jeans when the metal chain proved to be soaked. He pushed himself back and forth with his toes and Clare slowed to a stop. "This must have been yours," she said, and then laughed. "What am I saying? Of course it was yours."

He nodded to the small metal slide that stuck off to the side. A fat drop of rain landed on his wrist but he ignored it. "Broke my arm on that when I was nine. I was playing Superman and got a little cocky. Jumped off. It turned out I couldn't fly."

Clare snorted. "That's much cuter than my broken-bone

story, which is I broke my foot when I was twenty and completely wasted in college. I was running to catch up to Devi and tripped on a curb."

Logan winced. "I thought you were a nerd who didn't drink?"

"I was a nerd who didn't drink in *high school* because I wasn't cool enough. Even nerds drink in college, Logan."

She held her hand out and wrinkled her nose. A couple more drops of rain landed on her palm, although the light remained that impossibly clear, sharp contrast that could only happen before a summer storm. "Looks like it's starting to rain again."

"Did you want to go inside?"

She shrugged. "It's just water. And the thunder and lightning have moved on. We can go inside in a bit."

He smiled softly and stood, moving around the swings to stand behind her. He gave her a gentle push and she giggled. A few more raindrops pelted his head. "I feel like you're exaggerating how nerdy you were," he said.

"I'm really not. I was a Band groupie."

"Being a groupie for a band can be cool though," he argued.

She laughed, kicking her legs out as she soared away from him. "No, not *a* band. Band-band. Like, Marching Band."

"Wait, seriously?"

"Yes. I wasn't in it, but all my friends were, so I went to like, sporting events and stuff to support them. Hence, Band groupie."

"Yeah, okay, never mind. You were a whole ass dork."

"See? Told you." She laughed, and let him push her for a while. "I'm happy you invited me," she said, breaking the comfortable silence. "It's nice here. Not quite what I expected, but nice."

"What did you expect?"

"I don't know," she admitted. "But I didn't peg you for a farm boy."

"I'm not a farm boy," he protested.

"You're a lot closer to one than not," she argued.

On her next backswing he shot one arm out to catch her around the waist and the other to grab the chain, holding her still against his chest. Slowly, she lowered her feet to the ground and craned her neck to look at him. "Still think I'm a farm boy?" he asked in a low voice.

Clare's eyes darted between his lips and his eyes. The sky opened up and the rain came down in sheets, drenching them both, but neither moved a muscle. "I shouldn't," she murmured, and there it was again. Logan wasn't the right type of guy for her, and they both knew it.

But she made no move to shift out of his arms. "Do you want me to stop?" he asked, heart thundering.

"No," she breathed, raindrops clinging to her eyelashes. "I want—I want you to kiss me." Logan grinned and leaned forward to capture her lips in what he intended to be a quick kiss. But the moment their lips met, Logan knew he was lost.

He let go of the swing to cradle the back of her head, keeping her close even as she gradually turned in his arms to face him. The swing stayed trapped between their shins, her mouth welcoming his tongue, her hands sliding into his now-wet hair. She tipped her head to the side, deepening the kiss, and a soft noise that might have been a moan escaped her when he pulled back to take her face in his hands.

Logan's heart was racing. It had never done that before; not for a first kiss, anyway. And it wasn't even a first kiss for them, not really, but god, it felt like one. His limbs were trembling, and the world had been reduced to just her, the warmth of her skin under his palms and the taste of her mouth on his lips.

The rain was probably soaking through to his skin, but he may as well have been standing in the middle of a wildfire, for all he noticed.

He could have kissed her for ever, rain be damned, but all too soon she lowered herself to her heels and looked up at the clouds. Her hands were fisted in his shirt and she showed no signs of letting go. "Your dad will be wondering why we haven't come in," she said, and if there was a way to draw her voice, all raspy and wrecked, he would. He loved how it made him feel, soft and hopeful and happy, and when she smiled, he forgot the sun wasn't shining.

"You're right," he admitted reluctantly. He held out his hand and she took it, and together they sprinted through the downpour back to the house, laughing the entire time.

Chapter Twenty-five

Clare's RideShare driver pulled up in front of Aunt Peggy's large, South Minneapolis home and Clare got out, her aunt's favorite raspberry tarts in tow. Clare wasn't watching Kiki this weekend, but sometimes she and Aunt Peg had Sunday dinners together, just because.

Peggy opened the door as she came up the walk, keeping Kiki from bolting outside with her leg—Kiki couldn't be trusted with unlimited freedom—and Clare followed Peggy into the living room. She could smell the hot dish in the oven and her stomach growled. "The rose bushes out front look great," she observed, settling onto the large, cream-colored sectional.

"For how much I baby them, they better. Did you have a good weekend?"

Clare tried to hide her blush to no avail. "I did, yeah," she said as neutrally as possible.

Peggy wasn't fooled. "I see," she said mildly, and let Kiki jump into her lap for ear-scritches. "Logan?"

"Yeah," Clare admitted. "He's not what I expected."

"He's not what I would have expected for you, either," Peggy said. "How did you two meet?"

"We're neighbors," Clare said vaguely. "We'd seen each other around."

Peggy nodded slowly, clearly contemplating her words. "I'll admit, I don't know what you two might even have in common."

"Not much," Clare admitted. "But I think that's the fun of it."

"Fun," Peggy repeated. "I can see that."

"I know he's got, um, a bit of a reputation."

"To put it mildly."

Clare chuckled. "Like I said, he's a lot of fun."

Peggy pushed herself up as the oven beeped. "That'll be dinner," she announced, and Kiki followed them close on their heels to the kitchen. Clare helped her pour the wine and pull out plates and napkins, and the subject of Logan was thankfully dropped.

"Your boss is still behaving, I hope?" Peggy asked delicately, halfway into her chicken and mushroom hot dish.

"Craig? Of course, he's fine."

Peggy gave her a shrewd look. "No canoeing down the Mississippi lately?"

Clare laughed, although there was more discomfort behind it than usual. "My job is just a bit different, you know? That's what I like about it." Peggy made a noise that said she didn't agree, and Clare fell silent for a moment. "I do have a question for you, though. The other day, one of the guys on my team asked for my opinion on something. I've been trying to be more confident, so I said what I thought. But now I think it was the wrong call, because Craig seemed . . . I dunno, kind of weird about it."

"Weird how?"

"He just seemed hurt, I think. Which I get, our ideas are

really personal sometimes and things being shot down hurts, even if it's by a nobody like me."

"What made you decide to be more assertive?" Peggy asked. "I mean, why now?"

"Something that Logan said," Clare shrugged. "And, well, it can be a little lonely at work, you know? Everyone else is really tightly bonded and I'm trying to fit in, but it's not really working. And a lot of that is on me, but I thought if I said what I thought and didn't try and soften it at all, it might get their attention. But I went too far and hurt his feelings." That had been her big attempt at being more like herself at work, and it had backfired spectacularly.

Peggy frowned. "For one thing, I don't like how concerned you are about hurting your boss's feelings. But we'll put a pin in that for now. When it comes to being more outspoken at work, I see where Logan is coming from, but he can—let's say, he can suffer from an excess of confidence sometimes, and I'm not sure he's the right person to give you advice there. Not that he's wrong, but I don't need to tell you that women are judged differently than men for the same behavior. It's not fair, but it's the water we swim in, so to speak. That being said, do you feel like you aren't confident enough at work? You're usually very self-assured."

Clare shrugged. "Like I said, it's different there. I've wanted to work at Quest for so long, and now I'm there and there's a promotion available soon, and—I just can't risk it, you know?"

"There's being cautious because you're choosing your words deliberately, and being cautious because you're scared. The former is fine, but the latter—if it's like that, I would be worried. As for your boss's problem with your answer, I also know you, and I doubt you were cruel or even unkind when expressing your asked-for opinion on your boss's work."

"I wasn't," Clare agreed. She slipped Kiki a small piece of dinner roll and Peggy sent her a wry grin. "But I got a bad vibe."

"Which brings me back to my first point. Your boss's personal feelings shouldn't matter, especially if it's a work subject. I assume he doesn't care as much about *your* feelings?"

Clare thought for a minute. "Not as much," she agreed. "But that makes sense; he's got a lot of us to manage. And like I said, my job is a little different. Being creative is hard."

"If he's good enough to be a manager, he should be good enough to withstand some minor criticism from a junior employee," Peggy replied firmly. "You owe him nothing but courtesy, and if he can't handle it, well, that's on him."

"I guess," Clare said, but the pit in her stomach whenever she thought about work—and how work connected with Logan—remained. She forced a smile onto her face and changed the subject. It was obvious what Peggy would say if Clare brought up Craig's assignment, but what was done was done. She would just have to move past it now, and make sure she didn't fall for anything like that again. "But Logan has an excess of confidence, does he?"

Peggy grinned, eyes dancing. "It would be inappropriate for me to say much more, but yes, he is certainly sure of himself. It's charming, but it's not everything." She paused. "But you're happy with him? Sincerely?"

"Couldn't be happier," Clare said, with a certainty that surprised even herself.

Clare bounced on the balls of her feet, waiting. Logan had texted with a cryptic message about *having some fun,* and asked her to meet him in the lobby. Per his instructions, she was in comfortable shoes—although to be honest, she didn't really own any other kind.

Logan emerged from the stairwell in the same outfit he'd been wearing when he took her to the hospital: a pair of basketball shorts and sleeveless T-shirt that showed off an indecent amount of biceps and side torso muscles, which she hadn't realized was a thing she could be attracted to before that very moment.

But in his hands was a basketball, and she immediately shrank back. "No. No. No no no no no, we are *not* playing basketball," she declared.

He grinned a very unfair grin. "First you don't want to go to Uptown, now you won't play basketball," he sighed. "I'm going to get a complex."

"It's not my fault you like shitty things," Clare threw back, but even as she said it, she fell into step beside him. Logan held the door for her and she followed him outside. Twilight was fading and the streetlights flickered on. "Besides, what about me says I'd be good at sportsball?"

"Absolutely nothing. That's why it'll be fun. And if you're going to be with me, you're going to stop calling it sportsball and start calling it basketball."

Her heart literally—*literally*—skipped a beat at the way his voice dipped at the end. She had the absurd urge to reply *yes, sir*, and only barely stopped herself. Instead, she nodded and followed him around the corner, still running the words *if you're going to be with me* over and over in her brain. It made everything feel more real, and less like a very intense, vivid daydream.

She had made her decision, obviously. There was no way to pretend this was just a hookup, and she'd been lying to herself since before the kiss. She would just have to hope Craig didn't look too closely at her story and that Noah wouldn't bust her. Because *if you're going to be with me* was somehow the hottest thing she had heard, and obviously she was a goner.

In front of them was a park, although there wasn't much to it aside from a basketball court and a jungle gym for toddlers, with some patchy, yellowed grass in between. Clare had walked Kiki through it a handful of times, although her usual route took her north, toward the river. The night was warm and muggy, with the occasional hint of breeze that told her that outside of the city, it might almost feel pleasant.

Logan unlatched the wire gate and led her out onto the court. "The way I see it, I played your game, so it's only fair you play mine."

She gave an exaggerated sigh. "Fine," she agreed, and dropped her purse on the edge of the court. "But no mocking me about how terrible I am."

"Oh, I'm sorry, did you not get the memo? Mocking is the entire point of this," he said, bouncing the ball easily. The high-pitched resonance of the ball hitting pavement gave her an immediate flashback to middle-school gym class, and Mr. Zebrowski telling her she shouldn't ever count on a college scholarship for sports. (It wasn't like she'd ever thought she was a *good* athlete, but still, that was a crappy thing to say to a twelve-year old.)

He settled into a dribble that somehow looked graceful, something she didn't realize was possible until that very second. Everything about Logan felt like a revelation. His sweetness, his kindness, his talent, even his depth—none of it was what she had expected when she kissed him outside her apartment all those weeks ago.

"How much basketball have you played?" he asked, moving back and forth in front of her.

"The minimum amount required to not fail gym class in middle school."

"Not even in high school?"

"I worked very hard to avoid any gym class that involved balls of any kind, thank you very much."

Logan snorted at her phrasing and suppressed a grin. "So, it's been, what, ten years?"

"Longer."

"Okay then, I guess one-on-one is out, but you can manage a game of Horse."

"You have a very high opinion of me based on absolutely no evidence," she countered.

He shrugged. "If you embarrass yourself, at least there isn't an audience," he said, nodding to the empty park behind them. There were some small, quickly evaporating puddles on the far side of the court, and she could feel the humidity rising from the asphalt. The streetlights illuminated their side brightly, leaving the rest of the park in shadow.

A city of almost half a million people, and it was as if they were the only two who existed.

Logan kept dribbling. "You know the rules, right?"

She wrinkled her nose. "I need to make the exact same shot as you do, right? Same spot, same, uh, type? Form? Move? I don't know what to call it."

He shook his head fondly. "I'll go easy on you this time; just the same spot. You shoot however you want to make it."

"Is there a mercy rule?"

Logan caught the ball on its ascent and stepped closer to her, eyes dark. "No," he said in a tone that sent a thrill down her spine. "No mercy. We're done when I say we're done."

Clare licked her lips. "I thought you said you'd go easy on me?"

He leaned down until his nose was just brushing hers and tucked a lock of hair back behind her ear. "You can take it," he murmured, and then stepped back, leaving Clare breathing like she'd already played four straight quarters of basketball, assuming they had quarters, which she was reasonably sure they did.

No, she was not attempting to distract herself, not in the slightest.

Logan moved to a few yards away, just outside the curved line that inscribed a semicircle around the end of the court. He raised the ball, aimed, and with a small jump sent it straight through the hoop. Logan retrieved the ball and tossed it to her, motioning to where he had been standing.

Clare caught it—barely—and took her spot, elaborately shaking out her arms and legs and shrugging her shoulders to relax them.

"Are you dancing or shooting?" he called.

"I'm stretching," she replied primly. She finished and took the ball in both hands, surveying the distance critically. It was far. Too far. He'd picked this spot because she wouldn't be able to make the shot, she was sure of it. He wanted to goof around, and goof around she would.

Sinking into a squat with the ball cradled between her knees, she chucked it up and forward with all her strength, hoping it would at least hit the backboard.

It didn't. Her shot soared straight up and slammed back into the asphalt a good five feet in front of the basket. Logan let out a bark of laughter, catching the ball on its bounce back up with one hand. She bit her lower lip and shrugged. "Told you."

"Are you embarrassed? You should be embarrassed," he said, walking over to her and throwing his arm around her shoulders when she buried her face in her hands, laughing. He pressed an unexpected kiss to the top of her head and let her lean against his chest for a moment. She craned her head up, cheek still resting above his heart, and he smiled down at her. "Good thing you're cute," he added as he let her go.

Clare pouted. "Are you going to do that all night?"

Logan was dribbling and walking again, looking for another spot on the court. "Tease you? Yes, obviously."

She followed him and he stopped dribbling with the ball against his chest. Clare moved closer and watched the corner of his lips quirk up. "There's basketball-teasing, and then there's . . . teasing," she said, looking up through her eyelashes.

Logan smirked. "I thought you knew; I'm all about the anticipation," he said with a wink, tossing the ball over her head with barely a glance at the basket. "Nice try on the distraction, though."

She heard the ball swish through the net. "There's anticipation, and then there's just being mean," she replied.

"Like I said, you can take it," he said, but when she put her hand on his chest, he trapped it with his. Logan's other hand tipped her chin up and he brought his mouth down gently on hers, the kiss soft and sweet. But the moment she traced his lower lip with her tongue he pulled back, eyes dancing. "There. A little something to take the edge off," he said, and nodded his chin toward the chain-link fence behind the court. "Your ball."

Clare rolled her eyes and jogged to get it. Her legs and arms suddenly didn't work right, and eventually she slowed to what she hoped appeared to be a casual walk.

Logan hadn't moved from his spot and she bumped him with her hip to nudge him out of the way. "I feel like I should ask if I should, like, aim or something," she said, looking at him over her shoulder.

"Yes, aiming is the general point," he said drily, and then moved so his chest was against her back. "Here, I'll help," he whispered, lips brushing the shell of her ear.

"Isn't that cheating?"

"I won't tell if you won't," he replied, kissing the hollow under her ear. His arms came up to surround her, helping her lift the ball to straight in front of her chest. In a soft, deep voice he started talking her through the basic points of shooting a basketball, but to be perfectly honest she wasn't listening. She couldn't, not with him that close, sounding the way he did.

"Okay, go," he encouraged, and she ignored every instruction he'd given her and tossed it wildly in the vague direction of the basket, spinning in his arms and kissing him before the ball landed.

Logan stepped back at the force of her kiss and then caught her face in his hands, returning it eagerly. "You're still losing, you know," he managed when they broke for air.

"Do I look like I give a shit?" she said, fisting her hands in his shirt and dragging him down for another desperate kiss.

"You should make at least one basket before we go," Logan said, running his hands down her sides. "You made sure I had fun playing Quest for Sulzuris, so let me do this for you."

"It's fine, I had fun," she dismissed. It was true; she had never once liked playing any sport as much as she did right now.

But Logan shook his head and stood back. "One more," he said, retrieving the ball and stopping directly underneath the basket. "Come here," he ordered, and she couldn't help but comply.

Good lord, this man was sexy.

When Clare reached him, he crouched down, balancing himself with one hand on the ground. "Climb on," he said, and when she didn't, he looked back at her. "On my shoulders," he clarified. "I've got you."

Clare looked at his broad back dubiously. "I still might not make it."

"Then we'll be here all night until you do. Come on, Thompson. I believe in you; get on."

Gingerly, she arranged herself on his shoulders and squealed—half in delight, half in fright—when he stood. She was almost eye level with the rim this way. He kept one hand on her thigh and lifted the ball to her. "There you go, nice and easy," he said in a surprisingly soothing voice. Maybe he could feel her trembling, but that had nothing to do with nerves.

Clare tossed the ball the remaining couple of feet and it rattled noisily against the rim before falling through. She threw her hands up in victory, and whooped, while Logan carefully lowered himself down and ducked out from between her legs.

"I did it!" she screeched, way too excited for the situation, but Logan had a way of doing that to her. Everything was heightened with him; the colors sharper and the lights brighter.

"You did it," he echoed, scooping her up in a bear hug that turned into a kiss. Logan lifted her higher so she could wrap her legs around his waist. Her back bumped up against something and it took her a second to realize it was the post for the hoop. He pinned her there with his weight, one hand sliding under the hem of her shirt, gliding softly over her skin.

Clare gasped into his mouth, tangling her fingers in the hair at the nape of his neck. She could feel him getting hard, her jeans entirely too thick for her liking at the moment. Out on the street, tires slicked by on the still-damp pavement, and all at once her brain caught up with what was happening. She froze.

"Wait," she breathed, and Logan pulled back immediately, concern on his face.

"What's wrong?"

"We're in public. Someone could see."

He grinned. "Sometimes that's half the fun," he said, even

as he stepped back and let her get her legs under her again. He held her by the elbows until he was sure she was steady, then let go, but a blush was gradually crawling up her neck. Logan examined her closely and she looked away, worried he would somehow see the images that were flashing behind her eyelids every time she blinked.

Logan, kneeling in front of a chair.

A woman with long brown hair sitting before him, legs spread.

Her fingers splayed against the back of his head, holding him in place while her back arched.

"Or maybe you know that already," Logan added, turning her to face him with his fingers under her chin. His smirk had deepened and his eyes were molten. "Tell me, Clare, did you see something you weren't supposed to see?"

Her breath was coming in short, ridiculous pants. She probably wouldn't have been able to stand if it weren't for the metal pole behind her, rigid and cool. "You could have closed your blinds," she blurted, and then covered her mouth.

But Logan just laughed delightedly. "I knew it," he crowed. "I knew you saw us; you've been squirrelly about something this whole time."

"It wasn't long, I swear," she protested. "I just—well, your window is *right there.*"

Logan winked. "That was the whole point."

At this rate, she was just going to be permanently crimson. "I—you—she—" Clare sputtered while Logan waited with an air of amusement. "Do you—in public? Often?"

Logan shrugged and backed up, her lungs filling with air fully for the first time in ten minutes. Even still, she missed his warmth, his closeness. "Not often. Exhibitionism isn't really my thing, but it was Amber's, so . . ." He trailed off and ended with another shrug. "It felt like a good compromise."

He picked up the basketball and laced their fingers together, peeling her off the pole and towing her toward the gate. "You'll do stuff you're not into?" she asked, honestly interested. There wasn't a lot of exploration or experimentation in her sex life, and she found his attitude to be fascinating.

"Not everything. I've got some hard no's, but something like that? I'm up for it, if that's what gets her off."

Clare ignored the urge to squirm and rub her thighs together at his words. "Oh," she said, more to have a response than anything else.

He grinned at her and let the gate swing shut with a clatter. "Just something to keep in mind," he said with a wink.

Oh.

Chapter Twenty-six

It was hard to play a pick-up game with just three people—
Vince had to go home straight from work to Nicole and the
baby—so rather than the usual game, Logan and the Aidens
were just messing around on the court, challenging each other
for the ball and attempting trick shots. Sam called it playing
who's the coolest? and claimed it was a game that all unstruc-
tured physical activities involving men tended to devolve into,
and she wasn't wrong.

Didn't mean it wasn't fun, though. Brooks nailed a half-
court shot and fist pumped, following it up with a chest bump
from Aiden because sometimes, the Aidens were incredibly
predictable.

Not for the first time, Logan found himself feeling just a
little bit separate from them. They could be fun, but there was
an edge to their humor that he didn't always love. And they
could be super immature, which was sometimes funny but felt
less and less so lately. A few months ago, Logan thought maybe
they were changing, getting cruder and louder, but now he
could tell it was the opposite. It wasn't just Brooks hitting on
Clare, either.

He was the one who was changing. Leaving Clare at her door after their game of Horse was one of the hardest things Logan had ever had to do. He couldn't remember a time where he'd ever walked away from a willing partner, especially one who made him feel the way Clare did.

Well, no one had ever made him feel the way Clare did.

But that was why he made himself kiss her goodbye and leave, instead of waiting for her to offer to let him in. It all felt so new, so overwhelming, that some instinct had him holding back. *That's called being a grown-up, welcome to the club*, he could hear Sam say, complete with an accompanying eyeroll. But it was more than just personal growth. It was that Clare was special to him, and he wanted to be sure he was doing everything right. He might have started hanging out with her in a desperate attempt to salvage his job, but now he didn't give a damn about Schneider. He did want Peggy Roth to like him, but he didn't care if she fired him. He wanted her to like him because he wanted everyone Clare cared about to like him. Everything was different. *He* was different, hence the walking away.

But when he got home, he couldn't stop thinking about her. The way her lips tasted in the rain, the way her smile made his father's slightly dingy kitchen a few shades brighter. The way she gasped and moaned against him when he kissed her on the basketball court, the way her skin felt impossibly soft under his fingertips.

The way she couldn't meet his eyes when she admitted having seen him eating out Amber. The way he couldn't stop thinking about how Clare would taste.

Logan shook himself out of that very dangerous thought process just in time to see Aiden hurl the ball straight at him. "Think fast," he yelled, and Logan just barely managed to catch it before it slammed into his face.

"Go to hell," Logan sighed. He dribbled for a while, sizing up the hoop, and then drove in for a lay-up. He tossed it over to Brooks for his turn and stepped back, breathing a little harder now.

Aiden stepped up next to him. "She still on your case?" he asked.

Logan frowned. "Who?"

"Madame Vice President," Aiden said with faux-superiority. "Weren't you in trouble for fucking her niece?"

Logan swallowed back an unfamiliar surge of anger. "Not that," he said as evenly as he could. "It was work shit. Too much churn. Schneider being a dick, that sort of thing."

"But you fucked Roth's niece, right?"

Did they always talk like that? He shrugged, not really wanting to answer. Even though he'd originally brought Clare out with them he was now regretting it. He wanted to keep her separate from them if he could, and that was the first time he'd ever had that instinct. That was going to take some getting used to.

Brooks approached with a water bottle. "Her niece was that chick you brought out the other night, right? Cara?"

"Clare," Logan said tightly. "Yeah."

"She was cute," Brooks said, and Logan really didn't like the gleam in his eye. "You ever get sick of her, let me know."

Logan would rather let Sam shout at him for two straight hours on the topic of her choice than let Brooks within five feet of Clare ever again, but he did have to work with the guy and they were technically friends, so he just shrugged.

Brooks rolled his eyes and then crushed his water bottle in one hand. "Ready for me to kick your ass again?" he asked, catching the ball from Aiden.

"Bring it," Logan replied.

* * *

Logan turned on ESPN for a distraction, but after thirty seconds he was off the couch and pacing, eyes drawn to the warm yellow square of light that was Clare's kitchen.

He had been trying to take it slow, he really had. But tonight he had stopped by Clare's place to say hi; a thin excuse but she hadn't cared. *Hello* had quickly turned into making out on her couch, which was something Logan hadn't done since high school. Pulling himself away from her with another excuse about needing to go to bed had been maybe the most difficult thing he'd ever done, and that included the time Burt gave him an extraordinarily thorough sex talk at age sixteen, only for Logan to admit he was about six months too late.

He pulled out his phone, debating. Texting her and asking if she wanted to come over was against his better judgment, not to mention completely contradictory to what he'd just done, but Logan had never been a very good judge anyway. He was still arguing with himself and the voice in his head that sounded like Sam when his phone rang, startling him.

It was Clare. "Is everything okay?" he said upon answering, instead of *Hello* like a normal person.

Her laugh sounded oddly strangled. "No. You got me all worked up and then just *left* like that? What the hell is wrong with you?"

The sudden burst of anxiety faded, and he laughed. "I was trying to be a gentleman, okay? I thought you'd be into knights and chivalry and all that."

"Well, that's not actually what the code of chivalry is about, but that is seriously beside the point. The point is—you know, I don't know what the point is, I just know I'm extremely annoyed with you right now."

Logan leaned his shoulder against the window frame, peering down into her apartment. Resisting her was pointless, but

Logan was determined to exercise his long-unused willpower at least a little bit. He let his voice drop lower. "That would be extremely un-chivalric of me, wouldn't it, to leave you in an undesirable position?"

"You mean chivalrous, and that's not—"

"Do you want me to get you off, or not?" he snapped, smirking a little at the sharp intake of breath that followed. He'd seen the way her pupils dilated when he'd gotten stern with her on the court, and he was pleased to find his hunch was correct.

"Uh, um, yes please," she said with a breathy, awkward laugh.

"Where are you?" Logan asked. He could usually see her if she was moving around, but her apartment seemed still.

"Wait, are we—over the phone?"

"Trust me," he said cockily. "It'll be good. You in?"

"Yes," she said after a beat. "I'm in."

"Good. Then I'll ask again, where are you?"

"My—my bedroom."

He clicked his tongue. "I can't see you there, and we can't have that, can we?"

There was a long pause, and Logan's apology for going too far was on the tip of his tongue, but then she spoke. "You want me in my kitchen."

"I want you everywhere, Clare," he said, and there was a softness in his voice he hadn't quite intended. He cleared his throat. "But yes, your kitchen."

There was rustling as she got up and left her bedroom, padding across the darkened living room and toward her small dining table. He watched her sit down first in one chair, then hesitate and seem to change her mind before sitting back down. "Can you, um, see me?"

"I can," he said, and apparently, he would not be able to shed that gentle tone entirely. "And you want to do this?" he added. "You're sure?"

She was quiet again and he couldn't quite make out the finer details of her face, but he knew she was biting her lip. Clare looked up and down, scanning his side of the building. "Yeah, I'm sure."

"Good." Logan did his own check and as usual, all the blinds facing him were closed. "Take a deep breath, Clare," he said, and watched her shoulders lower a few inches, hearing a quiet exhale through the phone. "Like that," he said encouragingly. "I'd say you should close your eyes, but that would go against the whole point of this." He waited for her chuckle to continue. "Can you see me?"

She turned her head to face him, and after a moment her body followed. She was perched on a wooden chair with no arms, hardly the most comfortable place for this, but Logan was going to work with what they had. It was hard to tell if she was looking straight at him at this distance, but somehow, he could *feel* when her gaze settled on him. "Yes, I can see you."

His heart rate picked up, but he kept his voice steady for her. "You're standing at your counter," he started, but before he could continue, she interrupted.

"Wait, you want me to stand at my counter? I thought—"

He sighed, unable to stop his smile. "Clare. It's a fantasy," he said flatly, and laughed to himself when he saw her shoulders shake with her own giggles. "We're going to pretend."

He waited until she'd settled to start again. "You're at your counter, baking something."

"Brownies," she supplied, and god, she really didn't have to be this fucking adorable.

"You're baking brownies," he amended. "And I come up behind you, sliding my hands around your body. You think it's just a hug but then my lips find the nape of your neck and you moan, leaning back against me."

"Your hand moves up," she prompted, and he nodded.

"My hand moves up, moving your bra out of the way."

"I'm not wearing one," Clare corrects. "You spent the night last night, fucking me. I didn't bother with putting one on, because I knew—I knew—" she broke off.

"You knew I'd want to touch you again," he finished. "And I do. My thumbs start circling your nipples under your shirt, and you arch against me."

Across the building, he watched her slide her hand up her shirt, doing what he said. "You're forceful, but not rough," Clare said, and Logan pinned the phone between his shoulder and ear to undo the button of his jeans.

"So that's how you like it," he rasped. "Just hard enough to know you're mine."

He'd said something similar to that while screwing women before; it was a hot thing to say in the moment, and Logan had never really thought about what it meant. But the second the words fell from his lips, he realized how true they were with a clarity that scared him.

Clare whimpered on the other end of the line, and he shoved that realization to the back of his mind. He'd unpack that later. He reached down his pants and freed his aching cock, stroking himself just enough to take the edge off. "Pull your shirt up; let me see what you're doing to those tits," he growled.

Across the way Clare shoved her loose shirt up to bare her breasts, breathing hard into the phone. "You too," she gasped. "Take your shirt off."

Logan eagerly obliged, eyes glued to the tableau in front of him. "Touch yourself," he ordered, forgetting the entire fantasy thing he had been trying to create for her. "Touch yourself like I would touch you."

"Oh god," she moaned, and he tightened his grip on his shaft. Her hand was under her waistband now, pinned between her thighs. He wanted to be there, kneeling in front of her, tasting her again. He hadn't paid close enough attention the first time, and he was cursing himself for not burning every single second of that night into his memory.

"Tell me," he begged. "Tell me how it feels."

"I'm wet; so, so wet," she panted. "And my fingers—they're not enough. I can't—I need more."

"Are they in you?" he asked, making out her nod through the window. "Go deeper, I know you can," he urged, and her broken cry had his cock jumping in his hand.

"Are you—you're touching yourself too, right?"

"I am," he said, leaning forward to brace his forearm against the window. It was the only way he could get closer to her. "I'm so fucking hard I think I'm going to pass out."

She chuckled weakly. "If you pass out before I come, I'll kill you."

"Remind me to lock the door," he said, managing a laugh before another surge of need threatened to drown him. "Touch your clit," he continued. "Show me how you like it."

Her cry went up an octave and he knew she was close. If he was there, he would be able to feel her thighs tremble, see the sweat beading up on her forehead. As it was, he just had to imagine it. And even though he'd told her not to, he closed his eyes as heat pooled in his groin. "Tell me when you come," he said hoarsely. "I need to know."

"I'm—I'm close," she whimpered.

"Me too." He opened his eyes just in time to watch her palm her breast and saw her body seize up, arching almost off the chair when the moment came. There was a split-second delay between what he saw and what he heard, and he just barely had time to grab his T-shirt before he was on the edge himself, listening to her moan her way to her climax.

"I'm—" she couldn't talk anymore and honestly, neither could he.

"I know, I know," he managed. "Me too." He came with a groan that echoed hers, spilling into his T-shirt and collapsing into the chair behind him.

Clare's limbs went limp across the way, and his remaining shred of self-preservation and willpower was all that kept him from begging to come over and lick her clean, and then carry her to her bedroom and fuck her properly.

Logan caught his breath first. "Am I forgiven?" he asked, tucking his softening cock away. His hand rested on his bare chest, his lungs feeling like he'd just played the hardest game of his life.

Her laugh came out more like a sigh. "For everything. Consider this a blanket pardon for all past and future crimes committed."

A slow tendril of guilt unfurled in his stomach, but before it could grow, he quashed it. "Sleep tight, Clare," he said, leaning forward to place his palm on the window.

Clare did the same, and he could hear the smile in her voice better than he could see it. "You too, Logan. You too."

Chapter Twenty-seven

Clare closed the window of the prototype sent to her by Design, digging the heels of her palms into her eye sockets. She hadn't been sleeping well, unable to get Logan out of her mind.

Well, Logan and the fact that she had agreed to masturbate in front of a window while he talked her through it. She wasn't losing sleep because of the exhibitionism, although that was not within her usual comfort zone, but rather because of how it *felt*.

It felt good. Too good, maybe? The first time they had sex it hadn't been anything spectacular, but now he'd gone and given her one of the best orgasms of her life with his voice alone. She had known for a while that things were not what she anticipated with Logan, but just how different things were was really setting in.

She hadn't considered the possibility she would fall for him, much less that he'd appear to return her feelings. Clare probably should have admitted the truth to Logan earlier, but now it felt like the time for that had passed. Logan wasn't necessarily sensitive about his reputation, but he did have a vulnerability about him. And there just really wasn't a good way to frame what she'd done, so the kindest option was for her to just learn to live with the guilt.

Craig emerged from his office and caught her eye. Clare worked in the bullpen part of the office, which had some perks (there was always someone to roll her eyes at when someone gave incredibly detailed descriptions of their corns to their podiatrist) and an awful lot of negatives (she had to listen to incredibly detailed descriptions of her coworker's corns, and also, she couldn't avoid her boss when she didn't feel like talking to him).

"How are things?" he asked, perching on the edge of her desk. He at least seemed less annoyed with her than he had been, so maybe he was over the zombie thing.

"Can't complain; you?"

Craig shrugged. "One of my old Peace Corps buddies was visiting this weekend, so we were up late shooting the shit, swapping war stories, that sort of thing. Did I ever tell you about the time our truck got a flat tire and we had to walk all night to get back to our post carrying an entire truckload of medical supplies?"

He had. Several times. It was one of his favorite stories, although Clare couldn't help but notice that the amount of medical supplies had slowly increased from two backpacks' worth to an entire truckload. Not to mention that the first time she heard it, she could have sworn he was just carrying his own groceries.

Okay, so he exaggerates. So do most people, writers and creatives especially. "You've mentioned it," she said cheerfully. "I'm sure it was fun."

"The ten-mile walk, or the drinks with my friend, you mean?" he said with a wink, and she chuckled on cue. "Anyway, how goes the pitch?" he asked.

"It's good," she said, leaning back from her desk. "I got a mockup from Design of Captain Ellis Ravencroft, if you want to see? I've also been sketching out an outline for various ports she could take groups to, the sort of situations they could encounter, that kind of thing, if you want me to send it over."

He waved his hand. "I'll see it when it's done. I was just stopping by to see how life is going for you."

"It's good. Really good," she said, relieved that maybe things were getting back to normal with him. They could forget entirely about his little assignment and move on.

Craig grinned. "Oh, is it? Good for you," he said, and she shifted uncomfortably at his tone. "You deserve to live a little," he said, nudging her shoulder. "I know old habits die hard and all that, but trust me on this one, kid. Experiences like this— they'll make you a better writer in the end."

Clare smiled back weakly. *He's just looking out for me*, she reminded herself. And if it weren't for Craig's push, maybe she wouldn't have taken the chance on Logan at all. Craig looked around, noting that most of the rest of the team had headed out to lunch already. Clare was, as usual, the only one still at her desk. She normally had something to eat there while catching up on some fan fiction updates, and didn't really mind being left out of the rest of it. Much.

"Still planning to put your name in for Noah's Senior Game Designer position?" Craig asked. "We've started talking about names."

He seemed a lot friendlier than when he last mentioned it, so that was encouraging. "Did Noah get the Narrative Lead job?" Clare asked. If he had, she thought he would have bragged to the whole team about it right away.

"Not yet, but he's a shoo-in."

"Do you think I would have a good shot at it?" she asked.

"Noah's job?" Craig looked thoughtful. "Maybe. We'll need to see proof, though. That you're up for it, that you've got what it takes."

That was not particularly helpful, but Clare made herself smile. "I'll work extra hard, then."

"Have you talked to Noah recently?" Craig asked.

"About what?"

Another glance around. "How's his pitch coming along?"

Clare had chatted with Noah about his ideas just that morning. He was working on the horror movie pitch with most of the rest of the team, but if she remembered correctly, the pitch had been Derek's idea in the first place. "I think they're doing well," Clare said neutrally. "Why do you ask?"

Craig shrugged, but there was something in his tone that gave her pause. "I like to get everyone's opinions on how things are developing, especially when we have a couple of competing ideas. Do you think Noah's pitch is good?"

Clare wouldn't have called it Noah's pitch *specifically* since there were four other people working on it, but then again, he was taking the lead. And she still remembered how annoyed Craig had been with her for disagreeing with him. "I think it's got some really interesting approaches," she said as diplomatically as possible. "Our core audience will love it."

"Ah, so you think it won't broaden our appeal?" Craig asked with a smirk.

"Oh, I didn't mean it like that," Clare hastened to add. She didn't want to give Craig the impression she wasn't a team player, especially since he'd gone out on a limb to let her develop her own pitch. "I just meant, you know, it'll be a big hit with gamers and maybe would bring in some horror fans, too."

"But yours would be sure to bring in a new crowd, right?"

"I mean, that's my hope, yeah."

Craig smiled broadly. "Didn't know you were such a killer, Clare," he said, and she wished he hadn't goaded her into saying it. When she'd been hired, Craig had talked a lot about how they were a family and everyone had each others' backs, and she really did try to live up to that ideal. She might not love her coworkers, but she liked them well enough, and truly wanted the team as a whole, not to mention the company, to succeed.

But no matter how hard she tried, she never quite fit in. Maybe she could have tried taking up multiplayer video games, or hosted a horror marathon at her apartment, or something. She felt like a square peg being stuffed into a round hole; they were technically the same size, but she was the wrong shape.

"I didn't mean—"

"I know what you meant," he said with a wave of his hand. "I'm just teasing."

"Oh, uh, thanks," she said, and Craig patted her shoulder as he stood to go.

"Good luck, kid," he said, and when she first started the job, Craig calling her *kid* had felt like a sign he was looking out for her, like they were something approaching friends. But now it felt patronizing and discouraging. She scrubbed a hand across her face, sighed, and turned back to her desk, wishing she felt just a little bit better about everything.

Chapter Twenty-eight

Logan had barely started unpacking his meager groceries—several premade meals, a bag of salad, and four bottles of wine—when his phone rattled against the countertop.

Clare
Would you want to come over and watch a movie tonight?
Also I feel honor-bound to mention that I know you're home because I saw your light go on, but I promise I wasn't sitting in my kitchen staring at your dark apartment or anything

He grinned, deciding to simply embrace the softness in his chest.

Logan
Stalker
And next time just say Netflix and chill. It's faster

Clare
Fine you wanna come Netflix and chill?

Logan
I'll bring the wine

Even though he knew Clare didn't care—she really had the most appalling palate when it came to wine—Logan took his time choosing a bottle. There was no reason to feel like this was some momentous event to prepare for, but a pack of butterflies had taken up residence in his stomach and showed no sign of leaving. He hesitated before going to his bedroom and grabbing a condom, but it wasn't like he was giving her a condom bouquet or anything. What she wanted (and what he wanted, to be honest) was fairly obvious, but even so he felt more awkward than the first time he bought a pack at the pharmacy. As he was no longer fifteen there was no reason to feel that way, but everything about Clare had turned him upside down.

Clare opened her door and smiled up at him with a hint of shyness. *At least I'm not alone in feeling like this*, he thought, taking a seat on her couch while she opened and poured the wine. Her streaming service menu was called up on her TV, and Logan lifted his eyebrows when she sat down and handed him the glass of full-bodied Shiraz. "What are we watching?" he asked. He threw his arm over the back of the couch and leaned back.

"If you're letting me pick, *High School Musical 2*. It's my all-time comfort movie."

Logan chuckled. "Really?"

"Comfort movies are exempt from mockery, okay? And Troy really sings his heart out on that golf course. What would you pick?"

"If we're doing childhood comfort movies, probably *Shrek 2*."

Clare bit the inside of her lips, eyes dancing with laughter. "*Shrek 2*? And you're mocking *HSM2*?"

"You're the one who said comfort movies are exempt from mockery, and yes, *Shrek 2* is a banger."

Still glowing with amusement, Clare picked up her remote. "*Shrek 2* it is," she announced, and settled in.

She wasn't quite tucked into his side, so Logan decided to take matters into his own hands. He dropped his arm down from the back of the couch and pulled her closer, grinning to himself at her little squeal of surprise. "This okay?" he asked, bringing the wine to his lips.

She smiled up at him, taking a sip of her own. "It's perfect," she said, and snuggled into his side.

And it was. They were watching a goofy movie made for kids, and it was still the best date he'd ever been on. In fact, it was the first date he could remember where *Netflix and chill* wasn't just code for *come over and fuck me*. He was reasonably sure that was where it was heading, but Clare was content to sit and watch a movie with him first.

Because she liked spending time with *him*. Logan was getting a little tired of all these freight trains of realization coming out of nowhere and running him down, but there went another one. Even though he was on good terms with just about every woman he'd slept with, or at least the ones he'd kept in touch with, Clare was the first to truly show an interest in him as a person in years. She was willing to watch his dumb favorite movie from when he was a kid; she was willing to hang out with Burt; she was willing to sit and listen to him talk about drawing.

Clare must not have noticed that his world had changed all over again, because she stayed the way she was, curled into him like it was her favorite place to be. Logan idly played with the ends of her hair, and she sighed, melting against him a little more.

By the time the movie was over, Clare had moved from

leaning against his side to laying with her head in his lap, the better for him to stroke her hair. It was impossibly soft and silky, and he had long ago stopped paying attention to the movie on her TV. Instead, he played a game he hadn't played in a long time and considered what color he'd assign her.

It wasn't really a game so much as a thought exercise, but it was something he liked doing. His dad was a safe, enveloping, dark navy blue, and his mom—or what he knew of her—was the color of the sky in May, when it wasn't quite the deep blue of summer but still seemed brighter than the pale, icy blue of early spring.

Sam, with her prickly personality and habit of swearing like a sailor on leave, was a dark, bruised purple, and the Aidens were primary red. The credits began rolling, the light flickering off Clare's face, and Logan settled on a color.

Yellow.

The soft yellow of a newborn chick, or the yellow of butter on whole wheat toast. Clare was sunshine, warm and golden. He smiled softly, still stroking her hair, and she turned to look at him. "What's that smile for?" she asked, head still cradled in his lap.

"I picked your color." He'd never told anyone about that game, not even his dad. But telling Clare felt right. Her brow furrowed and he traced his finger down the short vertical line, trailing down across the tip of her nose.

"My color? Like . . . what color I'd look best in?"

"No, that's pink. Your color is more like . . . the color I associate with you."

"So, like my aura, or whatever."

"I guess, yeah. Although I don't see it around you, or anything. It's more about how you feel."

"Then what is it?"

Logan shrugged. "That's private," he said, the corner of his mouth lifting.

"Hey, it's *my* color," she protested, and pushed herself up so she was level with his face.

"How's this: if you can guess it, I'll tell you. But it needs to be the right shade, not just the general category."

She frowned again, thinking. "It's not pink, right?"

"Right."

"Is it *close* to pink?"

"I don't think I said anything about hints," he said sternly.

Clare leaned forward and captured his lips in a short, soft kiss. "I bet I can get it out of you," she murmured.

The dark, breathy timbre of her voice did something powerful to his chest, but he made himself look puzzled. "Are you seducing me?" he asked.

Clare grinned and sat up the rest of the way, slinging a leg over his hips to straddle him. "Yes, I am. I'm sorry, was that not clear?"

"Mmm, not sure," he said as he dragged his hands up her thighs to settle at her waist. "I'm not too smart; might need to make it more obvious."

He pressed his head back against the couch to see her more clearly, chin automatically tilting up as she took his face in her hands. "I don't like it when you say that," she said seriously. "That shit about not being smart. It's not true, and I won't let you talk about yourself that way."

Logan's throat was too tight to speak, so instead he nodded. Clare brushed her lips over his and pulled back, head tilting to the side. "Orange," she said, and he shook his head *no*. "Yellow, then?" she guessed. He could tell it was just a random stab in the dark, but he rewarded her anyway with a slide of his tongue alongside hers.

"Almost," he whispered. He let her control the tenor of the kiss, slow and searching and yet somehow igniting a fire low in his belly. His hands slid around to cup her backside, digging his fingers in and pulling her down against his rapidly filling cock. All thoughts of colors flew from his head, because all that was left was her.

She moaned into his mouth, but when he let his left hand dance across her thigh to settle between the apex of her hips she pulled away. Logan whined before he even realized he made the noise, missing the hot, wet taste of her mouth.

"What was that you told me about seduction?" she said, still holding on to his shoulders.

"I have no fucking idea," he replied honestly. All that mattered now was that she kiss him again and lower herself back against his aching dick inside his jeans. He craned his neck toward her and she pulled back, just out of reach.

Her face took on that look it had when she was about to teach him something, bright and playful and sharp as fuck. Christ, he loved that look. She skated her hands down to his wrists, curling her fingers around them. "I think it was *seduction is about getting the other person to take what they want*," she said, and pinned his wrists to the couch on either side of his ears. His heart was hammering so loudly for a second he thought someone was knocking on the door, ready to curse Peggy for yet again interrupting them.

Peggy. Right. He still had to unknot that mess, not to mention convince Clare to go on a double date with his worst client. He realized the only way he could pull it off was to be honest, and even if that was a big risk, it was one he had to take. Because his other option was lying, and he just couldn't do that anymore.

With the most impressive show of willpower he'd ever

possessed, he pulled away from Clare's mouth. "There's something you should know," he said.

"Is it that you've had a lot of sex? Because I thought we'd covered that, as I've already watched some of it," she teased.

Logan huffed out a laugh. "No, it's—Peggy."

"No offense, but I really don't want to talk about my aunt right now. And I know you work for her or whatever already."

Logan wanted nothing more than to pull her back against him and pick up where they left off, but a tiny voice in his head told him he would regret that for ever. So, he persevered. "No, it's more than that. It's about me, too. My . . . motivations."

Clare leaned back, sitting on her heels. "What about your motivations?" Her voice was sharp, suspicious; utterly unlike her. It pierced his chest like an ice pick.

"I—I have a churn problem. Clients like me enough to start, but they rarely stick with me for long, and Peggy—we had a conversation about it. There's one client in particular, who is a huge dick, by the way, but he's important and I have to keep him, or else I'm fucked. He's uncomfortable with, um, my reputation. And Peggy said I needed to show some maturity; prove I was someone she could trust, and that clients would trust. And then—"

"And then she walked in on you having spent the night," Clare finished. He couldn't read her tone, or maybe he just didn't want to.

"Yeah, that. And I—the first time, that had nothing to do with it. But I didn't want her to think I'm that sort of guy."

"Someone who sleeps around, including with her beloved niece."

"Yeah, that."

"Except that is who you are."

Logan ran his hands through his hair. "It is, yeah. Or it was,

I guess, because—god, Clare, I fell for you so fast. I've never— you're—" He stopped and sighed. "I've had women be interested in me before because they thought I was, like, damaged or something. Had some sort of secret pain, and they were going to heal it. But you—you didn't do that. You just like spending time with me. I mean, I think you do, anyway."

Clare chewed her lower lip and he wanted nothing more than to loosen it with his thumb, but he needed to be sure she understood him first.

She hadn't moved from his lap, at least.

"What are you saying, exactly? This was all . . . to impress Aunt Peggy?"

"No, not—not entirely. That first night, when we talked in the elevator, and then—"

"We fucked," she supplied drily.

He huffed out an awkward laugh. "Yeah, that. That was real, and there was something different about you from the start, I think. I never spend the night, you know. Not with hookups."

"But you did with me."

"Yeah. And then Peggy showed up, and with everything going on at work with that client, I panicked, and I thought, well, you're great, so it wouldn't be that hard to, you know, try and make this legit. And then you just blew me away, and I've been scared ever since." He was leaving out telling Schneider she was his girlfriend, but that was nothing. It was real now, so that didn't matter anymore. He could tell her that part later, once he was sure she understood.

"Scared that I'd find out the truth?"

"That you'd think of me the way everyone else does. As a good fuck, and nothing more. That you wouldn't want more, and I did. I do."

"Is that really what you think of yourself?" she asked softly.

"Isn't that how everyone sees me?" he replied, but she put her finger to his lips to silence him. The knot in his chest started loosening, unraveling with each brush of her fingertip. "I mean, I am pretty good at it, you know."

Her lips started curving into a grin. "Sex?"

"Sex," he confirmed. "And you would know."

"Is now when I should admit that I think our first attempt was at best a six out of ten?" she asked.

"What? Seriously? Even when I—" Logan spluttered until it hit him: if she was joking, she understood. And if she understood and didn't hate him, well, that was perfect.

"I'm kidding. Well, sort of, I think we both could have done a little better that night, but that's—"

"I'm sorry, you're going to have to skip to the part where you forgive me so I can fuck you properly," Logan interrupted.

Clare laughed and tucked her face into his shoulder. There was a sharp inhale, like she was preparing for a speech, but then she let it go and sat back up. "There's nothing to forgive, Logan. You're fine."

Logan let her kiss the grin off his face in response, losing himself in the elation of having her with him, warm and wanting. The kiss started slow, a gentle exploration, but when he took her face in his hands it started heating up, becoming less about what had just happened and more about what was to come.

Clare laced their fingers together and leaned her weight into pressing his hands against the cushion. "The other night was about what I wanted—needed, really," Clare whispered, and rolled her hips, dragging her core along his rock-hard length. "I think it's my turn to seduce you. Get you to take what you want."

Logan struggled to keep himself together. He would never

stop being surprised by her, never knowing where that mind of hers would go. "What if all I want is you?" He swallowed hard, shocked the words came out so easily.

Her throat bobbed as she took in his words. Her next question came out slow, hesitant. "Then what about what I want?"

"Are you complaining about something?" he asked with an arched brow. It was the sort of banter he was used to—charged and flirtatious—but it felt different, lighter and heavier at the same time.

She clicked her tongue, annoyed, but a shadow of a dimple appeared in her left cheek. He kissed it, just because he could, and Clare's eyes fluttered closed. "What if *I* want *you*?" she asked, eyes slowly opening. He could have sworn he saw fire in them, kindled deep in their depths.

"Then you should take me," he said, and the thin leash he had on his self-control snapped. He surged up to claim her mouth, welcoming her tongue with his as she once again rocked their hips together. She dragged her lips to just beneath his ear, her hot breath sending shivers down his spine.

Clare shoved his T-shirt up, greedy hands climbing his abs, and she shifted her weight back to let him pull it the rest of the way off. She ducked his elbows and overbalanced, tipping backwards. Logan's arm shot out and caught her just in time, slamming their chests together as laughter burst from both their lips. She rested her forehead against his for a heartbeat, but he was too impatient, too eager to taste her smile, and then they were kissing again, her nipples hard through the thin fabric of her tank top.

She let him shove her cardigan off her shoulders. The strap on her top fell and he nuzzled into the spot it had been, nipping at her collarbone and grinning to himself when she arched her back.

He scooted forward, getting his feet under him, and then hefted her into his arms as he strode toward her bedroom. He dropped her unceremoniously on the bed, gratified by her delighted squeal when he grabbed her ankles and yanked her to the edge.

It was short work to peel her leggings and panties down, and even shorter to bury his face between her thighs. He wanted to stay there for ever, maybe die showing her how good he wanted her to feel, but all too soon she tugged him up by his hair, hand going to his waist as she kissed him deeply.

By the time he was naked and rolling the condom on, his hands were trembling. Suddenly he felt like a virgin, all adrenaline and questions.

She reached up and stroked his cheek, her touch gentle. "Hey. It's just me," she said, "and we've done this before."

Logan rested his forehead against hers and laughed weakly. "And you just said it was mediocre," he replied.

She made him look her in the eye, which was surprisingly hard to do. "That was before we knew each other," she reassured him. "It's different now."

That's what makes this so terrifying. Logan took a deep, steadying breath. Clare's hand joined his, covering his fingers and easing the condom down. She smiled at him, so pure and light that it grounded him. It was easy to cover her with his body and nudge her thighs apart. Her hands roamed the skin of his back, her knee drawing up to his hip, and when he pressed into her, she threw her head back in the most perfectly curved column he had ever seen.

It's never felt like this before. The words popped into his head so clearly, he almost said them aloud. The realization wrapped around him, dragging his consciousness to the right conclusion as he drove into her, slowly at first but then faster, listening to her pleas and needing her to understand even if he couldn't quite speak. *Never. Felt. Like. This. Before*, he said with every stroke, every thrust. *I've never wanted anyone this much*, he said with his kiss, desperate and deep, tongue tangling with hers. *I don't know what it means to feel this way*, he admitted with his fingers searching out her clit. *I need you, I want you. I don't know what I'm doing but I want to learn*, he tried to explain as she came, walls clenching around his cock and pulling him over the edge with her.

I love you, his heart whispered. *I love you*.

Chapter Twenty-nine

Logan had the light next to her bed switched on by the time Clare came back from the bathroom. He was sprawled out like he belonged there, hands tucked behind his head and knee poking out the side of the covers, grinning proudly. Gone was whatever had taken him over just a few minutes before, the need in his eyes as he was inside her, like he was trying to tell her something in a language she didn't quite understand.

There was no hint of nerves anymore, no vulnerability. Just pure, unadulterated satisfaction. She was relieved, in a way. Vulnerable Logan made her heart clench in a way she was not fully equipped to handle. Clare grinned back as she crawled across the bed to him. "You really brought your A-game this time," she said. "I feel like we should high-five or something."

Logan snorted, swatting her ass lightly. "Good hustle out there." Clare tucked her face into his neck and giggled, letting him kiss her hair softly.

"Touchdown, Lakers," she said, and felt, rather than saw, him roll his eyes.

"You know there are no touchdowns in basketball," he chided.

She pulled back, one eyebrow raised. "Do I? You willing to stake your life on that?"

He laughed again. "No, I'm not. But it's important to me that you know that's wrong, okay?"

"If you say so." Clare propped herself up on her elbow to look down at him.

Logan swept his thumb along her cheekbone. "But really though, compared to last time, how was it for you?"

She kissed him first. "Spectacular, amazing, any other superlative that Lady Gaga uses in that one gif."

"Thought so," he smirked.

She traced the line of his eyebrows with a fingertip, his eyes fluttering closed at her touch. Clare wondered if she'd ever get tired of seeing him like this, soft and open and completely hers. "You never did tell me my color," she scolded quietly.

Logan kept his eyes closed. "That's because you didn't guess the exact shade."

"There are approximately one billion possible shades, how on earth am I supposed to?"

The corner of his mouth quirked up and he opened his eyes halfway, still hooded and dark. "Fair enough," he conceded. "Close your eyes."

"I—"

"Do you want to know or not, Thompson?"

Clare had barely recovered from their first round, but the tone in his voice had her thinking about a second. She obediently closed her eyes, still up on her elbow above him.

"Have you ever seen a baby chick? Like, right after it's hatched? And I don't mean a picture of it, I mean a real live one."

Clare thought for a moment. "Yeah, at the state fair."

"Okay, well, there's this softness to it, you know? Especially when you get them out of the incubator and into natural light.

It's yellow, but like—pure yellow. It's not garish or harsh or anything. It's warm and inviting and—well, it's you."

Clare opened her eyes, lips parted, and gazed down at him. "You're a hell of a romantic, did you know that?"

Logan still had one hand behind his head, relaxed and smug. "I am good at certain things, yes," he said, both of them temporarily lapsing into laughter. She walked her fingers up his ribcage, eyes zeroing in on the tattoo on the underside of his biceps she had never quite been able to read. *Art is a line around your thoughts*, it said in a tiny, neat script. She ran her fingertip over it, brow furrowed. "What does that mean?"

"It means I was twenty-two and drunk."

"This isn't a drunk tattoo, this is a thoughtful tattoo. A drunk tattoo is like, a heart with a girlfriend's name in it."

"Or barbed wire around my bicep."

"Or that," she conceded. "Why this one?"

Logan shrugged. "I really was just twenty-two and drunk. I googled 'art quotes' and liked that one the best."

Clare laughed, resting her forehead on his chest and letting him place a kiss on the top of her head. "If you say so."

Abruptly, he sobered. "About before. The stuff with Peggy."

"This may come as a shock to you, Logan, but I don't really want to talk about my aunt while I'm naked."

Half a smile flashed across his face. "I know, I just—I need you to know. That this is real for me."

Her stomach twisted. Logan had been honest with her earlier, and she'd known that was the moment to either come clean or take her secret to the grave. Telling Logan about Craig would serve no purpose, because when she really thought about it, her agreement with Craig was just a nudge that got them together in the first place. It felt shitty, but the truth would do nothing but hurt him; she was sure of it.

This would be her penance, then. She'd keep her secret and feel like crap about it, but it would spare his feelings, and she was discovering she was far more protective of Logan than she was of almost anyone, save Devi. Clare hadn't ever felt like this about anyone before, but she was going to do her best to make sure she didn't hurt him.

"This is real for me too," Clare said, and the guilt began evaporating because it was the truth. What they had together was more real than anything else in her life, and in the end, that was what mattered.

He caught her fingertips and kissed them, a gesture so sweet she thought she might pass out. He tangled their fingers together, face still serious. "I know we haven't talked about exclusivity, but I want to be clear—I'm not with anyone else."

Clare wrinkled her nose. "Oooh yeah, that's going to be a problem for me because I think I'm sleeping with like, ten different guys right now?" She failed at keeping a straight face and Logan playfully swatted at the outside of her thigh again.

"Fuck you," he laughed, cupping her cheek in his palm. "But for real, you're not . . .?"

"Seeing someone else? No, no. Of course not," she assured him.

He leaned back against her pillow, smirk returning. "Good."

"Good?"

"I like knowing what's mine."

Clare's eyebrows flew up even as a bolt of desire shot through her core. "Excuse me?"

"I'm an only child. Never really mastered the whole 'sharing' thing," he said with a lazy shrug.

"I'm sorry, I'm stuck on this *mine* thing," she argued.

"I don't think you are, actually," he said softly, catching her chin between his knuckles and tipping her face to his. "I think you like it."

Clare melted into the kiss, her train of thought completely scrambled. "I do?" she managed.

Logan's lips moved languidly, tasting her like it was the first time he'd kissed her and he wanted to memorize it. "You do," he said. There was a rasp in his voice that hadn't been there before. "I think you like being mine, Clare. You like it when I'm bossy and possessive, and I like that it gets you hot, so deal with it. You belong to me now."

She found her voice. "Then this is mine," she said, resting her hand on his heart again before dragging it down to his cock. "This too," she added, attaching her lips to the side of his throat. Logan groaned and pulled her on top of him, thrusting his hips up as she went.

"Yours," he agreed, sealing their lips together. "All yours."

Clare woke up with a languid stretch, rolling onto her side with a smile on her face that quickly evaporated.

Logan's side was empty. Her heart sank, but before she could do anything else there was a loud clatter from her kitchen and a vehemently whispered "Motherfucker!"

Snorting to herself she swung her legs over the side, snatching his shirt and shrugging it on as she left her bedroom. As she suspected, Logan was in the middle of a clear baking crisis, shirtless and wearing her apron, trying to fish a bowl out of her bottom cupboard.

She had never expected to see Logan in a *The North Remembers* apron, but she had to admit, it was working for him. Possibly because everything worked on him, up to and including a garbage bag.

Logan poked his head up over her counter and frowned. "Are you just going to stand there, or are you going to come rescue me?"

Clare leaned her shoulder against the fridge. "Just stand here, I think." She lifted her chin toward the stove, which currently had an empty frying pan resting on it. The counter was covered in flour, and there was a lone egg sitting out next to a muffin tin. "What are you even making?"

"Uh, pancakes?" Logan set the bowl down heavily on the counter.

"And the muffin tin is for . . . decoration?"

He ran a floury hand through his hair, giving him a distinct salt-and-pepper look. "I was going to make muffins at first, but then I decided pancakes would be easier, and in all of that I guess I decided to pretend I have done this before—which I haven't."

"You've never made pancakes?"

"I'm more of a take-her-out-to-brunch man, if I'm even there in the morning. Which, before you, I usually wasn't."

Clare's heart softened and she took pity on him. "Pan for pancakes is in the bottom left cupboard. I'll talk you through it."

Ten minutes later, their fourth pancake was sizzling softly in the pan, a stack of three on the plate nearby in varying levels of okay-ness. Logan wasn't a baker, that was for sure, but this was more fun than anything else, in her opinion. She prodded him to flip it, and he managed without major catastrophe, at least. "I, um, do have a big favor to ask," he said, focusing a little too hard on the pan. "There's this client."

"The jerk."

"Him," Logan confirmed. "He wants to make sure I'm someone who is 'settled,' and I guess he has some issues with my reputation, and he says he's leaving Loyalty unless I can prove that to him. I wouldn't ask, except it's basically my job on the line. Would you come to dinner with me? Help reassure him I'm, you know, responsible and shit."

Clare's stomach did a flip that didn't resemble butterflies. She had understood Logan last night; she knew him well enough to know that he tended to act on impulse, especially with his job on the line like that. But something about hearing this request in the cold light of day felt more mercenary and transactional than she'd like. But it wasn't like she hadn't used him at the start, so she put on a smile. "Just name the place," she said cheerfully, hoping she wouldn't regret it.

Chapter Thirty

Logan held open the door to the patio, letting Clare and Devi through first. It was a balmy summer evening, and the restaurant's picnic tables out back were nearly full. They found a seat at the end of one of the tables near a group that looked to be settling their checks, and when one of them stood up Clare surreptitiously slid her purse onto that spot to hold it.

Competitive patio seating was practically a sport during Minnesota summers, but fortunately Toni and Annie arrived just a few minutes later, forestalling the need for any more drastic measures. There was a flurry of activity as the server arrived and everyone hurried to get their order in, followed by a beat of quiet when she left the table.

Devi broke the silence, as Logan was rapidly discovering her role within this little group. She set the tone for their games and in their conversations. "So. Things. Happening. You two?" she said, pointing between them.

Annie giggled and Clare shrugged. "You could say that," she said breezily, and rested her hand on his forearm. It was a small gesture, but Logan preened inwardly anyway.

No one had ever really claimed him before. Logan covered

her hand with his and leaned forward. "Let's just cut to the chase. Do I pass the test?" he asked, making eye contact with each woman in turn.

Annie cackled and that set Toni off. Toni's laugh was infectious and drew the attention of several people around them, but Logan sat waiting Devi's verdict. She was considering him carefully, eyes darting between him and Clare. "You're a lot less boring than her last boyfriend, so yes, you pass," she said with a grin.

Toni wiped a tear of laughter from her eye. "God, yes, Reid was the *worst*. Sorry, hon, but we held it in as long as we could," she added to Clare.

"Okay, but that would have been useful information to have, oh, I don't know, maybe eighteen months ago?"

"He wasn't *that* bad, he was just, you know . . ." Toni trailed off and motioned with the pint glass in her hand, almost knocking the woman next to her in the face. "Oh shit, sorry," she said to her near-victim.

Annie picked up where she left off. "He was about as interesting as a *Politico* article about senate fundraising."

"As interesting as reshelving a set of World War Two biographies," Devi said.

"You know, my dad would probably like those," Logan interjected.

"I know approximately one billion, remind me and I'll give you some titles," Devi replied without missing a beat. "But seriously, Reid was . . . well, he was fine. But he was *just* fine, you know?"

"Wait, did I miss it? I have one," Toni said, turning back to them. "He was about as interesting as ordering hay."

Devi held her hand out flat and wiggled it in a so-so gesture. "Eh, I think Annie's was the best."

"As much as I love this comedy hour workshop, I'm not sure roasting my ex-boyfriend in front of my—Logan—is the best use of our time," Clare said primly.

Logan bumped her with his shoulder. "It's okay, babe," he teased. "You can call me your boyfriend."

"Babe? *Babe*?" Clare said indignantly. "Since when do you call me *babe*?"

"Since right now. Because I'm your boyfriend."

Clare stared him down and then sighed in defeat. "I feel like you're all ganging up on me," she whined.

"Because we are, babe," Annie replied.

"Oh no, please don't make this a thing."

"Too late, it's already a thing," Toni said cheerfully. "Babe."

Clare laid her head down on the wooden table with a theatrical groan. Logan scratched his fingers through her hair sympathetically, a smile permanently etched on his face.

They were halfway through the table's plate of nachos when the discussion turned to Clare's work. "Any news on the story launch, babe?" Toni asked around a mouthful of chips.

Clare rolled her eyes good-naturedly. "We're still working on things, trying to get it all in order before the big battle royale."

"And how's what's-his-face, your creepy boss?" Annie asked.

"Craig isn't creepy," Clare bristled.

"I don't know, I would be wary of a guy like that," Devi said carefully. "Cults of personality are usually a bad sign."

"It's not a cult of personality, he's just very engaging," Clare said. "Everyone wants to work on our team."

Annie made a face. "I just think he crosses a line sometimes. What about the time he wanted you to, what was it, go white-water rafting?"

"It was just kayaking down Minnehaha Creek, don't exaggerate."

"Okay, but like, he had some dumb theory about it, like you couldn't assign the right point value to rowing unless you'd physically done it. And then you went and did it, and you hated it."

"It wasn't about if I'd like it or not, it was about experience," Clare said stiffly. "And he was right. It helped to have a feel for how hard it was."

Devi intervened. "I don't really think it was necessary," she said. "It felt—well, you shouldn't have to do stuff like that outside of work, just to be able to assign a point value to something. You've never killed a dragonspawn either, but you can write that just fine."

"But I did need to take that archery lesson," Clare argued. "He was right about that."

Logan watched the conversation closely, noting the tension in Clare's shoulders. It felt out of proportion for the conversation, which itself felt far too tense considering the easy, joking atmosphere of just a few minutes ago.

"A lesson that you paid for," Annie pushed. "I just—back me up here, guys, Craig can be . . . too involved. He keeps telling you to do shit that has nothing to do with your job, or only vaguely related to it, and then you have to pay for it, or deal with the anxiety about kayaking because, don't lie, you were terrified of that, and—"

"Whatever, it's my job and my life, okay?"

Annie clicked her tongue and let it slide, and after another beat of awkward silence, Devi took charge and asked Toni about the new place she was boarding her horses. The conversation moved on, but the lingering tightness in Clare's posture didn't.

It was still there when they walked to Logan's car after dinner. The rest of the night had recovered easily enough, but he was too attuned to her now to ignore the way her smile didn't quite reach her eyes when Devi shared a story involving undergrad library workers, a frat party, and a TikTok stunt gone wrong.

"Everything okay?" he asked, pressing the ignition button. "That conversation about your boss got kinda . . . tense."

If possible, her shoulders climbed higher around her ears. "It's nothing. Craig's—I mean, yeah, he's probably too involved, but he means well, you know? Plus, I owe him. I didn't have the right resumé for that job, but he hired me anyway."

"What do you mean, not the right resumé?"

"Just something he let slip after I was hired. I wasn't supposed to know, but he saved me from being tossed aside before interviews even started. He said he could see the potential in my writing sample and wanted to give me a chance."

"And now he makes you do a lot of extra stuff?"

"Not extra," she said vehemently. "Just stuff that would make me a better writer."

Logan decided it wasn't worth pushing. He was no stranger to doing weird things to impress a boss, after all. He decided to drop it, but reached over and took her hand for a gentle squeeze before he pulled out of the parking lot.

Chapter Thirty-one

Kiki settled more comfortably in Clare's lap while Logan and Sam bickered about something to do with a coach. Mostly through osmosis Clare had learned that the NBA finals were happening, which was a big deal. The Timberwolves hadn't made it this year, she gathered, and a source of conflict between Logan and Sam was which team they were going to root for now. Logan went with the Lakers, since they used to be a Minnesota team, but Sam felt that leaving the Twin Cities for Los Angeles was an unforgivable betrayal, and thus was rooting for the Miami Heat. Clare was a little unclear as to why Sam had chosen the Heat, but it appeared Logan felt her reasoning was flawed.

"Their defense has been abysmal, you have to admit that," Logan argued. Kiki shook her head, tags tinkling softly, and rested her chin on Clare's knee.

"No, I do not have to admit that at all," Sam protested.

Clare scratched Kiki between the ears and held up her phone. "Hey, I just looked it up and it appears the Lakers left Minnesota in 1960. Is there a reason we're fighting about something that happened before our parents were even born?"

"It's the principle of the thing," Sam said vehemently. "They left; ergo, they are traitors and I will never support them. Also, my dad was born in '58, so suck it." That took them off on an argument about the validity of teams leaving various cities and states, although it seemed they were mostly angrily agreeing with each other that the SuperSonics never should have left Seattle.

The fight had been going on for what felt like ten minutes, and Clare decided to chuck a grenade onto the floor. That wasn't her usual approach, but she sort of liked watching them fight like angry cats. Clare glanced down at her phone and the new article she had just pulled up on playoff contenders. "What about the Milwaukee Bucks? Can't we root for them? Midwestern solidarity, and all that?"

"Don't be gross," Logan said sternly, while Sam made a face at her.

"Hey, at least she didn't suggest the Bulls," Sam said, and then they were off on a tangent about the playoffs two years ago and a bet that Logan may or may not have made on the Bulls' chances. Clare didn't follow half of it, but she did find it immensely entertaining to watch. This was a different side of Logan, not quite the brash charmer she first met in the elevator, but not the soft, sweet man she saw at his father's house, either. He was sharper with Sam than she'd seen him with anyone, but in a way that told her he was giving Sam exactly what she needed from him.

Clare had never considered that Logan was simply a people pleaser at heart. He had a way of figuring out exactly what people needed from him and becoming that person. Burt needed a supportive son, Sam needed a sparring partner who wouldn't flinch from her barbs, and Clare needed someone to gently push her out of her comfort zone. Logan had been able to read her Quest group, too, easily adapting to their humor and embracing the dorky vibe.

He was a chameleon, with an especially sensitive antennae for people's needs, down to noticing when Clare had gotten uncomfortable with Annie's characterization of Craig. Clare was still a little pissed at Annie for that, quite frankly. She knew Annie had her best interests at heart, but like Sam, Annie could be a bit of a dick. And the way she described Craig was unfair—it sounded accurate, but it wasn't. Craig was better than Annie had made him out to be, even if her criticisms had a ring of truth to them that Clare didn't appreciate.

Clare was very relieved she hadn't told the girls about Craig's suggestion regarding her sex life, since that would have sent Annie into one of her patented *go to HR* chants. She was usually right, but this happened to be a time when she was wrong. Clare was sheltered, and not willing to take enough risks, and when writing a game that was at its core about adventure, that wasn't the best fit. Without Craig's pushes, Clare might never have gone for it with Logan. Hearing Annie put Craig's habits in such blunt terms while sitting next to Logan had been unpleasant to say the least.

On the TV, the players arranged themselves on the court and the game officially began. Sam and Logan put a pin in their argument and both eyes turned to fixate on the players. Clare had watched a little bit of a game with Logan in the hospital, but this was the first time she could remember that she had sat down with the intention to watch an entire game of any type of sport, start to finish.

The game was both faster paced than she expected and slower, with a surprising amount of commercial breaks that allowed Sam and Logan to resume their bickering as if they had never stopped. And while Clare would probably never be into a game that had winners and losers—what she loved about Quest was that there wasn't a way to win or lose, and the best parts were collaborative—she did like seeing Logan so enthusiastic about something. His team made a three-point shot that was apparently quite tricky and he jumped off the couch with a whoop of joy. The smile on his face was so pure Clare couldn't help but smile too.

She took Kiki out for a walk at the start of halftime, and when she came back up Kiki trotted straight to Sam and settled next to her for a belly rub. "Hello, sweetie," Sam said in a tiny baby voice. "Did you have a nice walk?"

Logan sat down next to Clare with his arm draped across the back of the couch. "Kiki is how we first met," he said, almost wistfully.

"Really? I just assumed he picked you up on Tinder," Sam said to Clare.

Logan shook his head. "Clare's classier than you and me," he replied.

"I don't know if I'd say that," Clare interjected. "We did, uh, hook up after getting stuck in the elevator."

"Oh my god, Logan, you have *got* to chain up that libido of yours," Sam said, grinning.

"Still," Logan said dismissively. "You're different from me and Sam. You said yourself I was the exception to the rule."

"Yeah, but—"

"That's all I mean," he said, and shot her a grin that left her weak in the knees. Sometimes she wished Logan wouldn't be so insistent that they were fundamentally different, but at the same time, sometimes it felt good to be on his pedestal.

No, she'd made the right decision in not mentioning the Craig situation. She just wished she felt a little better about it.

* * *

The only thing better than hanging out with Logan was sex with Logan, in Clare's opinion. The blahs of their first encounter had faded to almost nothing, replaced by the spine-tingling memories of every subsequent bout. If it weren't for needing the occasional change of clothes, Clare wouldn't have even seen the inside of her apartment for the entire weekend.

Logan trailed his fingers down her shoulder, leaving a line of goosebumps in his wake. He had a habit of touching her after sex, she'd noticed, like he needed to keep contact with her or else she'd vanish. "That dinner with the client," he said, fingertips still tracking up and down over her skin. "Does next Thursday work?"

"This is the one where I show some guy that you're a responsible adult and not at all someone who sleeps around, right?"

"That one. It's going to be boring, though. Mind-numbingly boring. You'll hate every second of it."

"You're selling this very well," Clare said, biting back a grin.

"Good, that's how it was supposed to come across," he volleyed back. "But seriously, it'll be boring and I want to be upfront about that, but—could you make it? Next Thursday?"

Clare nestled closer to him and ran her fingers through the soft hair at the nape of his neck. "Sure." She fell silent, wondering how to phrase her next question. "I honestly don't mean to sound judgy, but is there a reason for all the sex? I mean, you've had enough that a *client* thinks you sleep around too much."

A laugh rumbled in his chest. "You're not the first woman to ask, but you are the first woman I'll give an honest answer to." He shifted, rolling to his back and pulling her with him. "I know a lot of women think that I sleep around because there's something broken or tragic about me. I've had a couple think that they could fix me, but the real answer is I just like sex. I'm good at getting women to want to sleep with me, I like flirting, and I like everything that comes after. That's it, really."

Clare absorbed his answer, her heart tripping over the idea that she was the only person he'd told that to, even if it was hardly a life-changing secret. "What have you told the other women?"

"That my past was too painful to talk about," he said with a mischievous grin. "Usually gets me another round."

Clare snorted into his chest, her smile so wide it made her cheeks ache. "You're incorrigible," she said.

"I'm going to take that as a compliment," he said, smiling against the top of her head.

Chapter Thirty-two

Logan couldn't stop smiling. It was a disease, really, and it was drawing attention at work. It wasn't that he was normally in a bad mood when he was at work—on the contrary, he spent a lot of time, probably too much time, goofing around with the Aidens—but even he had to admit, this mood was different.

Logan felt light and airy, and even the terror he felt when he considered the fact that he had, officially, let someone into his heart, couldn't outweigh his grin. Vince noticed first, commenting on his unusually good mood when they were in the break room waiting for the coffee maker to finish brewing Vince's cup of hazelnut and vanilla flavored coffee.

"What's gotten into you?" Vince asked, leaning his shoulder against the wall.

"Nothing," Logan shrugged. "I, uh, had a productive call with a client earlier."

That wasn't a complete lie, as he had finally connected with Bill Jefferson, an older client who Logan had suspected was wavering on remaining with him. It wasn't for certain, but it did seem more likely than not that Jefferson was going to stick with him for the foreseeable future, which should go a long way toward improving his metrics. The Schneider dinner was officially scheduled, and that would be his last major hurdle.

"Yeah, you've definitely got 'client grin' on, and not—" Vince broke off and narrowed his eyes, studying him. "Dare I say . . . 'met someone grin'?"

Logan shrugged and looked down. He hoped Vince wouldn't notice that his ears were burning, or if he did, that he wouldn't comment on it. "I've started seeing someone, yeah," he said.

"Really seeing? Or—your usual?"

"Really seeing," Logan said. He tossed a look toward the Aidens, who were spinning in their chairs and talking loudly about their last pick-up game. "But, uh, I think I want to keep it quiet, you know? Just for now."

Vince gave him a kind smile. "I get it. Secret's safe with me, but between the two of us? This looks good on you," he said with a friendly pat on the shoulder.

Logan watched his friend leave and loaded the coffee pod into the coffee maker. If he really was dating Clare, he was entering completely uncharted territory.

The thought was honestly terrifying, but he was still going to try.

Logan flopped down on his childhood bed, arm flung over his face. He didn't come home as often as he should, although he was doing it more so now that he was with Clare. He wasn't exactly sure why she made him feel like he should be a better son, but she did.

His dad was downstairs, puttering around like usual, and had sent Logan up to *clean out that closet of yours*. Logan wasn't sure what he was supposed to do with a ten-year-old varsity letter jacket or if the thrift store would even want it, but he dutifully placed it in a large cardboard box marked *donations*. His phone buzzed with a text; a warning from Sam that a rant was incoming. Three seconds later the rant began, mostly around the rumors that the Wolves were going to fire their coach at the end of the season and her strongly held opinion that the women's Gopher's coach was the perfect replacement but would never be given proper consideration due to her gender.

Logan agreed with her, but sometimes Sam just needed to vent without any response from him at all. He let her continue, phone buzzing every thirty seconds as he pulled half a dozen old hoodies and T-shirts out of his closet, tossing them into the pile for donations. His high school backpack—covered in white-out hearts courtesy of the girl who sat next to him in study hall, and still full of his notebooks and one very outdated science textbook—went straight into the black trash bag Burt had given him on the way upstairs.

He sat down on the edge of his bed and glanced at his phone, where Sam was still texting in all caps about the NBA's idiocy and misogyny. There was a soft knock on his door and Burt stepped through, surveying his minimal progress. Logan's phone buzzed three times in a row, and Burt lifted his eyebrows. "Sam angry with you?"

"Just angry in general today."

"She usually is," Burt agreed. "She's a hellcat, that girl."

Logan nodded, unsure of what to say, since his dad rarely followed him up to his room. But rather than ask a question, Burt pulled his backpack out of the trash and unzipped it, thumbing through the notebook. It was probably his history notebook, judging by the few random dates scribbled between doodles.

Well, they were more than doodles. Drawings; sketches maybe. Some were of things he could see from his desk in US history, like the oak tree in the courtyard that was crawling with squabbling, fat squirrels, or the pile of messy papers on the teacher's desk. Others were more imaginative, like the wing of a dragon curling protectively around a hatching egg, or a human stuck in an alien zoo.

Burt studied the sketches closely. "You really didn't pay attention in school, did you?" he said wryly.

Logan grinned reluctantly. "If I answer honestly, are you going to ground me?"

"I would if I could," Burt said, chuckling. "You're still spending a lot of time with that Clare girl, right?"

"Yeah, I am."

Burt sat quietly. He did that a lot, and it was something Logan wished he was better at, but he had gotten used to filling the silences over the years, and it was a hard habit to break. "I've never seen you that way," Burt said finally, and pointed to Logan's old notebook. "The way you are with her. It made me think of these."

"Clare made you think of how I was shitty at school?"

"No, how you used to be. When you were younger. You've grown into a good man, don't get me wrong, but sometimes I worry you've become a little . . . jaded. But with Clare, I saw— well, I saw you. The you that you used to be."

"I've disappointed you, haven't I?"

"Not at all," Burt said fiercely. "I just wish—" He stopped and sighed. "She would have been so much better at all of this." There was only one *she* that the Walsh men talked about in that tone of voice. "She would have been better at making sure you knew how much we loved you. I'm too much of an old bachelor farmer for this, too quiet. You haven't disappointed me, I just wanted to see you happy. And you weren't unhappy before, but I don't think you were happy, either."

Logan looked down at his old sketches. "Do you think she would have liked these?"

"She would have loved them," Burt replied immediately. "She loved art, you know that. All kinds, anything you could create or make, she adored and wanted to do it all, and nothing would have made her happier than knowing you have her talent." He studied the sketches closely for a long minute. "She always said that part of being an artist was putting your heart on display for the rest of the world, and I don't think I fully appreciated how brave that was until later."

Logan leaned his shoulder against Burt and let him throw his arm around him. "Being jaded is easier," he admitted. He thought about Clare pointing out that he refused to share his art because it meant sharing part of his mom with the rest of the world, and wondered how deep this instinct went. Because being jaded really was easier, and sometimes, when Clare would look at him and see him—really see him, even when he'd wanted her to—he had the instinct to run. To blow it up and walk away, because sharing that much of himself with someone else was terrifying.

"I'm sure it is," Burt said. "But there's a cost." Once more, he pointed to the notebook. "You'd lose this, I fear. And I don't want that to happen." He let Logan think about that for a few moments before continuing. "I don't want to butt in where I'm not invited, but Clare is good for you, and I hope . . . I don't judge your dating habits, I really don't, but I think you have a habit of—"

"She's special," Logan said, deciding to rescue his dad from the corner he'd backed himself into. No one, least of all Logan, wanted to go over his extensive sexual history with his father. "Different."

"She is," Burt agreed. "And I just wanted to say that I'm happy for you."

Logan glowed with pride at the same time his old doubts

resurfaced. There wasn't really anyone he could talk to about his fears. Sam would just call him a sentimental dumbass, even if she'd listen to him, but he and Burt were having a moment and he decided to risk it. Logan's eyes burned and he looked up at the ceiling, blinking hard. "What if she gets bored of me?" he said, throat tight. "I know she will. She's—you met her. She's deep, and I'm . . . shallow."

"I don't think I'd call you shallow," Burt replied softly. "More like a waterfall. A bit showy, perhaps, but deep in ways people don't necessarily expect." He sighed. "Your mother was the same way, you know. Bright, always the center of attention, hard to take your eyes off of, even for a moment. You've got a lot of her in you, and I know I've said it before, but it's true. Making people feel the way you do, the way she did, that's a skill. Maybe I didn't make sure you knew it well enough when you were younger, and that's my fault. But I don't want to see you scorn that skill or lose that spark."

"Clare gave me that spark back, you're saying?"

"I'm saying I think Clare helped remind you of where you'd hidden it away."

Logan leaned his shoulder against his father's. "It's still scary," he said.

Burt rubbed his back. "Everything worth having is."

Chapter Thirty-three

Clare arrived on the rooftop a few minutes before Logan. It had been a long day at work—Noah and Derek and the rest of her team had been kind of loud, and Craig seemed to be avoiding her—so Logan's suggestion of wine on the roof had been something of a godsend. She needed to unwind, and even if she probably couldn't go home with him the way she knew she'd want to (thanks to her team meeting tomorrow at the ungodly hour of eight o'clock in the morning), it would be nice to just talk to him.

Clare was curled in one of the chairs she now thought of as *theirs* when he appeared, two wine glasses in one hand, and a bottle of white in the other. He grinned down at her and her heart tumbled over because somehow, this astonishingly handsome man was hers.

Logan took the spot next to her, both of them facing the river, and poured her a glass. "How's the pitch going?" he asked, and it wasn't his fault—it really wasn't—but the small bubble of happiness she'd been feeling popped like a balloon.

"It's fine, I guess."

"You guess?"

"Well, we're supposed to be working on this as a team, you know? We're going to have the big all-hands meeting soon and the teams are competing on their pitches, but Craig still has me sort of . . . siloed off from the rest of the team, working on the Captain Ellis pitch while the rest of them do their horror thing. His idea is that a two-pronged approach would be better, give us a better shot of being the winning team. But . . ." She broke off and took a long sip of wine, desperately willing it to relax her. "But if that's true, then why am I on my own? Shouldn't I be working to integrate my pitch with the rest of the team by now?"

Getting the words out was like simultaneously ingesting and expelling a poison. It had been weighing on her for weeks, but she had been avoiding saying it out loud. Now it felt real, tangible; not just a figment of her imagination.

She hated it.

"You said Craig hired you?"

"He did. He took a chance on me, and my first big project didn't exactly pan out."

"And that was your fault?"

Clare shrugged. She hated thinking about that stupid online teaser and the humiliation that followed. Craig had been quietly sympathetic, but hadn't seemed interested in steering the rest of the team away from putting the failure on her shoulders alone.

"It wasn't so much that it was my fault, more that it was my first project, you know? We did what the company asked and it just didn't pan out. But it set a tone with the rest of team, and I've been trying to dig myself out of that hole ever since."

There had been red flags all over the project, mainly the fact that no one had any clear vision of the prospective audience. Theoretically, new players would find the one-shot, play the interactive version the web team set up, and then buy the game, but Clare had been tasked with crafting a story for players with characters who had already reached level twelve, meaning they had years of experience. If someone had years of experience, they were already playing the game, and if someone had no idea how to play the game, having no introduction to character classes, levels, or rules would be far too confusing. But Clare was too new at the job to point any of that out, so she'd done the best she could, and then bore the brunt of the failure.

In retrospect, maybe her problem was that she never managed to find her voice at work. She wanted so badly to work there that she had a tendency to make excuses for everyone else.

"And so that's why he assigns you extra work?"

"Something like that."

Logan frowned thoughtfully. "And this character is for a one-shot? But she doesn't fit in with the rest of the team's pitch?"

Clare shook her head. "Captain Ellis is a non-player character; someone to act as a guide to the world. I designed her as a sort of lady rogue, someone who sleeps around and has a paramour in every place the players could go. It's just a gimmick, really, but it's a different tone from a lot of our more recent stuff. She's more playful and light, and so the one-shot I'm designing around her has that same tone. There's a couple of different ports that players could call on, with some fairly loose storylines in place for each one if a Game Master is new at it or just wants to rely on someone else to call the shots for a little while."

"And the other one is a horror movie?"

"It's more complicated than that, but yeah. It's a gore-fest, which is a huge hit with a lot of our existing players, for sure."

"But it won't bring in anyone new," Logan ventured.

"No. Not in my opinion, anyway. We've already got them; why not branch out?"

"That makes sense from an economic standpoint," Logan agreed. "And yeah, I don't really see how those two pitches go together, or why no one else on your team could help you with yours."

Clare leaned back in the lounge chair, wine glass clutched tightly in her hands. "I just really think Captain Ellis would be good for the game," she said plaintively.

"You said she sleeps around, right?" Logan asked with the beginnings of a grin.

"She does, yeah."

He leaned over and whispered conspiratorially. "She's based on me, isn't she? It's okay, you can be honest."

Clare's stomach jolted uncomfortably. "I created her before we, uh, you know."

"Had sex?" Logan supplied helpfully. "We've had a lot of it, you know. You should probably try saying it out loud."

"Oh, I'm aware," she said in an attempt to match his playful tone.

She should have known Logan would pick up on her discomfort. He drew his brows together. "What's wrong?" he asked. "She isn't based on me, is she? I was just kidding, but—seriously, what's wrong?"

Clare licked her lips. This was as clear of a choice as she'd ever had regarding her Logan dilemma. If it were in a campaign, she knew how the group would push her to respond, and she also knew that lying to him now would be nearly unforgivable. She had been so sure that not telling him was the right thing to do, but that was before he had come so close to the truth. She was going to have to roll the dice.

Clare took a deep breath and set her glass down on the table between them. "Before I go any further, you have to know that this was all before I knew you." He lifted his eyebrows but didn't say anything. "When I first proposed Captain Ellis, Craig pointed out—well, I'm someone who is pretty monogamous, you know? That's not a secret. Anyway, Craig—he didn't say it outright, but, well, he said I needed more experience to handle a character like her."

"Your boss. Told you you needed to have sex," Logan said flatly.

"Of course not," Clare replied, aware of how defensive she sounded. "He just pointed out that I'm sort of, um, sheltered, and that I could use more life experience."

"And I was that experience."

"I—yeah. That day in the elevator. It seemed like exactly the sort of thing I needed to . . ."

"To try," Logan finished. His tone was hard to read, and he was staring fixedly out at the river rather than looking at her. "I was your proof you could write her."

"Yes," she admitted, and waited for the hammer to fall.

But it never came. Logan just looked out at the river for a long time before turning to her. "And that's why you wanted to keep things casual."

"Yeah, I didn't want to fall into old habits. I've never had sex with someone I wasn't dating, and I wanted to try something new. And with the Senior Game Designer position opening up soon, I really need to stand out."

"And I assume that means I have to be a secret at your work?"

Clare shook her head. "I never told Craig any details, just that I'd taken his advice. And we ran into Noah that once, but he never got your name."

"Well. There's that at least."

"I'm sorry if I—"

"You didn't hurt me," Logan interrupted, but his voice still wasn't quite right. It wasn't warm and playful, but it wasn't cold and harsh either. "I get it. We barely knew each other. And I'm, well, me."

"Right, and—"

"And there's that whole shit with my work, yeah." Clare wished Logan would let her finish a damn sentence, but she also wanted to tread lightly. "I guess we're even then, huh?" Logan said. "I did something kind of crappy, you did something kind of crappy, we both still have jobs, the end."

Clare bit her lower lip. "I am sorry," she said again. "I didn't know how to tell you without hurting you."

"I get it. It's fine."

"Are you sure?"

Logan smiled at her finally, but it didn't quite reach his eyes. "Positive."

Chapter Thirty-four

Logan was nervous. He was never nervous about anything before Clare, especially not before something as simple as a client dinner. He'd done dozens of these since he started working at Loyalty. This was the sort of thing he was made for; he excelled at small talk and at calibrating his flirting to the right amount of charming-but-non-threatening that usually delighted men like Schneider. And he did genuinely like talking to people. People were interesting to him, even the ones he didn't intend to sleep with.

He felt jittery, like he'd had a few too many coffees on an empty stomach. Sure, his job was more or less on the line but he could count on Clare. She cared about him and he cared about her, and he just needed Schneider to see that.

But Clare's confession from the other day kept resurfacing in his mind, like a piece of trash that kept rising to the top of a flood of water in the gutter. *I'm sort of sheltered and needed more experience.*

Logan understood. He really did. He knew what he was like, and he knew she had been aware of his reputation before they slept together. There was no reason to be hurt by this revelation, especially not since she had so easily forgiven him for his shitty motivations regarding her.

He'd meant it. They were even. They had to be, even if the knowledge that Clare wasn't really all that different from the other women he'd slept with stung like hell. In the end, she had just wanted him for sex. Sure, she wanted more now, but how much longer was that going to last?

He tugged at his waistcoat—yes, a three-piece suit was probably too much, and no, he didn't have any regrets, he knew how good he looked in them—and checked his watch. It wasn't like Clare to be late, and while she wasn't late yet, technically, he was anxious. They were meeting a good ten minutes before Schneider was supposed to arrive, but Logan wanted to be there to greet her at the door in case Schneider was early and saw them. Chivalry, and all that shit.

A car pulled up to the curb and Clare hopped out, waving cheerfully to the driver before turning to him. "Wow," she said, drawing up short. "You clean up nice."

"So do you," he said, taking her hand and pulling her close to drop a kiss on her cheek. She was in a nicer outfit than he'd ever seen her in, a fitted, dusky pink dress that brought out the tint of her lips.

"I changed in the bathroom at work," she explained, ducking under his arm as he swung the door open for her. "And did my makeup in the car."

"You couldn't just wear that to work?"

"Not if I didn't want to explain why I was so dressed up," she said.

Logan furrowed his brow and gave their drink order to the bartender. "And you couldn't just make up a reason?"

Clare looked unusually flustered. "I mean, I could have, I just—"

"I thought you said I wasn't a secret?" he asked, hating the note of suspicion that crept into his tone. He wanted to believe her, he really did. There was no reason for him to feel this way.

But god, it still hurt like hell.

"You're not, I just didn't want to tell them anything about my personal life, okay? I have to get through the pitch meeting first," she said sharply, and the hostess chose that moment to come over and escort them to their table. Logan took care of ordering the wine, figuring Schneider might be happier if he had a glass waiting when he arrived.

Clare studied the menu quietly while Logan studied her. He ran over everything he knew about her boss Craig in his mind, wondering what could have driven someone as confident as Clare to reach for his approval like this. She'd explained the whole failed-right-out-of-the-gate thing, and Logan certainly understood doing stupid things to get your boss's approval. But it still just didn't fit.

Or maybe he just didn't want it to fit. He didn't want Clare to be like him. She was supposed to be *better*.

Schneider arrived and interrupted his spiral. Logan jumped to his feet and Clare shook his hand politely, asking very sweetly about his wife. "Decided to stay in St. Louis with the grandbaby," Schneider said, sitting down across from them.

"Do you have pictures?" Clare asked, her face lighting up with what seemed like genuine joy. Logan knew her trick—*I imagine the baby pictures are cute dogs and react accordingly*—and he grinned softly, the pressure in his chest easing slightly.

They were fine. *He* was fine. He cared about her and their motives at the start didn't matter anymore, what mattered was now. Schneider passed his phone over and Clare cooed with delight, sending Logan a tiny secret smile that made him feel even more at ease. Logan steered the conversation to boating, something Clare knew a surprising amount about, thanks to her water-based work fiasco, and it seemed like Schneider was warming up. Clare was easy to like and he and Clare worked well together; Logan realized somewhere between the salad and main entrée that they had the almost effortless banter of a couple with years of history behind them. There was a slight tension to her smile that Logan knew Schneider wouldn't pick up on, but that was probably because of the overall pressure of the whole evening.

When Schneider asked Clare if she was going to order dessert, Logan knew he had it in the bag. *Suck it, Wimberley,* he thought, grinning warmly at Clare and covering her hand with his. His earlier nerves were completely gone; all he could think about were the ways he was going to pay her back for this. Repeatedly.

Schneider even lingered with them outside the door to the restaurant, eagerly talking to Clare about the biography of a medieval king he was reading. Clare dutifully wrote down the title in her phone and promised to read it, and Logan dimly heard him saying something about *I didn't believe it when he said he was seeing someone, but it was nice to meet you* and then they were finally able to say their goodbyes and walk away. Logan slung his arm over her shoulders as they went, unable to stop smiling. "Good thing I'm interested in a lot of the same things as retirees," Clare said cheekily, leaning into him comfortably. "That dinner would have been a lot harder if I had to fake interest in Louis IX of France. I mean, I still had to fake it—I both can and can't believe that man is a fan of someone who went on a *crusade*; gross—but it would have been more difficult if I didn't know anything about it."

Logan chuckled. "And since I know absolutely nothing about French kings except one got his head chopped off, I'm glad you were there. That's the most Schneider has ever liked me."

Clare fell silent for a few paces. "Silly question—when did you tell Schneider we were dating?"

Logan stopped. "A while ago, why?"

"Things are just so new with us, you know? And you said he was out of town for a while, so I was a little confused, that's all."

Fuck. He had left out this minor detail in his original confession, on account of having way too much to confess to, but now it looked like he'd hidden it from her. "I—okay, hear me out," he said, and Clare looked wary. "After we, you know," he said, gesturing between them, "but before we were, uh, hanging out, I sort of—slipped. I'd told him I was seeing someone and I swear, I was going to ask Sam to pretend to be my girlfriend, but then I said your name instead, and, uh, yeah."

Clare nodded slowly. "Okay," she said, and Logan let out the breath he'd been holding. That was it—there weren't any more lies between them, and Schneider would stay with Loyalty and Logan would keep his job *and* the girl.

He was so relieved, imagining Wimberley's sour face when he learned Schneider wasn't leaving, that when they turned the corner toward the gravel parking lot behind the building he didn't notice Clare's shoulders tensing up. She pulled away, looking intensely into her weirdly large, constantly full tote, like she'd lost something.

"Clare?" A male voice asked. A guy Logan vaguely recognized but couldn't place emerged from between two cars.

"Oh hey, didn't see you there," Clare said, but Logan knew her well enough to know she was lying.

Abruptly, Logan realized where he knew the man in front of them from. They had met before, that first night he took Clare out to Pour. *Neil? Noah.* Noah was on Clare's team; the golden boy who got away without any blame for that river-teaser thing. The one who's job she wanted. Clare had put a good two feet of distance between them, but Logan could tell Noah wasn't stupid.

"I don't think we introduced ourselves properly before," Noah said, reaching out to shake Logan's hand. "I'm Noah. I work with Clare."

"Logan. I'm—"

"My neighbor," Clare broke in.

Fuck. I guess I am a secret.

"Neighbor," Noah said drily, and Logan wanted to point out to Clare there was no possible way this guy was buying it, but he couldn't manage that without Noah hearing, and at any rate, she was also refusing to look at him.

Clare's face was beet red and her words came out in a rush. "Yeah, we ran into each other while we were out to dinner and since I don't have a car, he offered to drive me home."

"Got it." Noah gave them one last, long look and spun his keys around his finger. "See you tomorrow, Clare," he said, and headed off toward the sidewalk.

Clare waited for Noah to pull a few yards away before she turned to him. "Shit. I'm sorry, I panicked."

There was a roaring in his ears, but she looked genuinely apologetic. Logan made himself respond normally. "Yeah, whatever. I get it."

She looked slightly reassured, although he could tell she still knew something was wrong. She started to walk toward his car again, moving much faster than before, but Logan stayed put. She made it three paces before she noticed he wasn't following. "Logan?"

He couldn't do it. He couldn't pretend like everything was

fucking fine, when it wasn't. "You said I wasn't a secret," he said flatly. "And then you go and tell him I'm your *neighbor.*"

Clare blanched. "I'm sorry, I panicked," she repeated. "Things at work are kind of weird right now, and Noah's seen us together and if it comes out that I'm seeing someone before the pitch meeting, Craig could take the entire pitch away from me."

"Yeah, I get that. I mean, I don't, because you should just report Craig for being a fucking creep, but I get it." He finally started moving again, now walking a lot faster than she could comfortably manage in heels.

Part of him cared, but another part of him didn't. At all.

"Then what is it? I can tell you're mad, and I know it was stupid of me to say but—is this about what I said the other night?"

"What, that you slept with me for *experience*?" He hadn't meant to say it out loud, but once it was out there, there was no taking it back.

She stumbled in her heels. Logan shot his hand out without thinking, but she'd righted herself before he could help. "So, it is about that," she said quietly.

"It's not," Logan insisted. "It's—I don't know." He didn't want to have this fight, but he had no idea how to avoid it, either. Maybe there was a reason he'd never bothered with a relationship before.

Maybe he just wasn't cut out for this. Maybe his dad was wrong.

"Then what is it? Because you've been off all night."

Logan shrugged. They arrived at his car but neither made any move to open a door. He looked at her, wishing he wasn't so fucking pissed at her. The first time he met her in the elevator he thought she was cute and funny, and she just saw him as a chance to learn something new and prove herself to her boss.

It made him feel stupid and ashamed and a hundred other things that made his chest too tight. Logan had been so sure of where he stood with Clare, so sure of who she was, that discovering she'd originally slept with him for experience was throwing him into a spiral. And if he couldn't be sure of who she was, he didn't know where to go from there. What if she started seeing through him? What if she started thinking of him—or worse, already thought of him—like the other women he slept with? Like he was just an amusing guy to fuck for a while, before she moved on to someone real. He couldn't be sure she would keep looking at him the way he'd come to love, full of adoration and fondness.

"You were supposed to be better than that," he said finally. "You were supposed to be different from the others."

Clare took a step back from him, her normally soft eyes going flinty. "And what if I'm not? What if I'm not the woman you made me out to be in your head? What then? You can't hold me to some imaginary standard I never agreed to. I made a mistake, Logan, but so did you."

For some reason, her throwing his actions in his face made him angrier. "I told you about mine right away."

"You didn't tell me everything," she retorted. "You told Schneider we were together way before we were. If I didn't know you better, I'd say this was all just to keep his business."

She was wrong but she was also right, and Logan hated feeling that way. He didn't want to feel guilty, he wanted *her* to feel guilty. "Be honest: if I hadn't asked you directly the other night, would you have told me?"

Clare at least did him the courtesy of looking in his eyes as she broke his heart. "No. I wasn't going to."

"You would have kept on lying to me."

"It wasn't lying," she started.

"Sure as hell feels like it," he snapped.

"Why are you so mad?" Clare snapped back. "You only started dating me to impress Schneider. Don't act like you're so innocent in this."

"That's different."

Clare crossed her arms over her chest. "Oh yeah? How?"

It wasn't, and he knew it. He wondered if this was what drowning felt like, because there wasn't enough air in his lungs, and he was beginning to think there never would be. The thought of living without her was physically painful, but it was also coming one way or another. Better for him to end things now, rather than wait for the inevitable.

"Maybe I should have just listened to you when you said guys like me aren't interested in women like you," Logan said, aware he was blowing up the best thing he'd ever had. "Maybe it would have been better that way."

"You don't mean that," she said, the color draining from her face.

Logan had never been so deliberately cruel before, but he hated seeing her sad and he hated himself for hating it, but he had no idea how to pull out of the tailspin. All he could do was lash out. "How would you know what I mean? Is this how your character would react?"

"Stop it," she said, voice wavering. "It wasn't like that."

"How the hell am I supposed to know what it's like? I was just going along like a fucking idiot, thinking this was real, while you were taking notes for your stupid fucking game."

"Fuck you. You know that wasn't what happened. I was the one *risking* something by being with you," she whispered.

"Am I supposed to be grateful or something?"

"No, but I did just spend an hour charming the shit out of a gross old man for your job."

That barb hit home, but Logan couldn't let it go. "I guess we're even, then. You got what you needed and I got what I needed."

Tears welled in her eyes. "Logan, don't."

"Too late. I can't. We're done," Logan said and he climbed into his car, slamming the door behind him. He sped off out of the parking lot, leaving Clare small and forlorn behind him.

Chapter Thirty-five

"'But I didn't do it for you,' the Amethyst Queen says as the ash falls around you like snow and the Dragon Army's spell topples the Tower of Ibisk as if it were nothing more than a pile of children's blocks," Devi said and flicked the cover shut on her iPad. "Okay, now that that's out of the way, Clare, what the hell is going on with you?"

Clare barely had time to process that the Amethyst Queen had apparently turned on them and they'd lost the city before four sets of eyes were on her. "I'm fine," she lied.

Chase cleared his throat. "With all due respect, I'm only here about a quarter of the time and I can tell you're not fine," he said gently.

Toni nodded. "Yeah, he's right. What happened?"

Clare put her head down on the table, shielding herself with her arms. "Logan and I broke up."

"Why didn't you say anything?" Toni said, concerned.

"When did this happen?" Devi asked.

"Do you want me to kill him?" Annie offered. "My car's just outside."

"It was just a few days ago," she said, lifting her head slightly.

"And I didn't say anything because I don't know what to say. It was sort of my fault, but also definitely not, you know?"

"That's going to need a little more clarification," Devi said.

"I did a shitty thing. And hurt him." She took a deep breath. "The first time I pitched Captain Ellis to Craig, he, uh, implied I didn't have the right experiences to write a character like her."

"Jesus Christ, what a creepy asshole," Annie mumbled.

"Right experiences in what way?" Toni asked.

"He didn't say it directly, but—sex. Captain Ellis is a player, and I'm, you know, not."

"Oh my god, okay, new murder planned," Annie interjected.

"But the thing is, he was right. I didn't, and so I took his advice, and I went out and got some."

"Oh honey," Devi whispered. "Logan?"

"Yeah. I figured it was a one-time thing, but then we started hanging out more and I thought I'd just have to keep that original reason under wraps, you know? I didn't tell him right away, but then he sort of—well, obviously he didn't really guess it, but he was asking questions about Captain Ellis and I didn't want to lie, so I told him. He seemed fine and I thought we were in the clear. But there's all this other stuff too, with how and why he started trying to date me and his job and stuff, but—he told me about that a while ago, and I forgave him for it, but I didn't own up about the Craig thing."

"Ooof," said Devi.

"But he was honest about his side of things, or at least he was eventually, and like, yeah, we both did shitty things. But then the other day we were at this dinner thing for him, and we ran into Noah outside the restaurant, and then all of a sudden we were arguing in a parking lot and breaking up."

Toni furrowed her brow. "What happened with Noah?"

"I panicked. I said Logan was just my neighbor, and we'd run into each other, and he was just giving me a ride home."

"Oh yikes," Devi winced. "And Logan felt like you were embarrassed of him?"

"I think so, yeah. And then it spiraled, and I'm still not totally sure what all he's mad at me about, but he's definitely mad and we're definitely done."

"How sure are you about that?" Chase asked.

"He left me behind in the parking lot."

"Ooof," Devi said again. "I'm sorry," she said, and the rest of the group murmured the same thing.

"I also think we're severely underplaying how fucking disgusting Craig is. What the living fuck is wrong with him?" Annie said.

"Yeah, that's a whole lot of gross," Devi concurred.

"He didn't *specifically* say I—"

"He didn't have to," Chase said. Clare looked up in surprise, because Chase didn't tend to get involved in these discussions much, which meant whatever he had to say must be important. "Look, I know I'm only like, tangentially part of the group here, but you've idolized Craig since you started working there, and he took advantage of that. He was always pushing you to do extra things, like that time he demanded you learn about every single weapon, or when he made you go tubing down the Mississippi."

"I swear to god you guys exaggerate the kayaking thing more and more each time," Clare grumbled.

Annie shook her head. "It was still weird. And he doesn't give these assignments to anyone else on the team, right?"

"No, but they all have a lot more experience than I do."

"Define a lot."

"Derek was the next newest hire, and he'd been there three years by the time I joined."

Annie did not look persuaded. "Did he ever have to do extra credit just to be taken seriously at his job? And that's leaving aside the *incredibly disgusting* fact that *your boss* thought you needed *more sexual experience* to be able to write a goddamn character."

"I—I don't know," Clare said, thinking.

She'd heard plenty of stories from the rest of her team about things they'd done, but it mostly seemed to revolve around things they'd done *with* Craig—like gaming together on evenings and weekends, or laser tag outings she conveniently wasn't invited to, or even the time Craig and several of the guys went camping up in the Boundary Waters. It was all stuff she didn't really like doing, but the fact remained that the rest of the team were friends with him; they weren't working for Craig's approval the way she was. And before Clare was hired, there hadn't been a woman on their team for at least two years.

"No, I think I'm the only one."

"And that's bullshit," Annie spat. "Complete bullshit."

"Annie's right. I'd say it's HR-worthy, for sure," Devi agreed. "The bungee-jumping over a waterfall alone should have sent you there, but this is a no-brainer."

Clare cracked a reluctant smile. "Pretty sure you guys are going to be saying he sent me skydiving next."

Devi reached over and patted her hand. "What are friends for, if not drastic exaggeration?"

Chapter Thirty-six

Logan had never hated himself quite like this. He'd never hated himself before, period, because he wasn't someone who spent a lot of time second-guessing himself or examining his decisions. He trusted his gut, and, when that failed, he trusted his charm to dig him out of it. Logan was an easy in, easy out sort of guy, and handling this sort of lingering regret was new for him.

He was so out of it that he hadn't even gotten any joy out of crushing Wimberley, first with Schneider and then again on the court the other day. Wimberley and some of the guys from Confidential Wealth had challenged them to a game, and Logan had welcomed the chance to work out some aggression. He rarely played that aggressively, or that dirty, but it felt satisfying to watch Wimberley get more and more annoyed with him. Logan conceded every foul but smirked the whole time. It was a grim satisfaction to know he was beating him in more ways than one, but Logan couldn't quite forget what he'd lost in the process.

But that was because Logan rarely involved his feelings in anything. Sure, he loved his dad and he cared about Sam, but those were simple relationships for him. Neither of them expected him to try very hard; he just had to show up. The Aidens were easy; all he had to do was be his usual shallow self around them and they'd give him high-fives. He liked Vince a little more, but Vince had his own thing with his family and didn't seem too interested in a deeper friendship with him. Logan didn't begrudge him that, but he also made sure he didn't go out of his way to work on that friendship as a result. He had simply never had feelings for someone and wanted their approval at the same time.

But then he met Clare, and suddenly things mattered. She was smart and funny and kind and good, and Logan wanted to live up to her expectations. He really did. But he wasn't quite capable of it, so he'd taken the easy way out.

He blew it all up, because that way, at least it was his choice. But that didn't make it hurt any less, and it certainly didn't take away the deep self-loathing he was wallowing in these days. And it unfortunately didn't change the fact that no matter what, he still wanted her. More than wanted; he needed her.

Fine, he loved Clare. It was the first time he had consciously admitted it to himself, and of course it was too late. It would pass, he was sure, but goddamn it hurt. And in the meantime, there was no better way to punish himself than being on a double date with Brooks.

Logan frowned at his Martini like it had personally offended him. Brooks slapped him on the shoulder and leaned over to talk over the roar of the bar. "What crawled up your ass and died?"

"I'm out with you, aren't I?"

"Yeah, you're out, but you're acting like you've got your panties in a twist."

Logan's frown deepened. "Wow, that managed to be misogynistic and homophobic at the same time."

Brooks, never quite the brightest bulb, just preened. "Here they come," he said with a nudge and a nod toward the door. "And now that you're a free agent again, you should look a little less miserable, yeah?"

Logan started to roll his eyes again but stopped himself. Brooks had a point. And as he was the one who wheedled Logan into leaving his apartment, where Logan was spending most of his time alternately staring daggers at the closed shades on Clare's apartment and sending wistful glances that direction, Logan owed him. Even just seeing Clare in the lobby for a few seconds had sent his heart skittering for cover and he had to pretend he didn't see her to make it to the stairs. He didn't want to risk the elevator, and by the time he reached his floor he was thoroughly out of breath, but at least his heart rate had a reason to be that high.

When Brooks texted and demanded Logan "stop being lame and start being fun again," Logan had decided it was worth a shot. Given the obvious rumbling storm cloud over his head it maybe wasn't working the way Logan had hoped, but he was a firm believer in faking it until he made it. Besides, he couldn't hate himself *more* than he did now anyway.

Brooks' date was his usual; tall and blonde and just nice enough that she could probably do better. They had met on an app and she told Brooks she wanted it to be "more of a group thing" and was bringing her friend along, which was the reason for Logan's presence, Her friend, Steph, was a brunette with blonde highlights, with a job in marketing of some sort. Logan hadn't been paying much attention when she introduced herself, but at least she looked nothing like Clare, which was good. The last thing he needed was to go down another spiral of self-pity.

"What about you?" Steph asked, and Logan had to feign being unable to hear her, because he had absolutely no idea what her question was about.

"Sorry?"

Steph raised her voice. "I said, what do you want to drink? I'm going to go get us a round."

"I'll help," he volunteered, standing and helping push their way through the crush of bodies to the bar.

Logan was careful not to crowd her as they reached the front of the line. "What's the order?" he asked.

"A vodka Sprite and two gin and tonics."

Logan nodded and caught the bartender's eye, throwing her a practiced grin. "Vodka Sprite, two gin and tonics, and another Martini," he called, and she got to work.

"How did you do that?"

"I come here a lot. The bartender recognizes me," he said honestly.

Steph smiled and yeah, he could do this again, he decided. It was like riding a bike.

But that was about the last thing that went according to plan. Logan spilled the vodka Sprite down Steph's arm when trying to hand it to her, and when they made it back to the table his usual supply of easy-going chit chat seemed to have dried up. All his conversation starters landed with a thud, and within five minutes Brooks was sending him sideways looks and Steph was clearly searching for an exit.

Logan decided to give up. He announced that he needed to get going and let Brooks follow him to a few paces away. "What the fuck, man?" Brooks said. "What happened to you?"

The truth was, Clare happened. Logan was still furious with her, but he missed her too, and he hadn't the faintest idea of how to untangle those feelings. "I dunno."

Brooks narrowed his eyes. "Is this about whatsherface, Roth's niece? That little blonde."

"What about her?"

"You've been acting weird since you slept with her. Boring, mostly. And you were really fucking possessive of her that night at Pour."

Logan sighed. He was so sick of this shit. Sick of himself, sick of Brooks, sick of everything. "So what? Why do you even give a shit?"

"It's just pathetic, that's all. You can do way better than her. She's not bad looking, but come on, she looked like a—"

Whatever Brooks was going to compare Clare to, he never got the chance.

Because Logan punched him in the fucking face.

Chapter Thirty-seven

Craig took his seat next to Clare, casting her a sideways look. "Everything all right there, kid?"

Clare smoothed her hair back and fiddled with her stylus. She had taken extra care with her hair and makeup that morning, aware that she looked like an orcling corpse these days. She'd barely been sleeping since her fight with Logan, and the stress of Noah knowing the truth, and the upcoming pitch meeting hadn't helped things. It had been a long, grueling week, but she thought she had done a better job of hiding the way she had fallen to pieces. Just outside the window, thunder rolled and rain poured down in sheets, a perfectly melodramatic demonstration of her mood lately.

"Just nerves," she shrugged, and waited for Craig's usual encouragement. She needed him to come through now, and prove that she was right to have listened to him in the first place. Instead, he gave her a bland smile and turned back to Noah, who was laughing about something that had happened while they played Call of Duty together online the other night. He hadn't said anything about Logan either to her or in front of the rest of the group, which made her feel incredibly uneasy.

She couldn't tell if he was keeping her secret or waiting for the right moment to detonate it.

She couldn't get her talk with the group out of her mind, either. It was looking more and more like they had a point about Craig, but she also didn't know what she could do about it, and anyway, she still had to get through the meeting. Everything was about as terrible as it could be.

It was hardly the best mindset for the big pitch meeting, but she was just going to have to pull herself together and forget entirely about Logan's stricken face in the parking lot and the horrible things he said to her.

At the front of the conference room the leadership team called the meeting to order, beginning with a short summary of the vision they hoped to project with the new launch. There was a lot of corporate-speak, like "expanding our reach," and "new demographics," and "reaching out but also reaching in," which honestly didn't even make sense, and then they gestured to the Elfborns to begin.

The Elfborns' team lead, Natalie, stood up and began the introduction to their presentation. They had gone in a gentler direction than Noah and the guys, designing a portal world adventure that took players to alternate dimensions. Some of the worlds people could visit might be violent, others just silly fun. It was a type of one-shot world that Clare herself would enjoy, quite frankly.

The Mages were scheduled to present second. Craig had structured the presentation into two prongs; the first would be led by Noah, about several new classes of monsters and a one-off adventure based on slasher movies, followed by Clare's more character-focused pitch of Captain Ellis Ravencroft. Craig's reasoning was that the two would work well together, balancing the thrills of combat with her softer approach, and while she didn't totally see it gelling, Craig usually had a point, so she was going to assume he knew what he was doing.

Noah led the first part of the Mages' pitch. They had some goofy props to go along with it, something Clare hadn't been told about, and most of the room was chuckling along with their ideas. They were good ideas, after all, and as a player Clare appreciated the gorier aspects, knowing how much fun Toni and Annie would have on that type of campaign.

She called up the mockup image she'd had Design create of Captain Ellis Ravencroft on her tablet, waiting for her cue to come from Craig as Noah's presentation wrapped up. Craig stood, facing the leadership team at their conference table off to the side, and nodded. "Thanks for your time," he said, gesturing. "Take it away, Dragon Army."

Craig sat. Clare blinked. "Sorry," he whispered, as several members of the Dragon Army team stood up and moved to the front of the room. "Game-time decision. Looked like they really liked Noah's pitch, and I didn't want to undercut it by offering two."

"But you promised," Clare said quietly.

Craig didn't even look at her. "A character like that was never going anywhere."

"I—"

"Not now," he said, still whispering but with ice in his tone. "I humored you. Drop it."

Clare looked away, vision blurring. She blinked rapidly and breathed through her nose, doing her best to contain the sudden anger that threatened to swamp her.

It was all for nothing. Craig had never once taken her pitch seriously, and she would never be in the running for Noah's job. Everything she'd done for it, up to and including Logan, was now utterly pointless. She saw Natalie from the Elfborn glancing over their way, as if trying to puzzle something out, but whatever it was, Clare couldn't care less.

The Dragon Army team finished their pitch; Leadership made some meaningless noise about having a difficult decision ahead of them, and people began to leave the room in groups of twos and threes. Clare left on her own, desperate to escape to the bathroom to have a good old-fashioned anger cry. Craig was already rounding the corner up ahead, laughing with Derek, as usual. Noah caught up with her and she braced herself for everything to get much, much worse. She wasn't sure how much more humiliation she could take, but she suspected she was about to find out.

"I thought Craig had told you your pitch was out," he said, nicely enough. "I'm sorry you didn't get a heads-up."

Clare stared blankly at him. "I'm sorry, what? You knew?"

Noah furrowed his brow. "We all knew. Craig told us at the bar last night."

"You were at a *bar* last night? Who all went?"

"Just a few of us," Noah said defensively. "Craig thought it would be good for morale. Blow off steam before the big presentation."

"To not invite the whole team? And then talk about me?"

"It wasn't like that," Noah protested. "It was just, you know, the way he talked about your character and all, and the way he talked to us about it, I assumed he'd told you a while ago your pitch was cut."

It was like a veil had been lifted from her eyes. Everything that Craig did took on a new shade. It wasn't just the extra projects; Clare was the one constantly singled out to do menial projects like take notes at meetings, the only one on their team who would agree to wash the coffee mugs that piled up in the sink—because it was wash them or just live with the filth—and seemed to operate under a different set of rules from the rest of the team. Craig always seemed to want more from her than anyone else, something that just a few weeks ago she had written off as him urging her to reach her true potential.

But it was hard to see it that way once she knew he was literally laughing about her efforts with the rest of the team. She had been lying to herself this whole damn time, and what's worse, part of her had suspected it all along. She just didn't want to admit that her dream job could turn out to be so terrible.

"Yeah, well, no, he didn't tell me. What did you think I was doing, if my pitch wasn't going anywhere? Why wouldn't I have joined yours?"

Noah shrugged. "I didn't really think about it, you know? We were caught up in our thing, and your thing wasn't happening, that's all."

"That's all," Clare repeated dully. "Um, well, thanks, I guess."

He glanced around again. "And about that guy. Logan?"

Her stomach kicked the churning up another four notches, bile rising in her throat. She didn't want to talk about Logan with Noah. She didn't want any more associations of Logan with work, because all she had left was work, shitty as it was at the moment. "I don't want to talk about him," she said, far more sternly than she would have dared just a week ago. "My personal life is none of your business, okay?"

"Clare . . ."

"It's—whatever, Noah. Thanks for the apology," she said, turning on her heel and making a beeline for the women's room.

She stared at herself in the mirror. Her anger was now beyond tears, but her face was bright red with a combination of embarrassment and rage. She gripped the counter and took a deep breath, trying to figure out her next step. The door behind her swung open and Natalie walked in, drawing up short when she saw Clare's face. "Are you okay?" she asked hesitantly.

Clare blinked her still dry eyes. She wasn't okay. Nothing was okay, but she also had no idea where to begin to rebuild. "I'm fine," she said.

It wasn't true, but maybe one day it would be.

Chapter Thirty-eight

Logan ducked out of the rain into the lobby, wishing he'd thought to bring an umbrella. His client meeting had ended early, and it didn't seem worth it to go all the way back to the office just to leave again, so he'd taken the chance to come home a little earlier than usual. As an added bonus, it meant he had no chance of running into Clare, since she wouldn't be home for at least another thirty minutes.

But because the universe absolutely fucking hated him, the elevator doors were sliding closed when someone darted their hand out and jumped in with a dramatic sigh.

It was Clare. Of course it was Clare, looking for all the world like a drowned rat, but still somehow the cutest damn thing he'd ever seen.

Christ, he had it bad.

At first he thought she hadn't seen him standing in the back corner, but the slow crawl of pink up the back of her neck said otherwise. At least they weren't alone; a young couple with a baby in a stroller stood between them. All they had to do was make it five floors in each other's presence.

It's only a minute or two and we have a buffer, he told

himself, just as the doors opened on the second floor and the family made their way out. *Still just another ninety seconds*, Logan thought, completely ignoring the lesson he should have learned about jinxing himself the first time, because not ten seconds later the elevator came to a jolting, shuddering stop.

"Are you fucking kidding me," Logan muttered. He shoved past Clare without even glancing in her direction and tried to rip the doors open, only to once again see nothing but bare concrete.

He whipped out his phone, still with his back to her, and barked into it the second building management picked up. "Reset it now and call the fucking fire department. West elevator, between floors three and four."

Logan stuffed his phone into his pocket. His shoulders were tense and he could feel a muscle flickering in his jaw. "It shouldn't be too long," Clare said hesitantly. "They've been getting better at this lately."

"Don't," he said tightly. "Just—don't talk."

The muscle in his jaw was jumping dangerously now and she took half a step back. He hated making her shrink away, but he also didn't trust himself around her. He still wanted her too much, just as much as he knew it was pointless.

She sighed, and for the first time he noticed a line of red around her eyes, as if she'd been crying recently. He both hoped it wasn't over him and hated the fact that she might be crying about something else.

"Fine, then. We'll stand in awkward silence until the fire department comes."

She shivered, her damp blouse sticking to her skin. It didn't help that in these close quarters he could smell her perfume, which kept giving him flashbacks to lying in bed with her. Or not lying, as it were.

Logan's nostrils flared with his sharp exhale. "Don't do that either," he growled. "Don't—don't act like this is all on me."

"I didn't," she said, exhausted. "I was just pointing out that it's ridiculous to stand here, five feet apart, not speaking, for the next half hour."

He rounded on her. "What do you propose we do? Make small talk like you didn't break my fucking heart?"

Shit. He hadn't meant to say that out loud. She had a way of doing that to him, it would seem.

"My heart was involved too, you know."

Yeah, I know. This all would have been a hell of a lot easier if he could pretend she didn't care, but he had seen the hurt in her eyes that night in the parking lot. Logan knew full well how shitty he had been, hated himself for it, and hated her for making him feel things he thought he'd never have to feel. Logan crossed his arms. "And?"

"And?" she said incredulously. "*And? And* means you can't put this all on me. *And* it means you don't get to treat me like this."

"Like what?"

"Like I'm invisible," she said, and crossed her arms too.

Logan flinched. "You think you're *invisible* to me?" he said, running a hand through his hair desperately. "The problem is you're *everywhere*. I can't fucking escape you."

"It's not my fault we live in the same building," Clare said, curling her hands into fists. "Or did you want to draw up a schedule so we never accidentally cross paths?"

Logan turned away and then back to her, running his hand through his hair again. It must look terrible, but he was beyond vanity at this point. "No," he sighed, deflating. "I don't want that."

"Then what do you want?"

Every instinct in his body told him to turn away from her. If he did that, she would leave him alone. They would stand there in awkward silence, like Logan hadn't just spilled his guts on the floor, until the fire department came. It was the right thing to do, turning away. It was the practical thing, the smart thing.

But Logan was a fucking idiot. "I just want you," he blurted out, and then made the absolute worst choice he could possibly make.

He kissed her. It had been barely two weeks since they last kissed but it felt like ten years. It didn't matter that it was all wrong, that everything felt like some sort of funhouse mirror of all their firsts. Their first meeting in the elevator had been all light banter and charged innuendo, and their first kiss—their first real kiss, the one that changed everything—had been rain drenched and refreshing, a new, exciting beginning of something deeper.

But this couldn't have been farther from either of those. There was no charged innuendo between them now, just sadness and desperation. Logan kissed her like it was the last time he'd ever see her and Clare kissed him like it was their last night on earth. Rather than a rain shower washing them clean, their clothes were damp and cold to the touch as they clawed at each other. Logan got her blouse open first, trailing hot, searching kisses down her neck while she gave up on his shirt and fumbled with his belt buckle.

"I need you," she gasped as he pushed her back against the wall.

Logan pressed into her, trapping her hands between them. He rolled his hips, letting her feel how hard he was already, and bunched the hem of her skirt in his hand.

He rested his forehead against hers, breathing hard, and slipped his hand under the elastic of her panties, cupping her mound. "Is this what you want?" he asked, wanting—needing—to be sure.

She nodded and he delved deeper, pressing first one finger, then another, deep inside her. Clare whimpered, anchoring herself with her hands on his forearms, and his breathing hitched ever so slightly.

Fuck. He missed her so much. He went slow at first, gauging her every reaction, dragging his fingers in and out until she was a whimpering, soaking mess. Then he pinned her clit between his fingers, just this side of too hard, and flicked it with his thumb until she was keening and he could feel her thighs were trembling.

Clare came with a sharp cry that Logan muffled with a kiss, barely giving her a moment to recover before he was lifting her up onto the hand railing and shoving his own pants down around his thighs. He still had a condom in his wallet from his ill-advised, doomed attempt at getting back out there with Steph, and he grabbed it and rolled it on.

Clare let her underwear fall to her ankles and kicked them off one foot, leaving them dangling when Logan lined himself up and pushed inside.

It was like falling and coming home, and it broke his heart. Being inside her was the best thing he had ever felt, but it had to be the last time. He wasn't strong enough for this, and it was better for both if this was the last time.

Whatever they had before, it was broken now. Gone. Never coming back. This was a goodbye fuck, nothing more, and even as his heart shattered into smaller and smaller pieces, he let her pull him closer, filling his lungs with her scent. Logan nudged her cheek with his nose, clumsily finding her mouth, and he couldn't tell if the wetness was from her cheeks or his, but in the end it didn't matter. Logan came, spilling into the condom with a groan.

For the space of three heartbeats, neither of them moved.

Their breath mingled and he let himself pretend it wasn't the end. He let himself breathe her in, savor the feel of her skin under his hands.

But then reality sank in and he pulled out. Logan turned away, giving her time to wipe her face—and for him to wipe his—and they had just enough time to hastily rearrange their clothes before the fire department knocked on the ceiling and told them they'd be lowering them down soon.

They didn't speak again.

Chapter Thirty-nine

Clare watched as Kiki scrambled toward the door, almost losing her footing as she rounded the corner of the kitchen island in her haste to get to Peggy as she walked in. Peggy crouched to scoop Kiki up, letting her lick her chin enthusiastically before setting her back down and dropping her purse on the island.

"Did you have a good weekend?" Peggy asked, helping herself to a homemade donut Clare had sitting out on a plate. She didn't usually do anything that complicated—frying was not her best baking skill—but she had been in desperate need of a distraction to keep her from staring at Logan's windows.

It had been a miserable weekend, honestly. Between the wreckage of her pitch, fucking Logan in the elevator, and then realizing that both her job and her love life were probably ruined beyond repair, she'd spent most of the time crying and feeling sorry for herself. She had called out of game day, pleading a headache. Her friends clearly didn't believe her, but were letting her have her space. Kiki had been obviously concerned, spending more time than usual circling Clare's lap to try and find the exact right spot to settle in. Clare had appreciated the attempt, but she was beyond even Kiki's snuggles. Even her

Good Doggo photo album didn't help, which meant the situation was truly dire.

Clare's smile almost met her eyes. "Kiki was great. A little bit dramatic about human food when I wouldn't give her my entire sandwich yesterday, but otherwise she was delightful, same as always."

Peggy had briefly closed her eyes in pleasure when taking a bite of the donut, but the look she fixed Clare with afterwards was direct. "Everything okay with you?"

"Not really. You should know Logan and I broke up, but don't take it out on him or anything."

"I'm offended you think I'd do anything of the sort," Peggy sniffed, taking another bite. "But are you okay?"

"No," she admitted. "I feel like shit, all the time. But I'll get over it." Clare picked at a donut herself. She didn't have much of an appetite these days, which was not like her. Usually her sweet tooth was nearly uncontrollable, but lately everything she ate tasted like cardboard. But maybe if she forced herself to act normal, eventually it would *feel* normal. Or at least less shitty. "It takes time, you know?"

"I do," Peggy said wisely. "But I don't remember you being all that broken up about Reid, and you were with him much longer."

Clare frowned to herself. She hadn't really thought about it in comparison to the breakup with Logan, but that was probably because it felt so different. With Reid, she had felt rejected and sad, yes, but it was more about losing the *idea* of what she thought they could be. Reid had been . . . safe. He played Quest for Sulzuris, he laughed at her jokes, he liked *Avatar: The Last Airbender* as much as she did. They liked the same things, and they got along just fine, and Clare had assumed that was all she needed. But she hadn't ever bared her soul to him, not like she and Logan did that first night on the rooftop, nor had she ever wanted to. Deep down, maybe she had suspected Reid's soul just wasn't that interesting. When he broke up with her, she had been bummed for a while, yes, and hesitant to start dating again, but that was far less about Reid and far more about how she felt about herself in the aftermath. She'd been so complacent with Reid she didn't notice the warning signs that he was planning to break up, and recovering from that had taken some time.

Logan, though. He was a hurricane she never saw coming. He'd blown into her life suddenly, tipping everything sideways and making her reconsider everything she thought she wanted in a partner. They had nothing in common, but still she found him endlessly fascinating. And she found she liked teaching him things, like baking and gaming, almost as much as she liked listening to him talk about something he was passionate about. No, she'd probably never love playing basketball, but now she at least vaguely understood why it was fun to watch.

Life without Reid was more or less the same as life with Reid, but life without Logan was infinitely duller. He'd made colors feel that much brighter, like there was a vibrancy she didn't know she'd been missing. But she knew what she was missing now, and that hurt.

"Logan was different, for me," Clare admitted, studying the pattern on her countertop far too closely. She couldn't get his devastated face when they left the elevator out of her head, and maybe never would. "But we're done. He made that very clear."

Peggy looked at her sympathetically and picked up Kiki, handing her over to Clare for a quick cuddle. "I'm sorry to hear that."

Clare nuzzled her face into Kiki's soft fur and sighed. She'd just have to figure out a way to muddle through.

* * *

Clare held her phone out toward the center of the table. "I need help," she announced.

Toni sighed. "You can delete the Facebook app yourself, you don't need me to do it for you."

"Not with that," Clare said, rolling her eyes. "I've decided I need a new project."

Annie took her phone and widened her eyes. "You're on a dating app again?"

"It's time for me to move on."

"It is?" Devi asked.

"It is, because I want to," Clare said firmly. "But I want someone normal this time."

"Normal?" Annie echoed.

"You know, nerdy. Like us. Someone who would fit in."

"Logan fit in just—" Toni started, but Devi threw her a dark look and she broke off awkwardly.

"I know he got along with us, but he just . . . he didn't fit, you know?" Clare said. The rest of the table exchanged looks and she sighed. "Are you guys going to help me or not?"

"This is really sudden," Devi said cautiously. "Like, really sudden."

Clare knew they'd react this way, but she also knew the only way she could move on from Logan was to force herself to move on.

Or maybe she just knew that she'd never *really* move on from him, so she might as well figure out how to start faking it now.

"I'll help," Annie said warily, looking back down at Clare's phone. Sitting next to Annie, Clare could just make out what was on the screen. "What do you want me to do?"

"Help me find someone for a date. I'm bad at picking, obviously, so one of you should do it for me."

Annie kept her eyes on Clare's phone, frowning. "Wait, you want a date? These sorts of apps are way more about hookups than dating, you know. Are you looking for someone to date, or just someone to get Logan out of your system?"

"Hookup, date, whatever. I just want to find someone who will take me out for coffee and talk about *Star Trek* or something before making out with me."

"*Star Trek*?" Devi interjected. "Do you even like *Star Trek*?"

"Oh my god, are you on my side or not?"

"We are, we just want to make sure you're making the right decision," Devi said.

"It's my life and my decision, okay?"

"Technically, you're making it Annie's decision," Chase piped up from the other end of the table.

"Quiet, you," Clare snapped.

Chase shrugged and Annie paused with her finger above the screen. "Should I just swipe on the good candidates? What even constitutes a good candidate for you?"

"Nerdy but not incel."

"Good to see you're setting that bar real high there," Toni said drily, taking a handful of tortilla chips from the basket and sliding it down toward Chase.

"I prefer to think of it as casting a wide net."

"Okay then," Annie mumbled. She started swiping through the app, pausing occasionally to check someone's profile. "How many do you want me to—" Annie stopped and jerked the phone toward her in an incredibly unsubtle attempt to stop Clare from seeing the screen. "Sorry, uh, a guy had a picture of, um, himself with a dead deer and I wasn't expecting it."

Clare knew immediately. "It's Logan, isn't it? He's dating again?"

Annie looked at Devi desperately, and then nodded. "Yeah."

Clare affected a nonchalant look and shrugged. "He probably has his settings really broad. Women in their twenties and thirties in Minneapolis and Saint Paul. It's not surprising I showed up."

"Is it one of the ones where he can't see you unless you match with him?" Toni asked, leaning forward.

Clare didn't love how everyone was acting like she was some sort of fragile, breakable wreck. Yes, breaking up with Logan had been unexpectedly difficult, just like falling for him had happened unexpectedly fast. But she was a big girl, and she had gotten over heartbreaks in the past. She'd get over this one too. And moving on, finding someone who fit her interests better, was the easiest way to do that. She'd never done it this way before, but everything about Logan had been new and unexpected, so she was going to try to move on differently, too. It wasn't surprising that Logan had moved on too, especially given his history.

It hurt, but it was better this way. They weren't well suited to each other. He'd find someone taller and hotter, who already understood basketball and looked right on his arm. She would find someone who already knew how to play a tabletop role-playing game, and who didn't make people do a double-take when they saw them together.

She belatedly realized Toni was still waiting on an answer. "Yeah, it's one of those," she confirmed. "He won't know I've swiped left."

Annie hesitated. "Do—you don't want to see his profile, right? I can just make it go away."

Clare shook her head and held out her hand before she could stop herself. "No, I want to see it. It'll help."

"I think it'll do the opposite of help," Chase muttered.

Annie nodded. "It's your funeral," she said, slapping the phone back into Clare's hand.

It did hurt, to be honest. But maybe not as much as it could have, since seeing Logan's face when they left the elevator had felt like a spear being driven into her heart by a level-nine paladin. It was deep and piercing and nearly fatal, whereas this felt like a blow from a club wielded by a cleric who flubbed their attack roll—it still hurt like hell, but she knew she'd survive. She somehow could tell that Sam had taken the photo, maybe because the way he was smiling was the sort of carefree smile she'd only really seen on his face when he was joking around with Sam. It was like a weight had been lifted from his shoulders, or maybe just that she knew he could be himself around Sam. Clare forced herself to be the one to swipe him away. Logan's photo slid off the screen and disappeared into the ether, but when she closed her eyes, she still knew the exact shape of his smile.

Chapter Forty

"I'm going to need you to tell me more about how you punched Brooks in the fucking face," Sam said, leaning over and grabbing herself another slice of pizza.

"He was being a dick," Logan shrugged, picking a green pepper off a piece still in the box and biting into it. "You've said as much yourself a dozen times."

"More like hundreds," Sam grumbled. She was leaning against the other side of the narrow peninsula that constituted her kitchen's entire counter space, which also doubled as her mail room, kitchen table, and apparently, her office. Logan's elbow nearly knocked into her laptop as he talked, and the pizza box was sitting on top of a stack of unopened mail.

He honestly couldn't believe she lived like this.

"Right, so why do you need more information?"

Sam smacked his hand as he reached for another green pepper. "Eat the whole slice; don't just pick at it like a goddamn vulture," she ordered. "And I need more details about what pushed you over the edge this time, because you've been fine with him being a troglodyte for like, seven years."

When she put it that way, it really did throw Logan's personal judgment into question. He'd started hanging out with the Aidens in his early twenties, when that sort of bro-y behavior seemed to be what was expected. But their schtick had worn thin as the years went on, although Sam had been consistently disapproving of them from the start.

Logan pulled a slice from the box and steeled himself. "He was a jackass about Clare. Said she wasn't hot."

Sam's face stayed carefully impassive. "Hmm."

"Hmm? That's all you have to say?"

"Well, I'm trying not to get punched here," Sam said, tossing her crust into the box like that wasn't completely disgusting. Logan picked it up and threw it at her. She caught it and stuck her tongue out at him, dropping it back onto the counter. "I wasn't going to say she isn't hot, because she is. But she did, uh, break your heart? I feel like we had a conversation about that like, less than an hour ago. About how you couldn't forgive her for what she'd done—and, by the way, what exactly she did that was so unforgivable still remains extremely unclear to me—and how you were never going to speak to her again. Assuming all of that is still true, why do you also feel compelled to defend her honor?"

Logan sighed and planted his elbows on the counter. A stack of takeout flyers slid to the ground. "Because I don't want to talk to her again, but that doesn't mean I don't still care about her."

"Hmm," Sam repeated. "That does seem like a problem."

"Yeah."

"Yeah," Sam agreed, and they looked at each other over the top of the Pizza Lucé box. "You could always just, you know, see if she'd take you back."

"No," Logan said, shaking his head. "I broke us, and that's—that's that."

"Never took you for a quitter," she replied drily.

"There's a first time for everything."

Sam studied him for a long moment. "Well, then there's only one thing left to do. Give up entirely and move on. Make a clean break."

Move on. He'd been telling himself to do just that since the second he left her in that parking lot, looking devastated, but he couldn't imagine it, not really. He'd tried with Steph and only managed to fall apart. And then the other day he'd simply given in, letting his impulses run his life the way they used to, which naturally just made things worse. Logan could only imagine what Sam would say if he admitted he'd screwed Clare in the elevator, so he kept that to himself.

"Is it pathetic to admit I don't even know how to move on?"

Sam blinked, and Logan had the distinct impression she wasn't expecting him to agree with her about moving on. But true to form, she recovered quickly. "Everything about you is pathetic, but in this case, I get it. You're basically a dating virgin."

Logan rolled his eyes. "Okay, then how do I do it? Because I tried the other day and it ended with my fist in Brooks' face."

"That's because moving on isn't about just picking up where you left off; it's about taking some time to figure out how you've changed. Let yourself grieve the relationship, then move on."

"That's overkill," he argued. "It was like, three weeks."

"You literally just said you're still not over her," Sam threw back.

Logan fell silent. Maybe that was what he was so angry about; that Clare had come into his life barely a month ago but changed him entirely. She'd chiseled away the carefully constructed facade he had built for himself, and then had the audacity to say she hadn't even meant any of it in the first place. She'd upended everything he thought he knew about himself, turned sex from a fun physical activity to something meaningful.

She'd changed him, and he hadn't agreed to that. She was supposed to be a blip before he returned to his regularly scheduled life, but instead it turned out *he'd* been the blip to *her*. He wasn't anything more than research; a chance to stretch her wings and really nail a character in that stupid game that was more fun than it had any right to be.

"It'd be a lot easier if I didn't still lo—miss her," he said, catching himself half a second too late.

Sam looked sympathetic for the first time all night, possibly the first time in their entire friendship. "I thought as much," she said softly. "Are you really sure you want to let her go?"

Letting her go. Logan hated the idea, but he didn't have a better one. He looked at Sam and forced a resigned smile on his face. "I have to," he said, even though he had no idea where to begin.

Chapter Forty-one

Clare sat back in her chair, watching yet another meeting happen without her. In the end, Leadership had chosen the Elfborn's portal world adventure, and now each team was assigned a different world to workshop. The Mages, probably in deference to their horror-inspired pitch, had been given one of the Dark Worlds to create. Noah had an interview to lead the Dragon Army team scheduled for next week, but Clare didn't see any point in putting her name in for his job. Not now, anyway.

Horror wasn't her favorite genre—she'd seen a handful of slasher movies, but generally didn't like jump-scares—so this would have been a tough one to participate in to begin with, though Clare was confident enough in her storytelling abilities that she normally should have been able to propose a few ideas. But with everything that had happened, she didn't particularly feel like chiming in.

"I'm thinking we should do something with necromancy to start," Noah said, rotating his chair back and forth. "Zombies are always fun, and that got a decent response in the pitch meeting."

Derek spoke up. "We already settled on the sorcerer as an

NPC, maybe we could have him be the Big Bad, sending armies of monsters after the players?"

Clare decided it was time to try again. "We should probably establish how hard all the monsters would be to kill first, unless the goal of the campaign is to kill off players one at a time, in which case we make them nearly invincible."

"So nice of you to join us," Craig said, shaking his head.

Clare's chest burned with anger and she started scouring her brain for more ideas to throw out. If Craig wanted to make her seem incompetent, she'd make him work for it. "I like your idea, Derek," he added pointedly.

"If we're going with reanimated corpses, those should probably have the lowest hit points. If there's a horde, that would make it more challenging, and newer groups would have to learn to work together first," she offered.

"I guess we could work with that," Craig said reluctantly, and Clare wanted to snap. She wanted to shout in his face, but instead she plastered on a smile.

"And maybe we could work in a mystery, just as a bonus if someone wants to stretch the campaign out. Like, the sorcerer could seem to be on the players' side at first and then have a villain reveal if they uncover the right set of clues."

Craig shook his head. "Boring. And too much like Saruman and *Lord of the Rings*."

Clare wasn't about to let it go. "Does that really matter? We're not talking about creating a whole mystery game, just having this as an option for groups who want to go that way. It doesn't matter if the beats are familiar so long as you're doing something fun and interesting with them," she argued. She was done with being the meek pushover she had been. If Craig didn't like her ideas, well, fuck him. She was going to channel Yaen and not give a damn.

Craig waved his hand dismissively. "You'd be well served to learn how to take no for an answer," he said. "And you were the one who insisted on doing your own silly little pitch that wasted my time instead of working with the rest of the team, so I think you should sit back and listen rather than throw out useless ideas."

That was in no way what happened, and Clare blinked in surprise. She hadn't realized Craig was this comfortable outright lying, although she really should have.

He smirked. "Weren't you saying the other day you aren't even familiar with the horror genre? Maybe you should spend some time watching a few movies, then get back to us."

Clare snapped her mouth shut. She was abruptly aware that if she pushed it any harder, it could mean her job. "I'll do some research," she mumbled, cheeks burning with rage and humiliation. She turned her eyes to her tablet as the discussion moved on.

She couldn't do this anymore. She wouldn't resign herself to it, even though just a month ago she had been the one insisting that everything was fine. Everything was not fine, and Clare was fucking sick of it. Working for Quest Gaming—and for Craig in particular, given his near-legendary status within the company—had been a dream come true. She loved Quest for Sulzuris with her whole, entire heart, and Craig was dangerously close to ruining it for her.

Clare knew she could go to Human Resources, but saying "my boss is being a jerk" was probably just going to result in a bunch of awkward meetings and no real change. It wasn't outright harassment, or didn't look like it anyway, and Craig could easily say she was underperforming and he was just trying to get her up to the right level. It would be a huge battle, and Clare was sick of fighting.

But still. Something needed to change, and fast.

It felt like the meeting dragged on for an eternity, but in reality it was just another fifteen minutes. A handful of the Elfborns, including their team lead, Natalie, were waiting in the hallway as the Mages filed out.

Craig looked over his shoulder at Clare. "Why don't you type up a summary of how far we've gotten and send it out to everyone?" he suggested.

More out of habit than anything, Clare began to nod and moved aside to let one of the Elfborns into the conference room. But then she stopped and raised her chin. "No," she said, loud enough for Craig and everyone else in the hallway to hear. She was blocking the door to the conference room, and she could feel half a dozen pairs of eyes on her, but she kept her gaze directly on Craig.

He had the gall to look honestly puzzled. "No?"

"No. I am not the team secretary. If you want someone to be an administrative assistant, hire someone. I'm a writer, and you don't make anyone else on the Mages take notes, or wash the coffee cups, or any other bullshit job you give me because I'm the *girl* on the team, and I'm not going to do it anymore."

Craig rolled his eyes. He *rolled his eyes*, and started to turn away. "Don't make it a sexism thing," he chided.

But Clare stood her ground. "I will make it a sexism thing, because it *is* a sexism thing. When was the last time you made Noah take notes? Or Derek? Have you *ever* given any of them extra assignments because you think they can't understand something unless they do it first?"

Craig shrugged. "They're just better writers than you."

"Bullshit," she spat. She had probably just argued herself out of a job anyway, so she decided she might as well go all in. She had finally merged her home-self and her work-self, just in time to get her whole-self fired.

Logan would be proud, she thought briefly, before shoving that to the corner of her mind. "Bullshit," she said again, even more loudly. "I'm every bit as good as them, you just get off on ordering me around."

Craig tried another angle and fixed his face into a look of faux concern. "This is not the place to be having this conversation," he said quietly, although by that point you could hear a pin drop throughout the entire building. Everyone was watching them with bated breath.

"Why? So you can pretend it didn't happen? Like when you told me *I needed to have a one-night stand* to write a fucking *character*?"

There was a collective intake of breath around them. Craig's eyes flashed with worry, but his tone was casual. "You must have misunderstood me, because I have no idea what you're talking about," he tried.

This was the part Clare had been worried about. She didn't technically have any *proof* he'd made her sex life a condition of her employment, and he had been very careful about his wording. She probably couldn't make an official case for it, but if he was going to fire her—and he was going to, after this—the least she could do was go down swinging. Maybe damage his reputation in the process.

"I do," said a voice off to the side. "I know what she's talking about." Clare stared in amazement as Noah—Craig's golden boy—stepped forward. "You did tell her that. In front of all of us."

Craig stared at him too, mouth ajar. "I never—"

"You did. I suppose technically you just implied it, but then that weekend during Call of Duty you asked us if we thought she'd have the balls to follow through. And you do all the other stuff too," Noah said, and Clare could not have been more surprised if Golgath the Destroyer himself burst out of the ceiling and devoured them whole. Noah looked at Clare. "I should have said something sooner," he said, and it was the damnedest thing, but he sounded genuine. "I'm sorry."

"I—thank you," Clare stammered.

Natalie broke the silence. "Hey, Elfborns, we're going to postpone our meeting," she said in a surprisingly cheerful voice. Her straight brown hair was severely pulled back, and her navy pantsuit made her look more like an accountant than an employee for a company that made money off nerds imagining they were fighting dragons.

The smile she threw to Clare was nothing but friendly, but when she turned to look at Craig there was ice in her eyes. "How about we take a walk to Leadership?" she suggested to him. "They're going to hear about this sooner or later, so they might as well hear it from you."

Craig's face curdled. "You're not my boss."

"I'm not," she said, still chipper. "But you've been pulling this shit for *years* and I, for one, am sick of it."

Apparently, today was the day of surprises. Clare blinked, and Natalie lifted her voice for the rest of the crowd—which was now much larger—to hear. "For a decade I've been watching you hire women only to immediately declare them substandard and in need of your *guidance*. Remember Thea? And Katie? What about Amanda, or Brit, or Laura?"

"They were—" Craig started, but Natalie shook her head.

"All of them were perfectly qualified when we hired them, but you felt the need to send them on stupid, pointless exercises until they quit. I've never had enough for a formal complaint, even though it was obvious what you were doing. This should do it, though," she said, and looked at Clare again. "If that's all right with you?"

"Uh, yeah, sure. Should I, um, come with you?" Clare asked,

uncertain of how to handle this massive paradigm shift. She had started this thinking she would get fired, but now it seemed Craig might.

Natalie cocked her head at Craig like a dragon queen examining her prey. She was utterly terrifying, and Clare loved it. "Oh, I don't think that will be necessary. He's going to admit everything and face what's coming to him, aren't you, Craig?"

Craig didn't nod, but he didn't shake his head, either. Natalie turned on her heels and tipped her head down the hall, Craig shambling behind her like a corpse reanimated by dark magic.

The assembled crowd, much like Clare, didn't seem to know how to react. There was a smattering of applause, along with a lot of hushed whispers and one lone *Holy shit* that made the rest of them chuckle.

Lightness and a sense of unreality surrounded Clare as she walked back to her desk. A couple of people gave her high-fives, while a few others shot her dark looks. It wasn't going to be a cake walk, that was clear, but the situation was at least a whole hell of a lot better than it had been ten minutes ago.

There was just one more thing to do, and Clare 2.0 would be fully launched. Now was the time, when she was feeling invincible. She pulled out her phone and scrolled to the message she was looking for. She typed *Want to get a drink some time?* and hit send before she could second-guess herself.

Ten seconds later, the guy from the dating app—one with a Moffat-era *Doctor Who* joke in his profile—responded. *Sure thing, cutie* ☺

The *cutie* made her grimace, but she couldn't have everything. That was just life.

Right?

Chapter Forty-two

Logan glanced at the green square on his calendar with no small amount of trepidation. Meetings with Peggy Roth were fraught for him no matter the time, and despite his success with Schneider, Logan did not feel at all confident he was going to keep his job.

He had been doing better lately, at least. He had been paying more attention to client maintenance, and while it wasn't that unusual that he hadn't lost a client since their previous meeting—Logan's churn might be bad, but it wasn't *that* bad— he also hadn't gone out searching for new clients. That had been part of his problem, he had realized when he sat down and really looked at his metrics. He had gotten so used to the churn he was constantly hunting down new leads, which didn't leave him with much time for current clients. Settling down and paying attention to the ones he had was hardly ground-breaking, but at least he would be able to show Peggy he was meeting her expectations.

Whether or not that mattered was up to her.

The advancing line on his calendar app hit the edge of the green square, and Logan stood. Peggy's door was open, but there was already someone in there, a short, nondescript woman in her forties he vaguely recognized as being from HR. "Ah good, Mr. Walsh, come in," Peggy called, and his stomach sank like a rock.

He was about to be fired. That was the only explanation. He had thought Peggy might be willing to ignore the fact that he treated her niece like shit because he'd kept the Schneider account, but apparently not. Logan surreptitiously wiped his palms on his pants and sat down. He was reasonably sure Peggy and the HR rep—Linda, he thought—could hear his heart hammering.

Peggy tapped on her keyboard a few times and turned to face him, looking at him with an unreadable expression over the glasses perched low on her nose. "I'm sure you understand why I asked Linda to be here today," she said.

Logan started to nod and then stopped himself, because honestly, if he was going to be fired, he wasn't going to make it easy for them. "Uh, no?" he said, glancing awkwardly at Linda, who looked completely unperturbed.

"Given your personal relationship with my niece, I figured it would be better for both of our sakes if there was a neutral third party here to observe, especially with the topic at hand. Officially the company only has policies about immediate family members, but I thought this would be better for both of us."

Oh yeah, he was totally fired.

Logan made an understanding noise. "Oh, uh, got it," he added, when it seemed Peggy was waiting for him to say something more specific.

"First of all, good work on keeping the Schneider account. Whatever you did worked."

Logan hated thinking about that night and everything that happened after, so he just nodded.

Peggy nodded in return. "As you are aware, we also spoke

about slowing the churn in your client list. Have you made progress?"

Logan blinked. That didn't sound like a prelude to a firing, and it took him a second to find his footing. "Yeah, um, yes, I have." He pulled out his company-issued tablet and called up his client list, launching into his previously prepared presentation on the work he had done to prove he was someone trustworthy enough to stay at Loyalty Investments. It was the most thought he'd put into this job since he started it, and he had to admit it had made him better. He was being more deliberate and less impulsive these days, both in terms of paying attention to his clients and the choices he was making.

Peggy had a few questions as he talked, and a couple of suggestions when he finished, but otherwise the meeting was unremarkable. There was no addressing his relationship with Clare, outside that bit at the beginning, and Linda had nothing to say either. It was a completely normal, boring meeting. He wasn't fired. He was realizing that Peggy Roth—by-the-book, strict Peggy Roth—was not talking about his personal life when she told him to demonstrate some maturity. She'd never once alluded to his sex life; that had been Schneider repeating Wimberley's gossip. Everything she'd told him to do had been about work, not his personal life—Logan was the one who thought she would think less of him for sleeping with Clare.

In short, Logan had gone and blown up his life for no good reason. Sure, maybe he wouldn't have been able to keep Schneider without Clare, but maybe he could have. He could have talked Sam into pretending to be his girlfriend, or maybe just poured on enough charm that Schneider would forget all about that snake Wimberley. It might not have worked, and he might have lost his job anyway, but at least his heart would be intact.

Logan sat back down at his desk, pointedly avoiding

looking in the direction of the Aidens. He had overheard Brooks explaining his black eye as a basketball injury that Monday and decided to let that stand. Brooks had stopped speaking to him, and so had Aiden, but Logan didn't give two shits about that. He opened his email to start responding to a few clients and settled back into work.

* * *

Amber Green Dress
Wyd?

Logan
I take it it didn't work out with that guy

Amber Green Dress
Nope and I saw you're on tinder so 👀 wyd?

Logan
Just leaving the office

Amber Green Dress
This is late for you to be working

Logan
Turning over a new leaf, I guess

Amber Green Dress
I hope not too many new leaves
I was sorta planning on getting laid tonight

Logan
Buy a guy a drink first, damn

Amber Green Dress

😊

But for real my place or yours?

Logan paused as he pushed back from his desk. Most of the lights in the office were off already, and he and a handful of the higher-ups were all that were left. He had just finished making some notes in a client's file and had been planning on going home, nursing a glass of wine, and spending the evening trying not to peer into Clare's windows like a creep. Amber's offer, transparent as it was, would keep him from doing that. It was a return to his old form, which maybe was for the best. He wasn't really cut out for serious, and Amber wouldn't expect that of him. He could finally start the process of shaking off everything Clare had brought out in him. He grabbed his bag and headed for the elevators, typing his response as he stepped on.

Logan
Mine
See you there

"Plans for this evening?" Peggy asked as she stepped in just before the doors closed. She wasn't really someone he wanted to see right now, but beggars and choosers and whatever.

"Meeting a friend for, uh, drinks," he said.

"A lady friend?" Peggy asked mildly.

Logan was just petty enough to want Clare to know he was moving on, and he suspected Peggy was on a fishing expedition. "Yes," he confirmed.

She gave the barest of glances over her shoulder. "Must be a day for new beginnings," she said drily. "Clare's on a date as well."

Logan ignored the dagger that drove into his chest. "Oh."

Silence fell and the numbers above the door ticked down, far too slowly in Logan's opinion. "I probably shouldn't comment on this, but I never saw her as happy as she was with you," Peggy said, still not quite looking at him.

That sucked to hear. He liked it when Clare was happy, and he still hated making her sad. He was his best self around Clare, not because she made him someone different but because she let him be comfortable in his own skin. The panel above the doors glowed red with descending numbers. "Sometimes, it's just not enough," he said, and two months ago he would have been embarrassed by the rawness in his voice. Now he just didn't fucking care.

"That's a shame," Peggy said kindly, and stepped out of the elevator into the lobby. She looked up at Logan with that familiar shrewd look on her face. "In my experience, there are some situations where trusting your gut is necessary."

Logan had a vague idea of what she was insinuating, but he wasn't sure what she wanted him to do about it. Asking the severe Peggy Roth for relationship advice was not something he had ever seen himself doing, but there was a first time for everything. "And what do you do when trusting your gut means risking your heart?"

That was the softest he had ever seen her look. "Then you take the risk, Mr. Walsh," she said. "You take the risk because matters of the heart are always worth the risk." She smiled gently and turned to go, leaving Logan slightly stunned behind her.

Peggy was only five feet away when she paused again. "She's taking him to the rooftop of your building, by the way," she called, and he could have sworn she winked, but Peggy Roth was not a woman who winked, so that wasn't possible. "Just in case you needed to know."

* * *

Logan had entirely forgotten he had told Amber to meet him at his building, so seeing her standing outside the doors, idly scrolling on her phone, stopped him short. When Peggy had left him in the lobby, he had spent a good five minutes wondering what the *fuck* had just happened, before deciding to take her advice.

He was going to fight for Clare, and if that didn't work, well, he was just going to fight *with* Clare. Because not only was Clare on a date, she was on a date on the roof. As in the place they'd spent the night talking, the place he had just now realized he'd come to think of as *their* place. Maybe he'd fight her date too, what the hell.

But first, he had to deal with Amber. "What's wrong?" she asked, looking suspiciously at him.

"Nothing's wrong, something just, um, came up."

She crossed her arms. "Something, or someone?"

Logan decided blunt honesty was probably the best policy. "Someone."

"That was fast, even for you," she said drily.

"Look, it's complicated. I'm sorry," he said, and opened the door.

He had expected her to leave—Amber did not believe in wasting her time—but instead she followed him in. He was being an enormous dick, he was well aware of that. But his brain was only capable of processing one thing at the moment, and that was the thought of Clare on a date. If Amber was pissed at him, she was pissed at him. He'd deal with that later.

Logan pressed the button for the elevator and waited, Amber standing beside him with her arms still crossed. "Are you going to explain yourself?" she asked.

"Wasn't planning on it, no."

Amber snorted and tilted her head curiously as the elevator doors opened. "Wait, is she already in your apartment?"

Logan sighed. "No, but she is in the building," he said, stepping into the elevator. "I'm sorry, but I really do have to go. Now."

To his everlasting surprise, Amber stepped into the elevator with him. "I think I'll come with," she announced and let him hit the button for the top floor. "I want to meet the person who has you this worked up," she explained.

He hadn't really envisioned fighting for Clare's heart with Amber as an audience, but then again, until about fifteen minutes ago he'd given up on fighting for Clare's heart entirely. He was just going to have to roll with it.

The doors slid open, and he took off for the staircase that led to the lounge, dimly aware of Amber's heels clicking behind him. Logan burst through the door to the rooftop, eyes already roving the chairs to find her.

And there was Clare at a table near the edge, staring at him as if she'd seen a ghost.

Chapter Forty-three

"Um, Clare?" her date asked. "Everything okay?"

Everything *had* been okay. They were having a lovely, albeit slightly stilted, first date on the rooftop, which she had hoped would also serve as an exorcism of sorts of her memories of Logan. It hadn't been working very well, as she'd already managed to mentally compare Jason—no, wait, *Joey*—three separate times to Logan, although she'd chastised herself immediately after each time.

"Yeah, it's just—uh, my friend is here."

That was a straight-up lie, as Logan was not and had never been just her friend, and right now, he did not look particularly friendly. In fact, Logan was standing in the doorway to the stairs, looking positively thunderous.

"Really, Clare?" he called out in an unfamiliar voice. Even in the parking lot, he hadn't seemed that pissed off. "Here?"

A woman that Clare vaguely recognized—and then immediately placed, much to her eternal embarrassment—followed Logan out the door. So he was back to his old habits, it would seem, and even though she was trying very pointedly to move on, that didn't mean it didn't hurt to see him doing the same.

"You mean my building's rooftop lounge?" she said in an attempt at a cool, breezy tone. "Is there some rule saying I can't?"

Logan strode angrily across the roof, reaching them in an alarmingly few number of strides. His legs really had no business being that long. He looked at Joey with a frown. "Him?" he said rudely, his thumb pointing at a now very perplexed-looking Joey. "Really?"

Clare stood up, for all the good that did her. "I could say the same for you," she said acidly.

Logan's date looked at her sharply. "Watch it," she warned.

Clare didn't really want to fight with the woman, who in addition to being a solid six inches taller than her had a look about her that said *Don't fuck with me*. Besides, it wasn't *her* fault Logan was being a massive jerk.

Joey looked around, surreptitiously pushing his chair back from the table to put a little more space between him and Logan's towering stature.

"Am I missing something here?" he asked.

Both Clare and Logan ignored him. "I knew you'd move on, but I thought you'd do a little better than boring," Logan said, crossing his arms.

Clare did the same. "Don't be a dick. Just because Joey's nothing like you doesn't mean he's boring."

"Thank you. I think," Joey said under his breath. Logan's date moved to stand behind him, the two of them watching Clare and Logan with looks that were half annoyed, half amused.

Logan appeared to change tactics when he realized she wasn't going to agree Joey was boring. "But up here?" he said again.

"Just because we were up here together doesn't mean I can never come up here with someone else," she retorted.

"It's not what you think," Logan said to his date, who had raised her eyebrows interestedly. "We just talked."

"Honestly, that's worse," she said, making a face.

"Are you mad at me, or worried about what *she* thinks?" Clare snapped.

"I'm not—that's not—I—that's not what I meant," Logan replied.

"What do you want, Logan?" Clare asked, intending to sound irritated but landing somewhere around exhausted.

Logan's eyes softened and he swallowed hard, looking away from them all. "Not this," he admitted softly, and her heart lurched painfully.

His date clicked her tongue. "Okay, well, I don't usually like to watch." She nudged Joey's shoulder. "I'm Amber. I was planning on getting laid tonight but obviously that isn't going to happen here, so want to buy me a drink?"

Joey looked between them and pushed back from the table. Amber looked like she could eat him alive, and he looked like he wasn't sure if that was a good or bad thing. "Joey," he said, standing up. "And yeah. Let's, uh, leave them to it."

Clare could barely bring herself to spare them a glance as they left. She was trapped in Logan's eyes, drowning in their ocean.

He never even looked back as the door swung closed behind him. "I'm sorry," he said, finally closing his eyes. They had been glistening just a moment before, and the painful tug on her heart turned into a knife-sharp pain. "I don't know what I was thinking," he sighed, running a hand through his hair and scratching the back of his neck. He glanced at Joey's now empty chair. "I'm sorry I ruined your date."

Clare shrugged, all the fight drained out of her. "Sorry I ruined yours, too."

"Amber'll be fine," he said. "She always lands on her feet."

"We're messes, aren't we?" she said with a weak chuckle.

Logan's mouth curved up at one corner. "We really are."

She took heart from that. "So, why did you come up here?"

Logan collapsed into an armchair next to the table, elbows on his knees and his head hanging between his shoulder blades. "I was going to fight for you. I think. I don't know, I wasn't thinking at all. Because if I had been I would have cancelled on Amber, but we don't need to get into that."

Clare leaned back against the table for support. "What changed your mind?"

"Your aunt," he told the ground between his feet.

"Really? I never took her for a meddler."

"If I had to guess, I think we're a special case for her."

"And are you?"

Logan finally looked up. "Am I what?"

"Fighting for me."

"Only if you want me to," he said, swallowing hard.

She watched his Adam's apple bob up and down, his jaw clench and unclench. It was her turn to be brave. "I'm sorry I hurt you," she said. "I screwed up."

"I did too," he admitted. "I was feeling guilty and weird about everything, and I lashed out, I guess. And then in the elevator—I thought I could get you out of my system. I was wrong."

"I still miss you," she confessed. "I had to close my shades to keep from looking at you."

"And here I thought it was to keep from having to see me," Logan said.

"That too. But mostly it was because it hurt to even think about you." Clare took a tentative step forward. "I should have fought for you, too," she said, brushing the back of her knuckles against his hand. "I gave up too soon."

Logan caught her fingers. "I shouldn't have made fighting

necessary," he said, and brought her fingers to his lips, placing a soft kiss on the back of her hand. "I really fucked up."

"Me too. Does that make us even?"

Logan smiled weakly, trapping her hand against his cheek. "I still don't really know how to do a relationship. And I think you deserve better than having to teach me."

"How about you let me decide what I deserve?" she said, curling her fingers under his chin and lifting his face to look at her.

She was rarely in this position, standing above him like he usually loomed above her. Clare leaned down slowly, giving him time to back away, and when he didn't, she pressed her lips against his in a gentle, quiet kiss. Logan blinked, a tear falling down his cheek, and took her face in his hands, pulling her down onto his lap so he could kiss her again.

It was perfect. There was no other word for kissing Logan, because it felt right and good and warm and wonderful and *perfect*. Clare couldn't believe she had tried to convince herself she could move on, because there wasn't anyone out there who compared to the man kissing her right now.

She pulled back, rubbing her thumb against his cheek. "I love you, Logan Walsh," she murmured.

Logan smiled, that broad, sparkling smile that made her knees feel weak and her stomach all fluttery, and rested his forehead on hers. "I love you more, Clare Thompson."

"It's not a competition," she protested.

"I still win, though."

Clare's laugh died in her throat as he pulled her against him and kissed her again. Behind them, the sun sank down to the horizon, painting the Minneapolis skyline in a soft shade of gold.

Epilogue

Logan looked down at his sketchpad and frowned, erasing his last little bit of work and starting over. Frodo, Clare's obscenely large rescue mutt, sniffed at his leg and let him scratch his head absently. Hands still gave Logan trouble, so maybe the Amethyst Queen would be conveniently standing behind a cluster of Elfborn instead.

Clare and her friends had finally wrapped up their two-year-long campaign last week, and he wanted to draw them something to commemorate it. Their band of adventurers had soundly defeated the Dragon Army, saving Sulzuris from certain destruction. Vaildra had discovered a plot by the Crown Prince to betray Sulzuris to the Dragon King in exchange for sparing his own life, but the orcling Krysis, otherwise known as Chase, had assassinated the prince before he could go through with it.

Logan had drawn Krysis up in the left corner, holding a bloody knife in triumph, while Vaildra was down in the lower right, her black robes swirling with what Logan hoped looked like mystery and intrigue. Logan had put Yaen close to the middle, in an old-fashioned clinch with Ildash reminiscent of the romance novels he used to look at in the grocery store.

Ildash had fully redeemed himself, nearly dying in the process. He was saved at the last minute thanks to some quick thinking by Degar, who was standing to the left of the Amethyst Queen, his foot on top of a severed dragon head.

Drawing this tableau required a lot more blood and guts than Logan was used to, but he liked the challenge. He'd even included Keith the Ogre, tucked in behind the defeated Dragon Army. Logan had played just a handful of times in the last six months, and while he enjoyed himself immensely, he had quickly found that three hours every weekend was more pretending than he could commit to, so much like Krysis, Keith was now just a recurring player.

Clare came up behind him and leaned down, wrapping her arms around him and resting her chin on his shoulder. A year ago, just the thought of someone seeing him in the process of drawing would have made him flinch, but now he just rested his hand lightly on her forearm.

"What do you think?" he asked, as she pressed their temples together. Clare smelled like sugar and raspberries today, and he let her scent ground him as she scanned the sketch.

"I love it," she said, pausing before choosing her words carefully. "And I know it would be hard to do, since she's the Game Master and not really a character, but—"

"That's Devi," Logan interrupted, pointing to the mountain range that loomed up on the right side. "She's always given me a lavender vibe, and the mountain range is imposing but critical to your victory, just like her."

"Degar wouldn't have been able to hide the rebels without the mountain passes," Clare agreed. She kissed his cheek and Logan set down his sketch pad, tugging her around the chair to pull her into his lap. "I have to get the tarts out of the oven," Clare protested half-heartedly.

"How long ago did you put them in?" Logan asked, brushing his nose against hers.

"Five minutes," she admitted, and twisted to look at the timer on his oven. "Make that seven."

"Then we've got plenty of time," Logan said, dropping his voice into the register he knew she couldn't resist.

True to form, Clare squirmed on his lap. "Ten minutes is not *plenty of time*," she argued, even as he kissed the side of her neck. "And if I burn the tarts I'm making for your friends and the stupid game—"

Logan pulled his lips from her neck and made a mock-stern face. "Hey now, you agreed," he scolded. "And besides, Sam and Vince are your friends too now."

Clare smiled through her eyeroll and slipped her hand under the hem of his T-shirt, scraping her nails lightly across his skin.

God, he loved it when she did that. "And what are we watching today?" he prompted.

"Today's sport is . . . hockey?" she said, and Logan rewarded her with a lingering kiss behind her ear.

"Very good. And? Who's playing?"

"Well, I know it's *not* one of the teams with a racial slur for their name, at least. And thank god, because—"

"Stop stalling," he ordered, and she sank her teeth down into her full lower lip. Logan loosened it with his thumb and lifted his eyebrows questioningly.

Clare wrinkled her nose in thought. "The Minnesota Wild," she said, and he knew it was probably a stab in the dark but he kissed the corner of her jaw anyway. "And . . . the Colorado . . . Mountains? No, Avalanche."

"Final answer?"

She paused, and then nodded once. "Final answer. Hockey

game, featuring the Minnesota Wild and the Colorado Avalanche."

Logan curled his hand behind her neck and pulled her in for a deep kiss. He'd never get tired of kissing her, he was sure of that. "Be honest. How much of that was a wild guess?" he asked against her lips.

"How much trouble am I in if I say forty percent?"

"A lot."

"Then twenty percent," Clare said triumphantly.

Logan snorted but kissed her anyway.

Life might not be a game, but Logan sure as hell felt like he was winning.

Acknowledgments

This book was an absolute beast to write, and I could not have done it without the support of the people I have behind me. Thank you to Jess Dallow, for your endless rounds of brainstorming and emails as I tried to figure this out. I also owe an enormous debt to The Gaggle (Amanda, Brit, Laura, and Amber) for taking this vague pile of story-shaped ideas and plucking out the actual story for me. I mean it when I say this book wouldn't have gotten written without you.

To the team at Headline Eternal, particularly Kate, Sophie, and Jill—thank you for your work on this manuscript, and for taking yet another risk on me. Working with you all has been a joy, and I consider myself very, very lucky.

I want to extend my deepest thanks to my Tabletop Role Playing Reference Corps for their assistance. Claire (AKA Lady Stoneheart), John (AKA Swan Ronson), Other Claire (AKA Eirlando Baloom), Matt (AKA Aunuf Zeenuf), Debbie (AKA Lavinia Tosscobble), Josh (AKA Destyn Childe), and Wade (AKA Yoelow Swaggins), thank you for letting me sit in on a game and answer all of my questions, stupid or not. I took the liberty of using your ideas as much as I could, especially the detail about character-specific dice, and I promise not to tell anyone which 90s TV star you accidentally murdered in your game. Thank you, Thea, for your quick beta-ing and suggestions for Devi's descriptions. And don't worry about accidentally turning the whole thing into a Google Doc. It happens.

I'd also like to thank the random people on Twitter who would answer my questions whenever I wasn't sure something would "translate" to the UK. Thank you for serving as my on-the-spot references, and letting me know when specific basketball terms just really didn't make any sense to you. I need to acknowledge all the book bloggers and Instagrammers who read and promoted my debut too, because you guys made this second book happen.

To the usual suspects: I love you all, so much. I would not have made it through this pandemic without my Pocket Friends. Thank you, Erin, Brit, Chash, Alisha, Toni, Tina, Jeeno, Shep, and Lindsey. You kept me grounded when I really didn't think I'd make it through this pandemic/this book/literally everything. Alisha, thank you so much for answering all my questions about Chemical Engineering for the version of this story where Clare was an engineer. You were so thoughtful and helpful, and I hope you enjoy the Zutara mentions, as those were just for you.

It also would not have been possible for me to write this book without the help of our nanny, who wrangled my kids several days a week to give me enough time to get words onto the page. I firmly believe the world would be a better place if we could acknowledge that it really, truly isn't possible to "have it all" without outside help. Megan, this book owes a huge debt to your hard work.

I also need to thank my extended family for their love, support, and most importantly, the free childcare. Dad flying up so I could finish my revisions on time was a godsend, and

Mommy and Papa were able to gave me quiet time to write when I desperately needed it. Mom, thank you for reading to the kids whenever I needed a break. This pandemic has been terrible, but having family FaceTimes so often has been wonderful. Bobby and Lucy, I'm so glad we're neighbors and able to pass the kids back and forth whenever we need a breather.

I also want to thank my kids for being adorable and funny. Tdee Muay, whenever you call "have a good work!" as I go upstairs, I know it's going to be a great day. Tdee Bee, thank you for always wanting to "check on mama" to make sure I'm working. You're the best boss a writer could ask for.

To my husband: thank you for standing by me as I muddled through this mess of a book. The pandemic has been a lot to handle (to put it mildly), but with you by my side I always knew we'd make it out the other side.

And finally, thank you to my readers, because without you I would just be throwing words into the void. I sincerely hope you liked these particular words.

Victoria and Owen are bitter rivals.
Nora and Luke are friends online.
Who would believe these two couples have **anything** *in common?*

**All's fair in love and law in this
irresistible enemies-to-lovers rom-com!**

Order now from

HEADLINE
ETERNAL

HEADLINE
ETERNAL

FIND YOUR HEART'S DESIRE...

VISIT OUR WEBSITE: www.headlineeternal.com
FIND US ON FACEBOOK: facebook.com/eternalromance
CONNECT WITH US ON TWITTER: @eternal_books
FOLLOW US ON INSTAGRAM: @headlineeternal
EMAIL US: eternalromance@headline.co.uk